BOOKWORM

BOOKWORM

A Novel

ROBIN YEATMAN

HARPER PERENNIAL

NEW YORK • LONDON • TORONTO • SYDNEY • NEW DELHI • AUCKLAND

HARPER ● PERENNIAL

HarperCollins books may be purchased for educational, business, or sales promotional use. For information, please email the Special Markets Department at SPsales@harpercollins.com.

FIRST EDITION

Designed by Jamie Lynn Kerner
Book ornament image copyright © puckillustrations / stock.adobe.com

Library of Congress Cataloging-in-Publication Data has been applied for.

ISBN 978-0-06-327300-9

23 24 25 26 27 LBC 5 4 3 2 1

To all the writers who made me a reader . . . thank you.
And for my fellow bookworms, with love.

BOOKWORM

ONE

FRIDAY WAS VICTORIA'S DAY OFF. SHE LIKED HAVING FRIDAYS OFF
from the spa because Holly often did too, so they could visit and
gossip. But on the days Holly wasn't free, Victoria went to Café au
Lait, an artisanal coffeehouse several blocks from the apartment, and
read "her book." She always had one going.

She liked the café because it was warm, colorful, a little bit clut-
tered, and noisy. It was around the corner from a private girl's school,
so by late afternoon it was often infused with the noise of teenage
voices jockeying for attention, tables laden with backpacks and text-
books. It was run by an Eastern European woman with a beehive
hairdo and thick accent. She was always cleaning tabletops, leaning
her huge, wrinkled cleavage into the faces of her patrons. The rag
she used looked the same every time—gray and specked with crumbs.
Victoria was highly suspicious of the cleanliness of the café in general,
but the coffee was always hot and the foam on her latte was thick.

Her book propped on her table just so, she passed her Holly-less
afternoons here with a rather pathetic regularity.

Victoria was a great reader, thanks to Mrs. Herd, her ninth-grade
English teacher, who taught *Macbeth* and looked a little like one of

the weird sisters, with her black hair, prominent rump, and surprising cackle of a laugh. Mrs. Herd had opened the floodgates to the joys of literature with that sharp sparkle in her eye and the beguiling way she led the class into understanding the pages of a story. It was under her witchy instruction that Victoria discovered *The Handmaid's Tale* and *Siddhartha*. *Lord of the Flies*, too, one of her favorites. It spawned a lifelong love of the words people put on the page. These words had a power—to seduce, enrage, enlighten, in ways that television and movies could not. But a book served another function for Victoria when she was somewhere in public. It was a security blanket. Something to hide behind, a purpose no one would question. People tended to respect the barrier of an opened book, granting an invisibility that Victoria had come to count on.

She could see others, though, and not just physically. She could read people as well as any book. Often, Victoria would look up from her reading and play a little game. She could figure out anyone who walked into the café (or anywhere else, for that matter) in no more than a few seconds.

For example, today, the man at the counter, wearing the beret. Victoria could see at a glance that he was dreaming of a guy with a long, coiffed beard who worked in the ice-cream store on Monkland, fantasizing about his muscular forearms twisting with every scoop of gelato. Just by looking at him, she determined that he lived in the Plateau, in a trendy brownstone walk-up with his best friend and sister, who, vehemently vegan, was sufficiently distracted from her lack of sex life by her urban knitting club and two small chihuahuas, Felix and FrouFrou. The sibling devotion was comforting at the dinner table every night, but also very much stood in the way of a healthy social life, poor things.

There was the elderly woman at a table in the corner, who, once very beautiful, as evidenced by her large, warm brown eyes and elegant profile, now clicked her knitting needles together. In a reverie, Victoria was sure, she fondly remembered days with her husband before their marriage, when he'd been less serious and more interested in discussing art rather than his stock portfolio. He had once been so sensitive that way. She recalled his introducing her to Judith Leyster's work and the feminist interpretation of *The Proposition*. Oh, dear Harry.

And that Asian girl with the seven D&G bags, who always looked to be in a rush. Victoria assessed her easily: a clinical counselor, Type-A, who worked as a consultant for government organizations. A former teenage rebel, she'd lived in England during her formative years, in posh boarding schools. Spent that largely unsupervised time experimenting with drugs and men far older than herself—*Dog collar, Mom? You don't understand fashion*—before her parents realized that the money they'd spent on giving their child all the advantages wasn't exactly paying off. Now she redirected her addictive personality into her career and a wicked coffee habit. Sometimes, when she felt alone, she rubbed the spot between her toes where she used to shoot heroin with her tattoo-artist boyfriend. She dropped her shoe and did this now. This made her feel numb, and a little nostalgic at the same time.

Victoria, behind her book, took a sip of her latte. Just bitter enough. Caffeine really put an edge on things.

It was easy to get distracted by the people around her. On this particular Friday, Victoria had an albatross of a novel with her. It was one of the new releases everyone was raving about. *Rapturous! Resplendent! Unforgettable!* In fact, it was a long, torturous read, and the cover was equally terrible. On it was a picture of a man crying, either in ecstasy or pain, who cared. She couldn't *not* finish it, though. That's the kind of reader Victoria was. She couldn't release herself from the pain of a bad book until she'd read every last page. She liked to think it was due to an unrelenting optimism, the hope that anything could get better if she hung on just a little longer. But it was hard to say if this was true—hanging on rarely paid off. Often she came to resent the author with a near-lethal ferocity. She still hadn't forgiven Stephen King for "that scene" at the end of *It*, or Louisa May Alcott for making Jo marry the creepy old German guy in *Little Women*.

She was slowly forcing her way through another unbearable scene of apology and tears when she looked up.

That's when she saw Him. Light brown hair, dark blue eyes shaded by thick lashes. A laptop was open at his table, a shabby man-bag discarded by his feet, which were clad in scuffed work boots. These were all secondary observations, though. What drew her eyes to him in the first place was the book: the same book she was reading, the one with the crying man, was open in his hands.

Her world stopped.

She stared as though a dark Medusa charm had turned her to stone. Even if he had noticed her mouth-dropped gaze, she doubted she would have been able to pull herself away. She drank him in greedily in an attempt to memorize his features. Her heart hammered and then paused, then restarted vigorously, in a new, erratic rhythm. She realized this was a recognition. This was Him, He, with a capital *H*. This was the answer to her question, the filler for the emptiness. A color to provide the contrast. Her soul's counterpoint.

She watched him read. It felt very intimate, almost erotic, as she followed his eyes moving over the words, the page, perhaps the very same paragraphs she herself had moved over in moments recently passed. His minute expressions—she interpreted them to be disbelief or disgust; they had to be disgust, like she felt—manifested as a small creasing between his brows, as a light tightening at the corners of his mouth. He hates the book, too, she decided, as though this were confirmation of their cosmic connection.

He crossed his feet at the ankles. Every so often he reached for his coffee, without taking his eyes from his book. Perfectly, his hand reached the mug. His mug—it wasn't a generic one from the café. It had black lettering that could have been a Shakespeare quote, but she couldn't quite make out the words.

He wore a dark-blue pullover with two buttons at the top, and jeans. His chest looked substantial. Not muscles, exactly, but substance, strength. He had a little stubble on his face, which she liked. It was patchy in areas on his cheeks. She loved that too.

He turned pages, his eyes scanned the words, he sipped from his mug. Once, as he ran his hand through his hair, she let out an audible sigh and shifted conspicuously in her chair as she tried to pretend to read.

He didn't notice any of this, of course. Now he was looking through his bag and produced a phone. It was buzzing. "Yes," he said. "I'm on my way." Hung up without saying goodbye. She wanted to imprint his words on her memory, to have his voice with her, but it all happened too quickly, disappearing into the ambient noise of the café clatter.

Her heart leapt as he rose to his feet and she saw the length of him—tall and handsome—while he put on a jacket, sheathed his laptop in the bag, and took a last, deep drink from his mug. The book was under his arm, the handle of the mug looped by his index finger.

Look at me, she willed him telepathically. *I'm here*. But he didn't. He was already facing the other way, then was out the door, gone.

At that moment she became aware that her heart had been racing, was still racing, that her hands were trembling. Her eyes were wet with the threat of tears.

That whole afternoon she felt charged, as though something wonderful had happened, but she couldn't quite put her finger on it.

She moved through her usually mundane trip to the grocery store with an optimism she normally lacked. She took care with small things. She selected a more pricey sheep's milk feta, decided to try fresh *orecchiette*, aka "pig's ear" pasta. She made an effort to speak French with the woman at the checkout. When she had finished shopping, she gave her cart to an older man struggling to pull one free from the tangle, with a deliberately kind smile. In the car, she applied lipstick, something she rarely wore. It was a pinky nude color that Holly swore looked good on "anyone," during an overwhelming visit to Sephora some months ago. Victoria hadn't agreed at the time. She felt like an impostor with chalky, creamy lips. She had only bought the lipstick to appease Holly and to make the whole experience feel like a successful girls' shopping trip. But today she carefully, lovingly, traced the bows of her mouth with pleasure, deciding that it wasn't bad at all to take care of oneself like this. She should do it more often.

She closed her eyes and replayed the entire drama in the coffee shop, recalled all the details, rejoiced as each one appeared in her mind. She lingered on the memory of him, marveled at how content she had been just to have him in her line of vision, how she wouldn't change a thing about him.

She realized two things: she needed to see him again, and she loved him.

TWO

VICTORIA'S FACE WAS HOT, CONSPICUOUSLY SO, THAT EVENING. Her cheeks felt afire, radiated heat that had never resided there before. Her thoughts on Him, she went through the motions of making dinner. She poured vinegar into the rice instead of chicken stock and had to start over—*dammit*—the sour smell alerting her and shocking her back into the moment. Eric was home, with seven minutes cooking time left. She hated to make him wait.

"Cinderelli, Cinderelli," he said in a mocking tone when he entered the kitchen. His lips twitched slightly as he watched her hurry around, mopping up chicken drippings with a dishrag that she left unrinsed on the counter. She cursed as a few broccoli florets tumbled out of the steamer and onto the floor.

Her bottom faced him as she bent over to pick them up and toss them into the compost bin. She rose with prim modesty when she saw in a backwards glance that he was focusing on her backside with a bemused look on his face.

He watched her, curious. "Tough day at the office?" he asked.

"Oh, what? No, it was my day off." His irony was lost on her.

He continued to stare, irritated by her flitting movements, unusual for his calm wife, his spa girl. "Well, my day was fine, thanks for asking."

She stopped. Lifted her gaze. Her eyes met his as though only seeing him for the first time. "I'm sorry, Eric. So thoughtless of me. Can I get you a glass of wine?"

"You can, and may."

She made a quick move to the fridge and caught her hip on the corner of the white quartz countertop, a corner she had always thought was too sharp. "Shit." She held her hip as the pain pulsed and radiated in angry waves.

Eric's brows furrowed. "How about I get my own drink," he said. Opting not to watch her wincing, he poured them both the chardonnay he routinely ordered from a reserve winery in the Okanagan. "Something leather, cherries, and oak," he said superciliously, sniffing the bottle. He always described the wine in this manner before drinking it. It was one of the things that had annoyed Victoria early on in their relationship.

"Sorry," Victoria said, taking the glass. She was always apologizing. The pulsing was easing now, but she knew she was going to ache with a bruise.

"What did you do today, anyway?" he asked. He rarely asked, but today the question seemed warranted.

"Oh, you know . . ." She cleared her throat. "I went to the gym. I got some groceries. I went to the café and read my book. Not necessarily in that order."

She always called it "my book," after he had labeled it as such, regardless of which one she happened to be reading at the moment. "There goes Victoria with her book," he was wont to say. Eric never asked about details—books were all one and the same to him. That was fine with her. Reading was pleasurable for her precisely because it was solitary. She didn't need to discuss her reading with Eric—or anyone else. He had once suggested she join a book club, mainly because he wanted her to socialize with his colleagues' wives. She had attended only once. The evening was a test of Victoria's endurance. How long can you talk about a Nicholas Sparks novel and trade recipes?

Victoria belonged to a virtual "book of the month" club that sent emails with reading suggestions, which was about as communal as her reading life went. She was questioning even that now, as they were responsible for the latest crying-man door stopper.

"Did you talk to your mother?" Eric eyed her with suspicion after a prolonged taste of the wine.

"My mother? No. Why?"

"You seem . . . jittery."

She felt her cheeks, felt them licked red from inner flames, and wondered if he'd noticed. She stopped, took a breath, tried to smile. "Sorry. I don't know. Maybe I shouldn't have had that second latte."

"Maybe not," he said, disengaging her by looking at his phone in response to an email notification, announced by a British voice saying *"Gentlemen, start your engines"* with that Sean Connery–like pronunciation of "shtart." It was one of Eric's hobbies to collect ringtones and notification sounds that he found amusing or original. He'd had this one for at least a month.

Relieved that his attention was elsewhere, Victoria continued making dinner, but kept the man in the café in her every thought. He was with her in each movement. She felt as though she was suddenly repurposed, energized. Every other moment, she was hit with happiness but couldn't quite explain to herself why. There was something to anticipate, but what?

This is what hope feels like, she thought, just as the rice timer went off. Hope. It shimmered down her, from the top of her head to her steaming cheeks, giving her a tingly feeling. A giggle wanted to bubble in her throat, but she kept it a delicious secret, focusing instead on setting the table and plating the food.

And then the high took a dip, a slight one, as it occurred to her that she had no idea how to see Him again, this man she had recognized in the deepest way possible. This man, who had not even looked at her, or spoken to her.

Her whole being pulsed with the knowledge and the urge that she *had* to see him again.

She experienced this all silently amid small bites of tasteless chicken, rice, and broccoli. She was thankful that Eric didn't demand much in terms of conversation, because her thoughts were so huge, they took up her entire brain. I love him, I love him, I LOVE HIM . . . The words marched through her thoughts, which both shocked and enlivened her.

She went through the motions of the meal like a robot: fork to mouth, napkin to lips, plates to sink. She tidied up after dinner—she always cleaned up in the kitchen. The kitchen was her domain. Then, feeling aimless, she brought her book to her usual place on the couch.

"You're biting your nails again. God, Victoria, it's disgusting. Like you're *eating* your fingers."

Eric said it quietly, but with repulsion on his face.

She whipped her hand from her mouth. "Sorry."

She had been thinking about Him again and hadn't even noticed what she was doing.

"I can see you, you know," he said, his face a sneer. "I just ate. A little mercy, please."

Victoria pushed her hand down so far out of his sight she was practically sitting on it. She daren't apologize again; it made things worse. She stayed quiet and stared at the words on the page. He was in a bad mood. He normally didn't pay attention to her while he was watching television.

Eric hated it when she bit her nails. God forbid that she have a cold—nose blowing was akin to picking a zit or passing a big wet fart. Any bodily function was almost beyond his comfort level, and he expected her to attend to those things so they had no sensory impact on him.

Feeling the need, she cleared her throat—but the frog remained stuck in her. She tried to ignore it, but it persisted in a throaty, phlegmy gag until she cleared her throat again, louder, certain that she had succeeded in disgusting him. His back was to her. She saw the red, angry tips of his ears.

She mentally lashed herself. Up until now, the evening had been more or less a success. She had made one of his favorite meals—sliced organic free-range chicken breast and steamed organic broccoli on top of rice that had been cooked in organic chicken stock bought at the kosher butcher they used. Everything was the right flavor, temperature, quantity. His second glass of wine was poured with the timing of an Olympic relay handoff. She felt her words had been just the right ones too. That was always tricky. It was too easy to come off stupid, for her voice to echo shrilly against the tile backsplash, with only his judgmental blink as reply. That echo was the loudest thing she had ever heard. It hurt her ears.

No, she'd let him do the talking. He had lamented a bit about a case he was working on, using a bunch of legal mumbo jumbo that she was used to filtering into her "things I don't need to understand" category. She'd done that since childhood with her parents. It was a survival skill. Asking questions just prolonged things.

She thought she'd managed the evening as best as she could. But this was the seesaw she knew too well. It could begin on a high, and then with the equalizing force of gravity, topple down before her regretful, bewildered eyes.

His attention was back on the television. He was watching a

police procedural. Gillian Anderson, or someone who looked like her (she was so much more attractive now than she was in *The X-Files*) was wearing a smart pantsuit, and talking seriously in the rain with a skinny, cracked-out man.

Victoria stared at the back of Eric's neck and saw how slender it was. How tender and slight, how hurtable it was, with just a few muscles and a sheath of skin for protection over the bones. A miracle that he walked around all day without breaking it. Things fell all the time, didn't they? He walked downtown, by old buildings made of brick and stone. It wasn't out of the realm of possibility that, one day, the music would be in sync and a large cube of cement would come loose at the right moment and *down*, come down to bring his face flat against his chest at an acute angle, his neck bones splintered and divorced from each other, the break so sudden and sharp that the skin at the back of his neck would be pierced and the pearly bone poking out, ghostly white, almost plastic in appearance, protruding from the red hole, visible for only a handful of seconds before being drowned in a bloody pulse, a pulse that slowed exponentially to nothing, with each breath bringing her closer to the end, to the end of marriage, to freedom.

She saw herself being told the news—the doorbell ringing, her phone ringing, serious faces, kind voices, a hand on the shoulder. "He didn't suffer. It was instant. I'm so sorry." Her tears, her tears, so many tears, each tear healing an unspeakable hurt. The funeral. The eulogy. All the well-wishers. And then that night, returning to the apartment, she would shower and come to bed naked with her hair wet against the pillow, and she would look up at the ceiling and feel lightness in her heart, and sleep would come for her and sleep would find her so effortlessly all she had to do was to turn to her side with one leg pulled up to her chest the way she had done in her mother's womb and she would be gone.

When Eric had his fill of Gillian Anderson, he clicked the remote decisively and stretched before getting up. Victoria had already changed into her simple white Calvin Klein cotton pajama pants and blouse her mother-in-law had bought for her last month. The white pajamas matched everything in their white apartment.

She had already brushed her teeth, washed her face, and flushed the toilet, so Eric wouldn't have to see or hear any of it. They each had their own bathrooms, so it was unlikely that he would see or hear it, but it was their routine for her to ready herself for bed first, while he was still out of earshot.

When he made the decisive click, she raised herself from the couch with a faint smile, padded to the bedroom, and eased under the covers, careful not to disturb his side.

It took him about ten minutes to perform his nighttime skin-care ablutions. He appeared in his matching pajamas, turned off the lights, and rolled onto his side away from her, grunted "Good night." He fiddled with the box on his side table that contained his bright-orange ear plugs.

"Good night, Eric," she breathed, using her most serene spa voice, trying not to convey any weight or atmosphere in her tone, hoping that emotion wouldn't leak out, choking the words in betrayal.

She counted silently to one hundred. His breathing became heavy and regular. When she was sure that he was asleep, she sighed in relief, the first relaxed breath of the night.

Often plagued by insomnia, Victoria spent many nocturnal hours lying in despair. Her fight against wakefulness began in childhood. One of her earliest memories was of lying in bed, the cool sheets tucked so tightly around her small body she could barely move. Mummified, paralyzed, she stared at the moving shadows on the ceiling cast by the maple tree outside her window. They looked like killer rabbits with Nosferatu teeth. Her mother's narrowed eyes when she peeked in to see her daughter quietly awake. The hiss of her whisper: "Victoria, it's eleven thirty-*five*! Go to sleep!"

Her sleeplessness persisted in kindergarten class, during nap time. Mrs. Stanley had no patience for children who didn't nap, but despite the dark circles under her eyes, Victoria's body would never succumb to sleep in the classroom. Instead, Victoria would close her eyes and imagine that she could fly, up to the ceiling. She would *will* it. Once there, she experienced an effervescent lightness. She was a sparkling, floating fairy. She looked down at her classmates, and even herself, lying on the blue foam mats. She liked watching her friends, observing their descent to sleep, making little bets with herself about who would fall first. Who might twitch, who might suck their thumb. She once watched Mrs. Stanley pick her nose for a very long time. It took all she had not to laugh.

It was a game then. Now, it was her bedtime routine. Each evening after Eric fell asleep she closed her eyes, and in a deep meditative state, rose out of her body. As time passed, she got better and better at reaching the level of quiet, and then, the spectacular LIFT out of the heaviness of her physical form. Hovering over her bed, she was able to look down on herself. It's hard to say how long she would float up there. In this tall, expansive state, minutes and seconds did not exist. Possibilities were within her grasp. The lightness was exhilarating. Eventually, of course, she snapped back into her body, and the deep and dark velvet cloak of sleep followed.

Like the other nights, tonight she snapped back into her body. Like a child who had cried to exhaustion, she felt that same comfort knowing that sleep was inevitably pulling her under. She was powerless against its call.

THREE

I T WAS SATURDAY. THREE DAYS AFTER "HUMP DAY." YET VICTORIA was certain (barring sudden illness on his part, or unforeseen circumstances) they would have sex, probably around 10:30, after Eric had watched a few shows, one less than usual. She was certain because they had sex every single Saturday, like clockwork. They had since they were together. It was part of their routine. Saturday night.

Monday nights he played badminton at the club in his perfect whites. She didn't like hearing him say the word "birdie," and she liked "shuttlecock" even less.

Tuesday night he had *cinq à sept* with workmates and was usually unsociable and sleepy afterward. Wednesday he liked to binge-watch TV. Same with Thursday. Same with Friday, although by then he tended to turn in a little earlier, having gone through all his shows and complaining bitterly that there really is NOTHING on Netflix. Sunday they often had dinner with their parents. So Saturday was sex night.

To say she dreaded Saturday would be a little weak, though she never admitted that to herself. She once told Holly, who loved titillating "girl talk"—poor Holly never got much of that from Victoria—

that she was so relieved her relationship with Eric wasn't all about the sex, when in previous relationships it had taken up so much room! Holly nodded and blinked expectantly at this, as though preparing herself for an explanation. Victoria didn't really have one.

The truth deep down was that Eric slightly scared Victoria. He was tall and well-proportioned, and looked dapper, even elegant, in his three-piece suit. He had a good face and lovely blue eyes that contrasted with his dark hair ("He looks just like Archer!" gushed Holly on one occasion). Except there was something very, very cold behind those eyes—icy, even. As if he didn't, wouldn't, couldn't, look through them at her.

And, too, he approached sex with her with an off-putting, unsexy seriousness. "Okay, Victoria," he would say, as though about to set about doing a difficult but important task, like stripping wallpaper, or carrying an unwieldy object up the stairs. Her participation, though it was never stated explicitly, was equally serious, and would be nice— but it wasn't necessary.

Their typical coupling involved no heavy breathing. Heavy, flat kisses, cursory general sweeping of the hands over her body, pumping for a few minutes, and then over. Her breath was held the whole time as she lay, as passive and encouraging as a corpse. She was glad it was so quick. She was anxious for it to be over the moment it began.

The idea of her own climax was laughable. She found herself leaning away from him, hoping the whole time his nipples would not touch her. It had taken her awhile to understand what it was about Eric's body that bugged her so much: it was his nipples. They were unusually puffy. His chest hair, very black and thick, balded an inch all around his nipples, as though they repulsed the hair growth by their presence. She avoided taking off his shirt, even during sex, just so she wouldn't have to see them. Otherwise, she couldn't see anything else but their pink, too-vulnerable puffiness.

Of course, she always mentally lashed herself after noticing them. How could she judge him this way?

This Saturday, though, was different from all other Saturdays. She had met Him just the day before, and the thought of being intimate with her husband had her on the verge of panic. She wanted to avoid it if at all possible.

Eric was in the middle of watching a particularly engrossing episode of *Fargo*, during a scene in an elevator she was certain he couldn't possibly tear himself from, when she got up, yawning, and announced she was tired and was going to bed. Her feeble plan didn't work. He looked away from the screen, irritated by this deviation from their routine. He opened his mouth, as if to say something cutting . . . but then just clicked off his show and followed her into the bedroom.

Her heart quickened as she opened her pajama drawer, a signal to him that she wasn't interested. As she reached for the flannels, though, he was behind her, his hand on her wrist a little tighter than necessary, his breath on her neck, hot and yeasty. He turned her to face him. His eyes held a menacing challenge of sorts. Did she really think she could shirk her weekly wifely duty?

"Victoria," he breathed, his frown forbidding, his hand still clamped around her wrist. She looked down at it, saw the glitter of diamond from her finger. He released his grip.

Feeling a choking inevitability, she undressed.

He pulled off his underwear and moved around against her, penetrating her with some effort. Pausing as though for dramatic effect, he pulled off his T-shirt. She closed her eyes, pressed her face into the pillow, and tried to resurrect the face of the man in the café, but she could only see the red-black insides of her own eyelids. Bloody-branched walls of flesh, clamped shut. She was lonely and broken as Eric moved inside of her. Eventually he finished. He pulled out of her and out of the bed in a fluid move.

He always had a shower afterward, solo. His shower was perfunctory. Eric wasn't a dawdler. Besides, he was tired after his orgasm. Four minutes and he was back to bed. She had already used the bidet and slipped on her nightgown. She was on her side of the king-size mattress. Her back faced him, her eyes closed, feigning sleep. He got into bed quietly, inserted the orange ear plugs, adjusted his pillow, and turned on his side so both their backs faced each other. She counted down from two hundred, nice and slowly. By the time she hit thirty-nine, she heard it: his deep breathing.

She felt her body relax for the first time all evening. This was the time of day Victoria waited for, the moment she could breathe, stop holding her face in position, be herself, in the dark.

Tonight, she thought about Him. She recalled his face with ease. She replayed the moment she saw him. Her heart had pounded in her throat, in her groin. She felt the pulsing so strongly she had wondered if he could hear it. He was drinking his coffee, eating a cookie with pumpkin seeds on it. His jeans were worn looking, with whitish paint splatters close to the hem. She tried looking at her book, but she'd forgotten how to read. The words were just a collection of symbols. He sipped his coffee with a sensuous mouth. His phone rang, and as he answered it, she noticed he had a tooth on the side that was a little crooked, and she found herself loving that tooth. She imagined touching the tooth with her index finger, licking it. It was the perfect crooked tooth.

She realized then that even though she had noticed many of his physical details, she hadn't been able to read him like she did other people. Perhaps their connection went beyond such witchy tricks. Maybe she was meant to uncover him slowly, like unwrapping a gift. Good things didn't come easily, or that's what people said anyway.

At that moment she stopped herself with the knowledge that she had just been with Eric, only twenty-four hours after meeting Him.

The revulsion she felt for herself washed over her like bad news. Tears sprang easily, hot shameful tears, and she choked them out as silently as possible. How was it that she felt so guilty, so responsible, when she had not exchanged a word with this man, did not know his name?

The night was wounding, the heaviness of it smothered her. There was no relief, only wakefulness in which the seed of desire lodged itself in her mind.

FOUR

ALL THE GOOD STUFF AT THE SALAD BAR WAS HEAVY, VICTORIA noticed. Chickpeas, imitation crab, mini corn, beets, cottage cheese, macaroni, or potato salad. She didn't care too much about the price of her salad, but it bothered her to pay fifteen dollars for something she had to scoop herself, in line.

It was Holly's favorite place to eat, though, so they almost always went here. Holly was a girl who loved routine. If she found something that worked for her, she had no qualms about using the crap out of it.

Victoria strove to be on time for Holly, in order to avoid the r u still coming? text at three minutes past the appointed time, or the r u ok??? at five minutes. Holly was always there a few minutes before, with a big smile on her face, arms open for a hug and kiss-kiss on either cheek. Her blond hair was usually up in a French twist, her small blue eyes sparkling and expertly made up. If they were meeting on a workday, she was in a skirt suit. Holly had many of these, all the colors of the rainbow, with pumps to match. If meeting on one of her days off, she was often in workout gear—Lululemon pants and athletic bra (just barely containing her surgically augmented breasts), sports jacket zipped to her belly button. Holly, a dedicated gym bunny, loved the repetition and ritual of the gym, and her body was toned and shapely because of it.

Today was a workday, and Holly was in a pink-and-black tweed suit, something parochial schoolgirl, that she had found on a major discount at a cheap women's clothing store in the mall. Her lips were a glossy bubblegum pink that contrasted with her faux-tanned skin. As they hugged, Victoria could smell a whiff of Brando, Holly's dog, on her coat. Dog people always smelled a bit like dog.

They took their seats at a free table. They made a strange couple, Victoria mused. But Holly's eyes were clear, they always had been. They were small, they weren't deep wells of meaning, but they were steady and clear. Victoria had counted on that clarity for many years.

Victoria knew that Holly didn't really fit in with the idea her family or Eric had of "appropriate friend," but she'd been a constant since high school. Victoria had been surprised that Holly had picked her. No one had reached out to Victoria like that before. She didn't invite such things. She spent her lunch hours in the library and escaped from school as soon as the bell rang for the day. But Holly had been unrelentingly friendly, bubbly, and would do this thing that baffled Victoria at first, bringing a lump up into her throat—Holly would link her athletic, braceleted arms with Victoria's book-carrying ones. And Holly would look at her with her small, sparkly eyes. They were light blue, and completely absent of guile. She didn't understand *The Great Gatsby* (she actually thought he was a "creepy stalker"). She was a die-hard Jennifer Lopez fan. And she acted desperate around the popular boys, which embarrassed Victoria beyond measure. But when she linked arms, Victoria felt a sense of belonging that had been missing from her life.

And Holly had found a place in her too. After a remarkably

amicable-sounding divorce, her father moved back to England, leaving Holly with her rather humorless mother, who worked night shifts at the hospital. The divorce hadn't been his idea, and thus he licked his wounds in his home country, where his aged mother still resided. Holly was at loose ends, fatherless after thirteen years of unbroken adoration of the man. She never said a bad thing about him, but she would spend the rest of her teenage years and all her adulthood trying to replace him. Victoria often mused that it was his fault that so many men had seen Holly naked. Conservative, comb-overed, generously smiling Simon, who crossed the pond for visits every two years, would have been mortified to know that.

Holly had been with many men, it was true. She was on POF (Plenty of Fuckers, she liked to call it) and now, unfortunately, Tinder. She ignored Victoria's pleas to take herself offline and find someone the old-fashioned way. "That just doesn't *happen* anymore," Holly would argue in her earnest way. "It's easy for you to say because you have Eric."

Victoria didn't even want to know Holly's "number," though her friend would probably confide it to her with the same simplicity as she would her locker combination. She still had this innocence about her, a belief in people and possibilities, that both infuriated and endeared her to Victoria. Endeared because it was this exact innocence that she associated with the arm-linking of days past, but infuriated because she didn't seem to learn much from the rinse-and-repeat cycle she was on with unworthy men, some of them even seeming dangerous, likely to get into fistfights over football teams.

"So, how are things at the spa?" Holly asked, in her eternal expectation of hearing good news.

"Fine," Victoria said, stabbing at a chickpea with her plastic fork several times before spearing it.

"Yeah? I'm going to need a few appointments soon." Holly

showed her nails as evidence. "My mani is a mess and I probably need a facial too. And a wax . . ."

"Just let me know, Holl. I'll book you with Elizabeth." She was the coveted technician, even though her bedside manner was abrupt and her Hungarian accent a little harsh. Victoria never took Holly as a client, and Holly had never asked. The intimacy of massage wasn't something either of them desired.

Holly smiled at this. "Perfect. I need to be presentable for the next Mr. Right."

There was a big clatter of plates by the salad bar, something breaking. A heavyset male staff member hobbled over with a broom and dustbin to clean up the jagged ceramic pieces. A woman admonished her child, pulling him back roughly by the arm. "I TOLD you not to touch, Henry! Mommy gets the plates!" The child started to cry. Some people shuffled out of the way, others continued loading their trays.

Victoria dragged her attention back to Holly. "Sorry. Did you say 'the next Mr. Right'? What happened to Clyde, or Clive?"

Holly's face was free of expression. "Chad. Chad-the-Cad."

The child was now wailing, trying to pull away from his mother in a futile assertion of independence. The busboy was still sweeping up the plate pieces.

"What? What happened with Chad?"

Holly shrugged. "What else? What else happens when you meet a guy on Tinder. He found something shiny and new to catch his eye."

Victoria had an impulse to tell Holly that she was the shiniest thing she had ever seen. That she outshone any girl on Tinder. But she knew this would just embarrass them both.

"When did this happen?"

"Oh, last week. I called you but it just went to your voice mail. Not a big deal. I didn't actually want to bore you with it anyway. It's getting old, isn't it? Oh, don't look at me like that. I've already forgotten him. You have to cut away the negative things in life to make room for all the good. He did me a favor!"

Victoria felt a sinking guilt. She remembered exactly when the phone call had come. She had heard it ring, seven times. She had, in fact, suspected what it might be, on a Friday at 10:49 p.m. Holly had been stood up. Or got a text that was meant for someone else. Or had been unceremoniously dumped in a restaurant *after* one last roll in the hay. Victoria hadn't been in the mood for it that night. She didn't think she was that good anyway at helping Holly feel better. She had a hard time with platitudes. And much as she cared for Holly, it wasn't easy finding sympathy for a girl with all the freedom and possibility of a single life.

Chad-the-Cad (as he would be known from now on, with all the other hall of famers sporting hyphenated, rhyming nicknames) hadn't been around for long. He had that gym monkey look that Holly favored and Victoria loathed. The oiliness, the plasticky Ken-doll appearance, the too-orange skin. She couldn't help but imagine he had a tiny member with unnaturally yellow pubic hair.

"Well, I wouldn't say he did you a favor, exactly, Holl. I mean, you're good to be rid of him, but I'm sorry he was such a . . ."

"Cad."

"You deserve to be with someone nice. I'm sorry." Her words felt and sounded lame, generic, but she didn't have anything else to offer.

Holly's smile was hard, but determined. "And how's Eric?"

Holly always asked about Eric, but it was strange for her to switch gears so quickly. It was her ritual to dissect the demise of a relationship with minute precision. A cataloguing of he-said and she-said that started off with the salient and salacious but ended up an analysis of tone and intent. Then, interpretations of said analysis. The fact that she wasn't doing this made Victoria feel worried, and almost made her want to ask for the whole story. But she didn't.

"Fine, I guess. Busy with work, as usual," Victoria said, using her stock answer when asked about her husband.

"Gosh, that man works so hard," Holly crooned. She'd always been a fan of Eric's, though Victoria had no idea what he'd done to earn her adoration. He'd always treated her with just a shade up from contempt.

"Yeah, well, you know he's still trying to make partner. It's been intense for a while now."

"Partner," breathed Holly. She sounded like Marilyn Monroe, singing "Happy Birthday" to JFK. Like the word "partner" was the sexiest thing alive. Victoria wanted to tell her that there were, like, a hundred "partners" in his firm. But she decided to let her keep the myth of one man alive, even if it was only Eric. And the less they talked about him, the better.

"Look, Holl, can I tell you something that happened last week? Keep it between you and me?"

"Of course." Holly leaned on her elbows and pressed her large breasts together in a way that looked uncomfortable.

"I don't even know how to put it. I really don't . . ."

"You . . . you aren't pregnant, are you??" Holly interrupted, eyes bulging.

Victoria's mouth dropped, squinting with disgust. "Holly! No!"

"Okay, sorry, but don't look at me like that. It's not like it's out of the realm of possibility. You are married, after all."

Victoria resisted rolling her eyes. She glanced over her shoulder at the wailing child who had now spilled his glass of water all over the table, drowning his salad in the process. "Sorry to disappoint you, but it's not that. You're like the Jewish mother I never had. No . . . it's someone I met last week."

"Someone you met? Okay, who is it? A girl at work?"

"No, it was a *guy*, at the café."

"A guy." Holly's overly contoured eyebrows raised to a peak.

"Yes, a guy. You're not the only one who can meet guys, you know."

"I don't know what to say. You're not—are you—cheating on Eric?" she asked, incredulous.

The shock in Holly's face shamed Victoria. "No! Look—no. I don't even know his name, we didn't speak," Victoria said.

Holly's face relaxed a bit. She wiped her mouth with a paper napkin. "Oh, well then, what's the big deal?"

Victoria regretted bringing it up. There were no words, she realized, that would explain it in a way that Holly would understand. But she was in the middle of it now. "I just—I really felt, a *connection* with this guy. I know it sounds nuts. I saw him, and I felt like we knew each other. And I can't seem to shake it."

Holly looked upset. Her smile was gone. She had a bit of a grumpy expression, and her voice cracked when she spoke. "What about Eric?"

Victoria flushed and looked downward. She pushed around the chickpeas in her bowl absently.

Holly's voice softened, and her eyes became more benevolent. "I mean, most women would *kill* for a guy like Eric. You know that, right? And you're talking soul mates with a random guy at a coffee shop."

"I didn't say soul mates," Victoria said. "Never mind, okay? It's nothing."

There was a disapproving silence. "Just promise me you'll be careful. You don't want to go down this road."

Victoria suddenly felt as if Holly were sitting on her shoulder, like Jiminy Cricket. Jiminy Cricket with huge, fake breasts. She stifled the urge to laugh. She felt the flush of shame creeping up her neck, spidering up to her cheeks and ears.

She nodded. "Got it," she said, knowing full well she actually *did*.

Holly kept talking. "I mean, you couldn't possibly consider it . . . knowing about what happened with Eric's first wife . . ." She trailed off, with a significant pause.

Victoria nodded again. Eric's first wife had left him for her personal trainer. It was a source of shame for him, she assumed, as it was on the list of Things We Don't Talk About EVER. She had gleaned only a scant few things through the years about her husband's first wife, a woman named Carrie, with a dolphin tattoo on her cleavage, as evidenced by the only photograph Victoria had seen of them, on a beach, presumably on their honeymoon, which she'd found at the bottom of one of his desk drawers. They had been married three years when it happened. According to her mother, who had heard the story from Eric's mom, he had been shattered.

"Forget about it," Victoria said, interrupting Holly's monologue about how Chad-the-Cad sculpted his pubic hair like Hitler's moustache (a red flag, in retrospect), poking at spinach leaves ineffectually with her plastic fork. "I don't know what I'm talking about. I'll probably never see the guy again anyway. I'm just being silly. I've been reading too many romance novels." She laughed halfheartedly.

Holly's mouth smiled but her eyes didn't follow suit.

FIVE

THAT NIGHT, AFTER ERIC FELL ASLEEP, VICTORIA LUXURIATED IN the quiet. She conjured His face, and became lost in the beauty of His features, re-creating the scene as he lowered his eyes in reading pose, sipped coffee, crossed his legs at the ankles. She imagined his scent, a mix of soap and sweat, imagined the heat coming off his body and the slight roughness of his hands. She imagined zoning into his dark blue eyes, looking in them deeply, deeper than she'd ever gazed at another person before. So deep that her eyes eventually lost focus and she fell into him, weightless.

She noticed, then, that she had left her body. She was hovering above her bed, as she did most nights. But she wasn't looking down on her body. She was sightless, wrapped up in an embrace. Alone, but at the same time, all encompassed. She could smell Him, she felt His heat, she even heard His heart beating against hers, twinning the rhythm.

Comforted, she remained like this for a while until she felt released from the embrace. Instinctively, she reached out. His heartbeat was still close by, but getting fainter all the time. She floated toward it, a little bit behind. It was difficult to navigate, and sometimes she floated in the wrong direction, almost losing her way. She groped blindly in the dark, following the pulse.

She realized she had left her house when she looked up and saw stars glittering above. A remarkably clear night, Orion's belt shone. She didn't gaze upward for long, as she had to concentrate on the heartbeat, its steady, familiar rhythm guiding her through the night air. The urgency she felt to follow it dominated her thoughts, so it didn't occur to her to wonder at the fact that she had left her house, that she was floating through the air without her body.

She was at quite a height, floating at least twenty feet above the maple trees, avoiding telephone poles and rooftops with ease. In the neighborhoods she was passing through, a car alarm was tripped accidentally by its owner, a dog howled, traffic on the main thoroughfare that she crossed hummed, the people in their fall jackets and scarves on their way home from a nightclub or house party chatted. She admired St. Joseph's Oratory, a huge Catholic basilica with a green dome, as it passed under her, along with Brother André's preserved heart and all the discarded crutches of the healed.

The trip was timeless, dreamy, the heartbeat running through it. It wasn't until she felt the soft brush of branches and the caress of curtains against her arms that she understood she was in someone's house. In the gray-scale light of night, she made out bedroom furniture, a lone figure in the bed. The heartbeat was coming from the figure. As she got closer, she saw that it was Him. His face in repose was more beautiful than she could even have imagined. Seeing it with the luxury of being able to stare gave her a thrill of joy. She gazed at him with a Botticellian expression, serene and adoring. She wanted nothing more than to bring his heart up to hers, for the muscled pumps to beat closely together in raptured synchrony.

Hovering above the bed, she lowered herself and floated toward him. He was lying on his side. She mirrored his position to bring their chests together. His heartbeat entered her head, beating loudly in her ears, reverberating to her core, relentless and enchanting. She moved forward. Pressed close, she could feel the warmth of his breath.

With a ping similar to static shock, she found herself back in her body, in her own bed, alone with her own heartbeat. Eric was next to her in the bed, snoring.

"I was so close," she said quietly to herself, then curled up in the fetal position, hugging herself. She was hit by a pang of separation, but the memory of his face, of his warm breath, made her heart swell, and she allowed a heavy sleep to claim her, darkening her consciousness with its powerful anesthetic.

SIX

She slyly peeled back the sleeve of her white cotton coat.
The tiny numbers on her watch told her five more minutes. Clocks
were forbidden in the spa, where time was not supposed to be an
object—though customers paid by the minute. Even her watch had to
remain hidden, to be glimpsed only at opportune moments.

Her client's body was heavy in relaxation, as was always the case
by the end of a massage treatment. Victoria pressed her aching hands a
last time into the thin shoulders, which were warm and moist from the
oil. The air was heavy in a sleepy, opium-induced way. It smelled like
lavender and peppermint from the essential oils diffusing discretely at
the back of the room.

Five more minutes. Victoria stretched her fingers, which felt
rubbery and cramping. She was tired. She liked to give her clients
their money's worth, and the last thing she wanted was a complaint
to management. Although it was unlikely that this client would have
the guts to complain if she noticed her treatment was five minutes
short.

She was a tiny woman who resembled Shelley Duvall, with
stringy, long black hair and a face that often wore an expression of

horror, not unlike Wendy Torrance's in the bathroom scene in *The Shining*. Her name was all wrong: Bernadette. She looked much more like a Maude or a Mildred, or maybe even an Olive, given her appearance. Victoria decided she was too insubstantial to merit three syllables, the name too weighty for her.

Bernadette now lay on her back, head wedged in the black circular resting spot on the massage table, and had the appearance of being asleep. In this supine position, her small breasts were flattened to an almost androgynous status. Only the triangular outlines of her brassiere visible through the sheet hinted at their existence.

From the moment she was introduced, Victoria understood who Bernadette was. It took only a few moments to see that she was a mouse, a quivering, pathetic creature who had been living with alley cats her whole life. Victoria saw Bernadette as slave to a domineering mother, an obese woman who wore a wig and lay, day and night, on a sagging, flowered couch. She'd hurled demands and insults at Bernadette as a child, and still did. Bernadette was single, had never been paid the least attention by men (unless you counted Uncle Pete, who was dead now, thankfully), and was so lonely she took to people watching using an old telescope she'd found in a box in the upstairs closet.

Bernadette had been Victoria's client for about eight months now, at her doctor's insistence, and in that time had been in three car accidents. None of which were her fault, all rear-enders. She wasn't suited to the aggressive style of Montreal motorists. After each of the accidents, she arrived wearing the Wendy Torrance eyes, showing slightly too much of their whites. Her anxiety was palpable, an invisible millstone burdening her slight frame. Victoria felt, in addition to irritation, pity for the woman. After Bernadette's third accident, Victoria decided to add something to her massage treatment. She used the last five minutes of the session to teach special relaxation techniques, in the hopes that Bernadette might take them to heart and eventually learn to try them at home. Doing this also had the hidden bonus of relieving Victoria's hands from five minutes of deep tissue massage.

Victoria turned off the background noise of whales and waves that had been playing. She lightly touched Bernadette on her three main chakras, then said: "Your body is at peace. Your body is at rest. Feel each of your limbs, where they lie. Your arm—you feel your bicep and shoulder resting in its socket, you feel your elbow holding your forearm just the way it should all the way to the wrist. That wrist in all its intricacy, its lacework of bones, is perfect. It links to your hand, then the fingers. You can even feel your nails. Feel this in all your limbs, how rested and perfectly laid out they are. Your organs. Your hair . . ."

She noticed Bernadette's breathing became even deeper during this exercise. Her childlike rib cage rose higher with each intake of breath.

"Once you acknowledge your wondrous and rested and perfect body, set it aside in your mind. Set it aside like a heavy object that you have been carrying a long time. A bag, with handles that cut into your palms. A burden that is causing you distress. Set aside your lovely body. Let it lie there in repose, in deep, sentient rest. Let it continue breathing. Let its heart continue to beat. It is contented and calm. It can lie by itself in its heavy rest. You can leave it behind. You are light, so light you cannot be contained by this body. You are like a bubble in a glass of carbonated water. You cannot be weighed down."

Victoria glided noiselessly through the room as she put used towels in the hamper for cleaning. She leaned against the smooth white cabinet, both hands tightly gripping the glossy surface.

"You are a helium balloon, unconcerned about the weight you carry. You are a child's laugh, surging forward without holding back. You rise up, up, up so light, lighter than air. You can see your body lying in repose below you, you can see it is okay in its weight, and that you are free of the weight. You, and all that you are, are light, and love, and peace."

Victoria fought the burning in her eyes, fought it, but it was inevitable. Her eyes stung painfully and she squeezed them shut, two large tears tumbling down shamefully and splashing onto the disdainful white veneer. She swallowed a silent, painful sob. One hand quickly brushed the telltale wetness from her eyes. Two deep breaths. When she knew she could trust her voice again, she gently opened her mouth. "Just light, and love, and peace."

THE STREET OUTSIDE THE SPA WAS CROWDED WITH PEDESTRIANS, A struggle to navigate. Victoria was always in the wrong place. Her shoulder was bumped by a man rushing by, her foot barely escaped the wheels of a bulldozing stroller being pushed by an unrepentant nanny. Victoria, needing a break, stopped in front of a dreary busker who was doing a bad rendition of "Bird on the Wire" by Leonard Cohen. She gave him a dollar anyway. Victoria always supported street artists. One never knew what a bit of encouragement could mean to a person.

Bernadette had been her last client of the day. This was fortunate. Victoria's nerves were shot. She felt as if she had transferred her strength into Bernadette and traded it for her current delicateness. The Wendy Torrance eyes were now lodged in her sockets, as if she were seeing through them, frightened and frightening. She knew she should follow her work shift with a visit to the gym. That was her usual routine, to work the neediness of her clients off. But she didn't have it in her today. She hated the gym, only went because Eric stressed the need for cardio and core strength. They never worked out together; his routine was much earlier and more intense.

Each step felt deliberate; her mind had to remind her body to do each thing, like a mother encouraging a toddler. Keep going, it's okay, yes, one foot in front of the other. Yes, you can tuck that hair behind your ear, that's better. Stop to wait for the light to change.

Something in her told her to walk to Café au Lait, where she had been the first time she saw Him. She had the book in her bag. It would be good to read something, good to steady herself with a hot, milky, caffeinated beverage.

The ding of the bell as she opened the door, the checkered floor tiles, the smell of coffee beans, all provided a welcome-home feeling for her upon entering the café. The woman with the beehive hairdo nodded kindly in her direction, midwipe with her usual cloth. Even the dirty cloth gave Victoria a sense of comfort.

She found a place to sit with an unobstructed view of the entire café, realizing just then that she was really here in the hopes of seeing Him again. She hadn't given much thought to her appearance, and panicked, searching through her bag for the enamel compact mirror Eric had brought her from one of his business trips to Europe. "So you can check your makeup and freshen up a bit during the day," he had suggested helpfully. "Your eyeliner sometimes smudges. And you don't want to be looking like a raccoon, do you?"

The mirror told her that her eyeliner was fine. It was almost four, about the same time that she had seen Him the other day. Perhaps he, too, lived by a predictable schedule? She hoped not, but at the same time, it would be convenient if he did. She wondered if he would see her this time. His face lighting up with recognition. "Oh, it's You," he would murmur. Then, shyly, "From the other night?"

The idea of his recognizing her seemed the most natural thing. After all, she had recognized him, hadn't she? He might even remember their nocturnal meeting. Granted, he never opened his eyes the whole time she hovered by his bed, even when she lay next to him, so he wouldn't know her face. But maybe it would be enough for him to inhabit the same room as she did. His heart reaching out to hers as it had that evening. Her pulse beckoning him in a familiar pace.

She took her book out and tried to read. It was difficult, because she kept looking up hopefully every time someone came in or out. It also didn't help that she hated the book. She was close to the end, and knew that the redemptive ending she had been hoping for was not going to come, and this infuriated her. She hoped He would bring the book with him again, so she could commiserate with him over the experience of being manipulated by the author. Surely He felt the same way. How amazing it was that readers could be led by the hand to feel and react. Like drones, gobbling page after page of words, coerced into feelings, concocted into a brew that convinced, assured, and spoon-fed the phoniness so gently it was accepted and, yes, loved with devotion! Independent thought swept aside, the seduction was complete.

The crying man was in his bathroom again, performing more self-harm. Sick of the book, Victoria looked up, only to witness a grotesque, prologued nose-picking session by an elderly man at a nearby table, who could have fit a fist up his extraordinarily large nostrils. When he finally found what he had been digging for, Victoria looked away. She turned the book over to read the enthusiastic blurb declaring the book to be *A towering monument!* She dug her nail across the words, a rebellious act of book defilement.

In an effort to self-soothe, Victoria directed her thoughts to a familiar scenario. One that involved Eric, traveling by plane for work, something he did several times each year.

She imagined him, smartly dressed, in first class, sipping from a highball glass and eyeing the female flight attendant's comely figure—*A little more ice, if you don't mind?*—before returning his serious concentration to a file laid out on the tray table in front of him. Eric adjusting his neck pillow fussily, making a few decisive red-

inked check marks on the top sheet, then confirming the time on his
large fancy watch and sighing. He wouldn't have time for a shower
before the meeting with Reginald. And then, with a whoosh, a sudden loss of altitude that wasn't correcting itself. A woman, screaming.
His drink, rolling down the aisle toward the front of the plane. Fast,
fast, fast, all happening so fast. One bird's fall from the sky and another, soaring free.

Before the airplane had a chance to reach its fiery destiny, Victoria shook herself out of the vision. Why did she keep bothering to go
there anyway? She knew she couldn't soar, not in this situation. No. It
just didn't sit right with her, the demise of all the other people on the
plane. The woman with the yappy dog, the newly immigrated family
from India, the schoolteacher with a passion for botany, the twin boys
in matching sweaters on the way to visit their ailing grandfather. She
just couldn't do it, not even in her private thoughts. It wasn't their
fault. They shouldn't have to pay the price for her freedom.

She kept lifting her empty cup to her lips, every so often for-
getting that she had finished her latte at least half an hour ago. The
optimism that she had been experiencing, the optimism that had had
her jerking her head up every time the door opened with its welcoming chime, was transforming into disappointment. She would have
to leave soon, she was already cutting it close. Dinner still needed
making and she only had about an hour before Eric would be home.

Inwardly, she willed Him to appear at the café's door, using her
father's motto, "I think, therefore I am." He had injected this saying
into many a lecture, with his long index finger pointed in the air theat-
rically, in a misguided attempt to instill some kind of self-sufficiency
in his daughter. He never seemed to know that Victoria thought *all
the time.*

She knew her father wouldn't appreciate her using his favorite
saying in this case, but what he didn't know wouldn't hurt him.

At any rate, it didn't work. He didn't appear at the door. She put her things in her purse, tossed the empty coffee cup, and left the café in a staccato, self-loathing clip. There was barely enough time to get to the store to pick up the chicken Eric favored.

Under the fluorescent lights near the entrance of her neighborhood IGA, Victoria veered her cart, which had a wonky wheel that tugged to the left, toward the organic aisle. Eric preferred his food to be organic. She had a vague belief that eating organic didn't matter all that much, but never voiced this thought. It's not like they couldn't afford it, so why argue? She picked up organic blue corn chips and a twelve-dollar jar of organic salsa. She already had the free-range chicken in her cart. Eric loved chicken. She grabbed cereal, the most joyless bark mulch she could find, and a carton of coconut milk (Eric was "off" soy milk these days, thank goodness, but fancied himself dairy-sensitive, so no cow's milk this month). She had some mangled-looking carrots already in her cart, still wearing their dirty green tops, as well as a few lackluster tomatoes and a rock-hard avocado.

She could do grocery shopping with her eyes closed, almost. It didn't vary all that much. Lots and lots of chicken, a smattering of accepted, grotty, free-range vegetables, and organic snacks. Eric wasn't all that adventurous. But it wasn't like she was Julia Child. She could live with it. It could be a lot worse.

The truth was, Eric was a white-bread guy raised by a mother whose cuisine came from the backs of several boxes, and who was reluctant to introduce "different foods" to the dinner table. Eric's mother was a fifties housewife, for all intents and purposes, who made a wicked Jell-O mold, Velveeta cheese sauce slathered on steamed broccoli, sweet potatoes topped with marshmallows, neon-orange macaroni and cheese, and, of course, chicken. Now that Eric was an adult, very health conscious, and (let's be honest) aware of eating trends, too, he took that palate and mashed it into the organic aisle. No more marshmallows or Jell-O (unless they were eating at his parents') and the mac and cheese had to be Annie's brand, if it entered their house at all. Occasionally, he asked her to prepare something "exotic," like eggplant, kale, or, more recently, starfruit. But he liked the idea of gastronomic adventures much better than the reality.

Sometimes Victoria longed to bring home a frozen pizza, or make sloppy joes with seasoning from a package. She thought she'd like to see the look on Eric's face as she poured him a tall glass of kumquat Fanta from a glugging, green two-liter plastic bottle. He might have a stroke.

Victoria continued to aimlessly push her cart past the refrigerated section, which contained a smattering of premade vegetarian options. Between the tofurky and paleo lasagna, she closed her eyes and tried to keep from judging Eric. She was being so unfair. Of course everyone was influenced by trends and the world around them. It wasn't like she was immune to such things. Eric was really very healthy. It was a legitimate interest of his. He exercised every day, he played badminton a few times a week at the club. He stayed away from processed sugars. He read articles on health that he forwarded to her every week or so. Just yesterday, in her in-box: "Fine-tune your stomach floor with probiotics!" That was thoughtful.

It did her no good to focus on the negative. She needed to accept Eric, everything about him, even his puffy nipples—because that's what you did when you loved someone. And he wasn't going to change. She needed to accept Eric and their life together. Once she did that, her heart and mind would be at peace.

She practiced positive thinking as she walked home. It was after five, so the sidewalks were full of people heading to their cars or a metro station. The sunlight had that fleeting, magical, golden quality just before it dips away for the night. There was a coolness creeping into the air. She didn't have a long way to go; their building wasn't far from the grocery store.

As the handles of her reusable bags cut into the creases of her palms, Victoria reminded herself of all Eric's good qualities. He was clean. He was good at his job. He provided a great standard of living. He was predictable. Her parents liked him. Holly liked him. He didn't require sex very often. And a hand-job now and then took care of things.

She continued these thoughts on a loop, hoping that her heart would feel warm and that the pervasive heaviness that had emerged during her session with Bernadette would lift. It didn't.

However, she maintained a clear, uncreased expression on her face and managed to smile at Bert, the building's concierge, greeting him by name as she always did when he opened the elevator door for her.

The lobby and elevator were like an extension of the spa, in Victoria's mind. Both spotless, both decorated with flawless white tiles and sterile lighting. At the fifteenth floor, she got out and the white world continued. It was Thursday, so the apartment smelled faintly of cleaner. Molly cleaned every Monday and Thursday. She could also detect the air freshener that Eric insisted on using in the bathroom. It had an artificial, floral smell that Victoria hated. She preferred essential oils but Eric didn't, complaining from time to time that she came home smelling of her work.

She walked through the sparse, spacious hallway to the kitchen and began to prepare dinner. It was 5:35, which meant she was on track for dinner being ready by 6:20, which was about five minutes after Eric would return from work. Which was fine because he usually took a three-minute shower upon arrival, or made himself a drink and relaxed a few minutes while reading the entertainment news on his phone. Knowing how much Eric appreciated routine, she set herself to work, preheating the oven, peeling the carrots, seasoning the meat lightly. She appreciated the quiet of the apartment. She moved with care, unobtrusively, barely disturbing her surroundings with a clang or a staccato of chop.

Eric's arrival was marked with the click of the door at 6:13. He wordlessly beelined to the bathroom. The shower hummed seconds later and she heard the swish of the glass door as it closed.

When he emerged, in a new white polo shirt and dark-wash jeans (his usual après-work attire), dinner was steaming on the plates and Victoria was just setting them on the table.

"Wine?" she asked. She held the pinot gris in her hand, with an inquisitive expression, hesitating over his glass.

He nodded, businesslike. She poured the wineglass to about half full.

He sniffed it, closing his eyes as though in prayer. "Pink grapefruit, charcoal, just a hint of basil. But really, quite fruit-forward."

They ate, and she tried to keep her noises to a minimum, because hearing her chew disgusted him. His jaw clicked slightly when he ate, something that irritated her, though she knew she was being unreasonable, that it was out of his control.

She was going to ask him how his day had been, she sometimes did that. But she did not perceive an invitation to chat, so she kept silent.

When he was finished, he looked at her. "Thanks," he said. She smiled demurely and nodded, a response he tended to like.

He rose and brought his plate to the sink.

He looked a little less serious as he paced across the room to their large cream-colored Italian leather sectional, which was made custom for them and cost a fortune. He turned on the television and happily surveyed all the shows in queue that he had recorded.

Eric liked his shows. Not network TV of course. Nothing so pedestrian as *The Mentalist* or *Everybody Loves Raymond*. He watched all the "good shows" on independent channels. And he really watched them all. He kept up with them week to week, and binge-watched those he missed. His favorites were (but not limited to) *Breaking Bad*, *The Sopranos*, *Game of Thrones*, *Nurse Jackie*, *Fargo*, *The Fall*, *Luther*, *The L Word*, *Legit*, *Better Call Saul*, and—she couldn't think of the rest. Victoria didn't have much interest in television, and that was okay with him. He preferred it to be a solitary pleasure, as her reading was to her. He talked about shows to colleagues, clients, and people at the club, even his parents, perhaps to show that he was connected to the world or on the cutting edge of pop culture. She often heard him make comments to colleagues and friends that began with "Oh, that's like a scene straight out of <insert TV show name>." It succeeded. People usually laughed and agreed heartily. Or it became an opportunity for Eric to fully explain the show and make a fun recommendation, giving a canned plot summary ad nauseam.

When he watched his shows, Victoria read on the other end of the vast white sectional. It had taken awhile for her to learn to concentrate on her book with the television blaring in the background, but it didn't bother her anymore. It was better to be there, sociably, in the room. It made the obsessive television watching seem almost normal if she was there with him. If she didn't, he seemed embarrassed, almost petulant at the end of the evening, as though she hadn't been interested in his company.

If he laughed loudly while watching a show, she would smile with him absently. If he reacted with shock, she would meet his eyes briefly in consolation. Mainly, though, he watched, engrossed and in his own world, keeping a running commentary. *Would you believe that? Oh, I knew it, I knew it, I knew it, I knew it. What'd I tell you?*

Classic Coen brothers! Just classic! And she read. She read book, after book, after book.

He encouraged her reading. He bought her a tablet and gave her carte blanche to purchase ebooks to her heart's content. He didn't, however, wish for her to purchase physical books, because he hated the accumulation of things, and he also didn't see the logic of it. "Would you read it again?" he asked. "I don't know—I might," she had once ventured tentatively. He shook his head dismissively. "Dust collectors," he said.

Victoria preferred paperback books, ones that she could carry in her purse, ones that she handled in the most loving way, ones that had her notes in the margins and highlights over gasp-worthy phrases. But she respected Eric's need for streamlined living. And, as he had pointed out, there were "so many more good things" about ebooks. Price, for one—although that wasn't an issue for them. The ease with which she could store so many dust gatherers in such a small place. The ability to look up words and to copy and paste quotations on social media. He encouraged her to carry her tablet in her purse so she could read wherever she went. So, she did. For a while.

Victoria just couldn't stay away from real books, though. She needed the sensory experience. The sometimes musty smell of the paper and ink, the visual progression as the dog-eared pages she had read became thicker than the unread, the frequent glance at the cover or the author photo. She borrowed the books from the library, much to Eric's bewilderment. "Who knows who touched those books," he said once, disgust creasing his brow at a battered copy of *Ethan Frome*. "It's probably covered in mold and larvae. And God knows what else."

That evening, in a quiet stolen moment, she had wiped both sides of the cover on his pillow.

SEVEN

VICTORIA VISITED THE CAFÉ THREE MORE TIMES. THREE CARE-fully chosen outfits, three different shades of lipstick, each picked out at the drugstore, solely selected for the name of the shade. Midnight Kisses had her looking like a late-blooming goth, its dark burgundy tones bleeding in spidery legs outward from her mouth. Bewitched, which was far too purple, stood out insolently against the mauve of her blouse, and had her hoping that he wouldn't show up to see her looking so clownish. Soul Mate was a lot less notable, a more sensible color. But it didn't do her any good in the end.

Looking at the colorful, unfamiliar gashes left behind on her coffee mug had been truly depressing, and raised her self-awareness regarding her level of desperation. This man had a life. He certainly didn't haunt cafés, day in, day out. He wasn't looking for her, or for anyone. He had other things, other people, to occupy him in a meaningful way.

Nevertheless, this unsuccessful stalking propelled her through the week, gave her impetus to rise from her bed, made the days dreamlike with the fantasy of Him always so close at hand. His face was her mind's screensaver. She might lash herself for being pathetic, but she had to admit, her life was better with Him in it, even in this tiny, desperate capacity. What that said about her life before Him, she didn't want to acknowledge.

Part of her—a very small part of her—was relieved each time her attempts to see Him failed. Then, when she returned home, she could honestly say she'd gone to the café that day and read her book. Nothing more complex than that. A clean, unsullied sentence. "Not much, just read my book." Something in her knew that these sweet, truthful declarations, as innocent as a single daisy offered by an out-stretched hand, were precious, even if the flower might be rife with tiny, larval-stage aphids.

So, as was her habit, she stopped in the café, not planning to stay long that day. She needed a coffee and thought she'd make a quick sweep of the place, a fast check to satisfy her addict-like curiosity. In line, a young girl with frizzy brown hair and a rumpled private-school kilt pushed past her on the way to the bathroom. Fourteen and already servile to a nicely entrenched eating disorder, birthed from devout kosher practices at home, and a father who pinched her waist every time he hugged her. A girl hard to pity because of her strident need to be loudest and first all the time. Thus she tended to follow people around rather than earn their concern. She was going to be a nightmare when she started dating, though that wouldn't be for a while—her body was still prepubescent. Victoria was almost certain the girl's name was Rachel. She looked exactly like a Rachel.

Victoria was giving her order when she heard a man's voice in line behind her. His voice.

"I told the guy we needed him Thursday. He hasn't gotten back to me. I know. Yeah. I know. Look, he's an asshole but he can afford to be one. He's got work lined up around the block. Yeah. Yeah, I know. Give him another day, then hound him. Okay. Bye."

The barista with the triple nose piercings hardly disguised a frank look in his direction, her rosebud lips parting, tongue resting against her front teeth in an unconscious, universal signal. Victoria bristled, narrowing her eyes and sticking the barista with imaginary voodoo pins. There would be no change plunked in the tip jar today.

She didn't have to turn to know, but she did, involuntarily. It *was* Him. Her legs went limp and rubbery, like they had in elementary school when she'd been bullied by a tall, pimply girl whose family was Jehovah's Witness. She felt perspiration under her arms, even though she didn't usually sweat. The nose-pierced barista asked her a question, looking at her expectantly. She fumbled through payment. In order to access her wallet, she pulled out her book, and placed it on the counter. The crying man book was so thick it barely fit in her purse. Eric didn't like women who carried big purses. They represented clutter to him. He hated watching women rifle through their bags, never finding what they were looking for.

Two customers behind her, He was waiting politely in line, looking at his phone. He didn't look up at her or notice her book. She was too harried to feel disappointment over this. She was too panicked to feel elation at his sudden proximity. She felt as if she were the only actor in a play, and the rest of the world spectators. She felt a paranoia that there was something hanging out of her nose, a crust at the corner of her mouth. Or, god forbid, her eyeliner was smudged in that way Eric hated.

She moved to the side counter to pick up her coffee order. She surreptitiously swept her sleeve over her nose and mouth. Her hands felt enormous and hot. The barista called out names. A man wearing a fishing vest pushed past her, unapologetic, smelling of alcohol. A woman in cream-colored pumps and white jeans reached over Victoria's shoulder, harboring an irritation that Victoria realized was due to her close presence at the counter. The rest of the patrons waited a considerate two steps back from the counter and moved forward only once their names were called. Victoria, embarrassed at her coffee-shop gaffe, slunk back two steps. She knew better than this.

"Hey. Excuse me? Miss?"

It was Him. HE was speaking—to HER.

Her purse suddenly slipped down her shoulder as though it had shrunk in width and could no longer accommodate the leather strap. She clumsily adjusted herself, stammering a response. "Yes?" So hopeful, it was pathetic.

He smiled slightly. "You left this, over there." It was her book.

His voice sounded to her like refreshing, cold water over gravel and reminded her of biting lips, or maybe she just wanted to bite his lips? She remained mesmerized, staring at the cover for a moment that dragged.

"Oh . . . thank you," she managed, recovering. She reached for the novel. "How could I forget *this*."

Her attempt at irony missed its target. He nodded. "Yeah, power-ful stuff," he said. "I'm reading it too. Not so far along as you, though. I'm a slow reader." He indicated to where her bookmark lay, close to the end.

Powerful stuff? Powerfully bad, she thought. Like an emetic. So powerful it makes me want to vomit, makes me furious that I'm stupid enough to continue reading this torture porn. Sure, powerful.

"Pack a few Kleenexes," she heard a strange, smiling version of herself say. "It gets really intense." She patted the book (fondly? really?) before shoving it into her purse.

He nodded. "Yeah, for sure."

"Victoria, vanilla latte, nonfat," shouted out the barista.

"That's me," Victoria found herself cooing, trying to sound cool, again having the sensation that every move she made was a carefully analyzed stage direction. The two steps she took forward felt forced and unnatural. Reaching forward and taking her coffee felt like play-acting in the worst possible way. She wondered if he was looking at her rear. Wondered if everyone was looking at her rear. Eric, in an earlier, playful moment during their courtship had joked that it was one of her better assets.

She fiddled with stir sticks and lids and was putting a sleeve on her to go cup when she heard the barista again.

"Luke, americano."

He advanced, the perfect two steps. Of course, Luke. Of course, americano.

She waited, childlike and paralyzed by the stir sticks, holding her cup with both hands. But his was in his own mug brought from home and he didn't require stir sticks or a sleeve. So he just grabbed it from the counter, consulted his phone again, and with a quick nod of his perfectly barbered head as he passed, exited stage right. He left her agape, feeling like an understudy who had forgotten her lines.

Victoria stayed in the café for several minutes longer. She sat by the fireplace on the rock hearth, waiting for her heart to slow to a manageable pace. She knew his name. He had spoken to her. She had spoken to him. They were in each other's lives, however minutely. That she had not conveyed her disgust about the book was of little importance. That he had seemed to like it was nothing to focus on. Perhaps he was being polite, as she had been, thinking that she was enjoying it. Why else would she carry it around and read it to the last page? Maybe one day this would be the great joke, the great ice-breaker of their relationship, when they both laughed about how they had been too nervous to be honest in their first meeting. They would keep their copies of the book out of sentimentality. They would always be grateful for that horrid book.

No, none of that was important now. What was important was that they were no longer strangers. Had she sensed a glimpse of recognition in his eyes? He had called her "miss," a rather formal way of addressing a stranger. Had he already forgotten their nocturnal meeting? Was that possible?

EIGHT

MONTREAL'S ONCE LONG-AWAITED SUMMER WAS FINALLY OVER. The city was experiencing rare days of temperate coolness, static in the air. If the seasons were a family, winter was the big, dominating brother. Spring, the weakest of the siblings, would appear for the briefest glimpse before the heavy, humid air of summer took over. But not before bringing forth determined greens and blooms that had been suffocated under snow and ice the previous six months. Spring's reign, though short, would bring the city back to life with a necessary aggression. Summer was moody, heavy, humid, the air pregnant with the possibility of storm. The city awhir with AC units. People flocked outdoors despite the suffocating humidity. Music festivals, street markets, a day at a man-made "beach," lunch on a *terrasse*. And then, the relief of autumn arrived. No rain, just cool, cleansing air, which released the shock of color in foliage for the precious days before those very leaves became garbage collected in orange bags on the side of the road.

Victoria hated the inevitable path to winter that autumn paved, but adored the dry, startlingly blue sky of October. It made her believe in beauty, in spite of death hovering close by.

It was the first Sunday of October, and Victoria was doing battle in the kitchen, chopping and slicing. The "parental units," as Eric called them, were coming over for dinner. Both she and Eric had type-A parents who were still very much involved in their lives, so it made sense to kill two birds with one stone. Initially, they alternated having dinner with their respective parents every two weeks. That quickly became too much, and since their parents actually knew and appeared to like each other, they decided to combine the separate dinners in an all-in-one evening. The frequency was diminished as well as the intensity of concentration. The parents were too distracted by each other to focus solely on their progeny.

Victoria felt a great deal of anxiety preparing for this particular meal. Not only did the preparation of something "suitable" concern her, but she had the most worrisome and persistent thought that she should broach the subject of leaving Eric, even just temporarily, if just to find herself again. She suspected that either her or Eric's life depended on it—and she had to at least *try*.

She had inherited her mother's perfectionism but not her flair in the kitchen. She was also limited severely by the white-bread palate of her husband and her in-laws. She was always in search of a slightly original way to prepare chicken that did not include excess spice or root vegetables. There was also a nix on mushrooms, and—this was new—a minimum of dairy, which apparently now gave her father-in-law terrible flatulence.

Victoria's mother, Deirdre, offered to prepare the meal with her once, but it turned into a two hour drilling-for-information session as well as a delicious Thai curry that was inedible to Eric's family. A complete disaster. Since then, Victoria had taken the burden of the meal on herself. The result was more bland food and another opportunity for her parents to blink in mystification at her, but it was still better that way.

Deirdre and Mick Cavanagh probably believed their only child had been dropped from the sky by aliens, rather than having come from a miraculous and complex mix of their DNA. It was glaringly obvious to anyone that they had very little in common with their daughter, and that they were baffled by who she was on a regular basis. Physically, Deirdre and Mick looked almost like siblings. Both were lean and tall, with Nordic coloring—blond hair and fair, almost invisible eyebrows. Deirdre was slender with small breasts. Victoria, almost a half foot shorter than her mother, had darker hair and a curvier figure.

The Cavanaghs were powerful lawyers and had met in law school. Deirdre was a well-known family lawyer who dealt with high-profile divorce and custody battles, and Mick was a high-end personal injury lawyer. They both loved what they did and had a continued passion for law. They had assumed for many years that their daughter would follow suit, and that the only question was what type of law she would practice. But their hopes grew thinner and thinner as she progressed through high school. They had marveled at her "lack of direction." They were disappointed at her average grades, despite the tutors. They were unimpressed with her interest in literature, at her tendency to hole up in her room reading a book. Fiction was *entertainment*, her father was known to observe, when finding his daughter "in the stacks" of her bedroom. A book, he would declare, is no more than an old-fashioned movie, before movies existed. Not something to focus one's life on. But it had been the yoga that had turned them catatonic. It made literature look a hell of a lot better.

Once she had turned thirty, her parents had given up on "getting" her direction. Because it was their nature, lecturing was something they continued with no real hope for change. But ever since her marriage to Eric, they had been relatively content. They saw Eric as Victoria's direction, and they approved of him. She may not have found a career they could be proud of, but at least she'd married someone with one—success by proxy.

As a child, Victoria had fantasized about being an orphan. After reading *Anne of Green Gables*, Victoria fell in love with Anne Shirley and her story. She wanted to be like her, down to her red braids and straw hat. She loved the idea of an orphan's life, hopping from home to home before finding wonderful parents like Marilla and Matthew. It seemed like a reinvention of life. Of course, she didn't think much about the bad parents she could end up with, like Mrs. Hewitt, who beat Anne and made her slavishly care for her thirteen brats. She didn't think about the cruel power of chance, and how Anne could have ended up with a completely different story. But she liked the idea of having a new life. Even then, she felt mismatched with her parents, as though she had been dropped off at the wrong door.

Deirdre and Mick always arrived first, and they did so now, with aggressive punctuality—i.e., half an hour early. They brought with them an almost violent energy, like two Vikings dressed in severe business attire.

"Hello, daughter," Deirdre said at the door, with a formal air kiss on both cheeks, pressing a jar of pickled herring into Victoria's hands. After unwinding his cashmere scarf and draping it over the back of a chair, Mick wordlessly performed the same air kisses.

They preceded Victoria into the kitchen and perched on the bar stools, much like vultures. The chicken was roasting, and the smell was pleasant and warm.

Victoria busied herself with ice and gin, her parents' traditional drink before supper.

"Thank you, darling," Mick said absently, receiving his glass.

"Where's Eric?" Deirdre wanted to know, her eyebrows arching her forehead into an omega sign.

At that moment, Eric entered the room, accustomed to the Cavanaghs' early arrivals. He was wearing a navy sweater that came to a slight V close to his Adam's apple, with a white shirt buttoned to the top underneath. It had the appearance of choking him.

Deirdre smiled approvingly. "Well howdy—*partner*, is it?" Her teeth were long and her wide smile showed her canines, wolflike.

Victoria busied herself with place mats and cutlery while they talked. She hadn't had a chance to set the table before her parents' arrival.

Eric smiled, too, in mock bashfulness. "Ah, not yet, I'm afraid. The announcement was postponed till next month."

Both Cavanaghs' expressions clouded. "What? Well, that's vexing. But you'll get it, Eric. I can't see why not."

Eric smiled again at Deirdre. "That's the plan," he said, taking his drink from Victoria and inspecting it for fingerprints before taking a sip. "Wexler had to go out of town, and I think they postponed the announcement for when he returns."

Her parents nodded knowingly. Mick slapped Eric on the back. "Sure, sure. They want to get away with paying you your pauper's rate for another month before you really start to rake it in."

They both guffawed.

Eric always made this part easy. He was gifted at talking with her parents, asking about the big legal cases they would enjoy expounding on, delivering a well-versed comment about the stock market, making a wry political comment that was both intelligent and noncommittal. They loved him. They delighted in him. Victoria was certain that they had wished to have this kind of relationship with her, but had been cruelly thwarted, their hopes dashed when they had discovered their child was an alien, speaking a different language. Now Eric was their child. It suddenly occurred to her that they prob-

ably came early so they would have a chance to dote on him, uninter-
rupted, before his parents arrived.

This didn't really sting Victoria. She didn't mind having their attention diverted, laser-beamed on someone else. It was a relief, really,
to assume the role of mute caterer for the evening. It wasn't always
this way, of course. Sometimes her parents would arrive, bees snugly
in bonnets, armed with a barrage of questions, some magazine clip-
pings from the business section of *The Gazette*, and maybe an email
address of a friend of a colleague who would be good to talk with
about her stalled career—after all, what was a degree in literature
good for, if it wasn't for getting into law?

While they continued to trade anecdotes and bathe in mutual admiration, Victoria prepared a couscous salad (for her parents, who
needed more culinary stimulation) and a basic green salad (for Eric
and his parents). She plated a side dish of red and yellow beets that she
had picked up at Première Moisson that afternoon. A little cheat she
didn't think anyone would mind.

She had just recently finished reading *A Thousand Acres* by Jane
Smiley, in which the main character finds out her sister had an affair
with her lover, and she is devastated. She gives her sister sauerkraut
that she seasoned with poisonous herbs, and then anticipates her sister's death, a delicious, dark waiting game that appealed to Victoria's
sense of drama. The beets made her think of the poisoned sauerkraut.
She wished Eric liked beets.

Her mother was asking Eric about his recent badminton tournament, giving his bicep a sensual squeeze that made Victoria's stomach
turn, when the doorbell rang. She escaped the scene to answer the
door, letting in Joan and Dick.

Joan brought a bouquet of white lilies, as usual. Victoria wasn't
crazy about their cloying pungent smell, but she accepted them with

a gracious thank you and pressed her lips against the older woman's cool, powdery cheek. Joan smiled broadly, exposing a line of coral lipstick along her teeth. She always had lipstick on her teeth. "You have a little . . ." she used to say, with a gesture to her mother-in-law, who would grimace and bring out a small mirror, using her fingers to swipe and smear. After a half dozen times, Victoria just gave up.

Joan had never worked. She had been the support to Dick his entire career in the banking world, his "right-hand woman" as he liked to say. Short and plump, she wore twin sets in bright colors, and for decoration, always, always a brooch. She also wore flesh-toned nylons. Even when she was doing nothing at home.

Dick was a tall man with a head too small for his body. Victoria thought "pinhead" every time she saw him. She found herself analyzing his head while zoning out of conversations. He would have been much more attractive if his head were bigger. Like the grinch's heart, his head was two sizes too small.

He was ready to retire but hadn't just yet. Some of his investments needed to "perk" a little while yet. The boat was expensive to maintain. A few more years, a few more bonuses, and they would be "footloose and fancy-free." He could be a little bit creepy, with how he often rested his eyes on her breasts. It was a subconscious thing, Victoria told herself, and fairly indiscriminate.

"Sorry we're a little late, love," Joan crooned to her son as they entered the kitchen. The clock read 6:07. "Your father insisted on a parking spot he found just in front of your building, then spent about ten minutes trying to read the signs and gave up in the end. We parked a mile away."

Dick grumbled a little, though his eyes were smiling. "Ten of your mother's minutes is about two in real time, as you know, son."

"Oh, my Dick," Joan said adoringly, as she rolled her eyes. She always referred to her husband as "my Dick," which embarrassed everyone, but she was totally innocent to how this sounded. If someone laughed or tried to make a joke about it, she never noticed.

In this room, however, there was no giggling or snide comment. The specter of a glance passed between Deirdre and Mick that only Victoria detected.

Victoria murmured something comforting about how difficult it was to find parking, it was the bane of her existence.

Then, with the efficiency of a skilled geisha, Victoria quickly assembled the meal on the table, and it proceeded like every other monthly dinner. Except that, for Victoria, there was a glimmer of hope in her heart. She didn't quite know how to name it, but it was there, lifting her mouth into a natural smile, allowing minutes to glide by easier than usual. She wondered how and when she would suggest the personal reprieve she had been thinking about.

Sitting opposite each other, as per tradition, the parents approved of one another. Dick and Joan had known both the Cavanaghs by reputation and from the many functions that they mutually attended during the year. The Cavanaghs knew Dick well enough too. He was a fixture in Montreal's financial industry. He'd made his presence known for decades and had done very well for himself. So they always had plenty to talk about.

The fact that Eric's parents' money was aged by four generations did create a fissure in the otherwise pristine niceties of their relationship. Victoria's parents were self-made and proud of it, as was demonstrated by their comparatively ostentatious style and demeanor. Deirdre wore oversized, glittering jewelry; Mick drove a banana yellow, Italian sports car; and they decorated their home like a Roman palace, complete with replica statues of *David* and *Venus de Milo* flanking their large marble fireplace. Dick and Joan, by contrast, tended to wear their wealth like a comfortable coat that was never quite shrugged off. Joan's jewelry was all heirloom, their house filled

with tasteful, valuable antiques. They were also of an older genera-
tion, and seemed old even for their vintage. They had had their only
child later in life, when Joan was forty-two, declaring resolutely in the
face of her doctor's concern: "No child of *mine* will be a mongoloid!"

Inevitably, the parents' talk came around to something in which
they all had an undiluted, common interest: their children. The focus
was primarily on Eric. And then it was usually Joan, like a 1950s
model of etiquette, who turned her inquiries to Victoria.

"And so dear, how is it at the spa?" she asked now. She would always say it like "the spa" was in air quotes, as though it was amusing
for her to say. She wasn't being unkind, though. She didn't actually
care about Victoria's lack of vocation. In her mind, Victoria's place
was to support her son and provide babies when the time was right.
"The spa" was, to Joan, a temporary and even healthy diversion.

"Oh, I can't complain," Victoria answered. Her words never
came easily. She felt a reticence that she had to fight against, an un-
willingness to talk. "I keep busy and my clients are happy, I think."

"That's so nice, dear." Joan smiled absently, following the other
conversation between Dick and Eric about the stock market and how
a recent comment made by the president, sterling man of character
that he was, had caused a significant dip in some of their investments.

"Though, I was thinking . . ." Victoria struggled to find the
words and the courage to say them. "It might be a good idea for me to
take a . . . hiatus . . . maybe . . ."

"A hiatus?" asked Joan, still smiling, but the smile was more frozen in place, her attention, once divided between the two conversations, now on Victoria.

"Yes, well, I was thinking it might be good, to take some time,
you know . . . for me," Victoria said, feeling her face get hot.

Joan's face became more serious. "I don't understand, dear. I
thought you were happy at the spa."

Victoria squirmed. "Oh, I am. I don't know. I was just thinking it might be good to have a little break, from everything . . . for a little while. Get out of Montreal, even."

"Oh, a vacation! Didn't you lovebirds come back from a cruise, just last year?"

"Oh, right, that's right," Victoria said vaguely, recalling the endless casino nights and the tacky "black-tie affairs" on the ship, as well as the seasickness that had confined her to their stateroom for three days. And then, without even realizing, she blurted what she'd been thinking about for days. "No, not a vacation—at least, not for Eric. I was thinking I might go somewhere. Just me. You know, to—regroup. It might be good. That saying—absence makes the heart grow fonder?"

By now, Joan's smile had completely faded. Her brooch, a Halloween-themed spider in black rhinestones that came out every October, appeared to be crawling up her shoulder. Her face took on a very knowing and disapproving expression. "Don't think you can pull something, young lady. The only person you'll hurt is yourself."

As if she cared, Victoria thought.

Joan's front teeth, stained coral, were visible as she pulled back her lips, smiling in a way that was all but feral. Victoria saw the resemblance between mother and son for the first time. "Let me tell you something. Not *one* person at this table will support you wandering off. And not *one* will welcome you back, if you do. Think about that."

Victoria, shocked, found no words to reply. The usual jovial Joan had shown her colors—and not just on her teeth. And, more to the point, she had spoken the truth.

A "hiatus" was not in the cards.

As her mother-in-law leaned away from her and into the other conversation, Victoria felt her presence at the table descend to a butler-like status. She was watching glasses carefully and offering more baguette when the lulls in conversation allowed it. Now she shifted back and back and yet further back, almost into an invisibility, a game she played every month at these dinners. She wondered if one day she would be able to disappear completely.

She watched, as if from a distance, her mother-in-law chewing with such a satisfied expression on her face, her perfectly manicured nails gripping the utensils. She was happy, and why shouldn't she be? She had orchestrated Victoria and Eric's union a few months after the demise of Eric's first marriage. A modern, arranged marriage, with all the parental pretalks and interferences. Cornering Deirdre at the Women in Business awards luncheon, Joan had cozily taken her by the arm for "girl talk." Deirdre couldn't possibly imagine what Joan had in mind, but was delighted when Joan, probably again displaying her lipsticked teeth, had suggested they get their "kids" together. It was perfect. Dick and Joan needed a stop-gap, a new story to tell, a girl who wouldn't go anywhere, and it helped that she was from a good family. Deirdre and Mick got the son they'd never had, and doubted they'd ever would. And they had been able to assure Eric's parents that indeed, Victoria wasn't going anywhere.

Sometimes Victoria wondered if Joan and Dick felt they got the short end of the stick in the bargain. But it was during these monthly dinners that she knew any shortcomings she brought to the family were more than made up for by the golden aura of her parents' success. A marriage is between more than two people, this was the harsh truth.

Her hope, she realized now, as a most daring thought unfolded in her mind, was that this could be her last parental dinner. That she might not be a fixture in this house for much longer.

"Victoria, looks like we're all out of water," Eric said, waving the green bottle in her direction. "Can you get another Perrier from the fridge?"

Victoria smiled and accepted the bottle with a nod, then retreated to the kitchen in graceful compliance.

NINE

T HE NEXT DAY, ERIC CONFRONTED HER. HE MUST HAVE SPOKEN with Joan on his way home from work, something he did fairly often. She liked to be kept "in the loop."

Of course, he didn't alter his usual routine. It was after he had his shower and changed into his après-work attire that he found Victoria in the kitchen.

After he had poured himself a glass of wine, he said, "So, what? You need a break from me?"

Victoria had just finished breading chicken cutlets, and her fingers were sticky with egg and flour. Her head snapped up to meet his gaze.

She struggled to orient herself enough to respond. She knew her face spelled guilt. She turned to the sink to rinse the gluey mixture from her hands. "Eric, I don't know—"

"Oh, don't play Miss Innocent with me. Making plans for a little vacay, are you? Solo? What made you think I wouldn't find out? Wouldn't know what that really means?"

His nostrils flared a bit, unattractively. He screwed up his eyes into slits. She imagined laser beams coming out of them, shooting right into her heart, sizzling and scorching it into a well-done steak.

"I just thought—" She floundered for words.

"Thought *what*, exactly? I'm all ears!" He threw his hands up in false expansiveness.

Her heart was pounding now, her head full of its drumbeat. It was the moment, the dreaded moment, and he had brought it to her on a silver platter. She had to take this opportunity. She had to say it.

"We aren't—well, we aren't that happy, Eric," she said softly.

For a moment, he looked genuinely stricken by her statement. She could see the little boy in him briefly, a boy dressed by his mother in a pair of perfectly ironed jeans. She felt emboldened to continue.

"It's no one's fault. But, don't you think we both might feel better, I mean, we might be better off, if we—"

"Better off?" He barked a mirthless laugh. "You'll be better off without me, is that what you think?"

She watched as he sauntered with deliberate slowness over to a chair by the sectional, sat, and swiveled around to face her. He had recovered from his moment of vulnerability and reassumed a sure-footed scorn.

"You obviously haven't given this much thought. Let me remind you, this life you don't enjoy, it's all yours through *me*. Remember the prenup you signed?" He swirled the wine around in his glass, with the air of a cheesy theatrical villain.

"Money isn't everything," Victoria said, barely audible.

"Funny how the people who say that tend to *have* it. Well, you might sing a different tune, Victoria, renting some flea-bitten apartment off-island. And how would you pay your rent, if you don't have a job?"

Victoria bristled. As luck would have it, Eric's parents were close friends with the DiMarcos, who owned and ran the spa she worked at. Currently, Victoria was something of a pet there and could cherry-pick her schedule. That would all change easily with a phone call from Joan.

"Oh, silly me. What was I thinking? Don't worry about your job. You can always go live with your parents again. I'm sure they'd love to have you." Here, another cheerless bark of laughter.

Their eyes met, his in a glittering threat, hers already in retreat.

"Let's not do this, okay? It was just an idea, Eric, a little time away. I wasn't planning anything extreme," she finally said, after a wave of nausea passed. She picked up the tray of chicken and slid it into the hot oven. "I do enjoy this life."

TEN

Victoria moved the strap out of instinct. Eric had left his gym bag on the entrance floor by the front closet as usual. But this time, the strap was looped out in an invitation, a questioning curve that presented disorder, perhaps more. She stopped, after tucking it safely away, and imagined Eric entering in a rush, maybe having forgotten a file or his umbrella, nipping in for a moment. He wouldn't notice the beckoning noose on the ground. His foot would nestle right into the top of the figure eight. His other foot would advance a step. And then the strap would tighten, and hold his foot and leg hostage, suspended for a moment while he, cartoonish, would reach out to grasp—what? There was nothing to grasp in this minimalist house. Nothing but air and a wall too far away to reach. His body would hover imperceptibly at an angle before it swiftly whapped to the ground. It wouldn't be a soft landing. White marble tiles would meet his skull, forehead first, and then a delicate crack, like the sound of an egg breaking. Clean. The blood would pool in his brain and would not sully the beautiful floor, until it eventually made its way out of his unseeing eye in a small, thin trickle. Not with a bang, but a whimper.

She smiled to herself and pulled out the strap once more.

"He was knocked out cold, miss," she imagined the paramedic telling her compassionately. "He didn't feel anything. He didn't suffer."

"And, it didn't ruin his looks at all," her mother-in-law said, suddenly part of the scene. "He can have an open casket. Just a little makeup to cover the bruising. Funeral homes deal with these things all the time. I know one that will do an excellent job."

She could see it, Eric's face, with an excellent layer of concealing makeup, lying in a limousine of a casket, looking quite natural indeed. Picturing it, she'd never liked him so much as now. She'd never felt more understanding of all his faults. She'd never had so much generosity.

Victoria walked away from the bag. Served him right for leaving it out.

ELEVEN

I T WAS STRANGE HOW SOME WOMEN HELD THEIR WEIGHT, LIKE A
faux-pregnancy, all out front, yet their rear ends were snubbed,
flat, forgotten nothings. The bottom of the woman in front of Victoria
at Canadian Tire made not even a curve in her white cotton pants.
Just a longitudinal line of sorts, down the center, delineating right
and left.

It was all Ian McEwan's fault that she was here. She had been
thinking over her morning coffee about his Shakespeare-infused no-
vella, *Nutshell*. She often mused about books she had read when she
had quiet time. This one was pretty daring: Hamlet played by the ultimate nonactor, a fetus. It had delighted her. It had spurred her on to
read several more by the author, but none had impressed her as much
as *Nutshell* for its audacity.

It was also educational. In McEwan's story, the baby's mother
and uncle conspired to poison the father by putting antifreeze in his
smoothie. Apparently, in addition to tasting pleasantly sweet, antifreeze also does not show up in blood tests unless it is specifically
tested for. Once she remembered that little nugget, and saw that her
afternoon was blissfully client-free, Victoria ceased waxing poetic over

McEwan's literary prowess and found herself at Canadian Tire behind a woman with no ass.

The drive there, even the search for a parking spot, felt innocent enough. Turning the car left, then right—there was nothing intrinsically wrong with that. Pulling in front of the store was also no big deal. Even going to the automotive section and taking the four-liter container from the shelf was a normal, blameless action. People bought antifreeze all the time and it was not noteworthy.

Her head, though, felt disconnected, fuzzy. Her stomach had dropped five stories in a mixture of dread and fear. The container was heavy, straining her arm muscles as she walked to the car and put it in the passenger seat next to her. When she turned the car on, it beeped with an alert meant to remind the passenger to put on the seat belt.

She looked over at the antifreeze, and for a moment it took on a dreadful sentience. Gingerly, she pulled the seat belt across it. "There you go," she said in an unnaturally high singsong as she clicked it in.

Leaning back against the headrest, she took a few deep breaths. *Get it together*, she told herself. She closed her eyes a moment and then started her drive back home. She imagined doing something similar to what the woman in the McEwan book did, like buying Eric an iced coffee—wait, would antifreeze react strangely in something iced? No, it wasn't worth the chance, and besides, she never bought him those things. It would have to be a health shake from the gym. They came in white plastic cups so he wouldn't be able to see it had been diluted. She'd give it to him on his way out somewhere. He'd take it with him in the car, to work or a meeting.

It was pretty fast acting, she'd read, and he was a fast drinker. She imagined that he'd have had at least half the cup before starting to feel that something was not quite right. She imagined the liquid snaking through his intestines as he started to feel the first symptoms. He'd feel a bit slow, dizzy, like he was drunk. His eyelids would droop and chin bob downward. Then he'd feel sick but unable to re-act quickly enough, vomit in a chunky spray all over the steering wheel and dashboard of his car. Hopefully by this point, cardiac arrhythmia would be in full swing, clenching and unclenching his heart in a death dance. She imagined a smack of metal on metal, the floury, strong poof of airbags deploying, his wide eyes and slack jaw open with lolling tongue on display.

She would tell people how much pressure he had been under of late to make partner. It would be so reasonable. His associate Jim Moon had died of a heart attack just last year, and he was Eric's age. It happens.

What didn't make sense was the big plastic jug on the kitchen counter, something that didn't belong in the house. Neither Victoria nor Eric tinkered with their cars. Eric barely knew where to put the washer fluid.

That evening, when he returned home from work, Eric's foot-steps echoed in the foyer, past the gym bag and its loop of temptation and promise. A few moments later she heard, with a hollow heart, the crumpling sound of the gym bag being lifted and shelved.

After dinner, when he returned his plate to the sink like a good boy, he noticed the jug for the first time. He stared at it blankly, reading the label to be sure of what he was looking at.

"Antifreeze," he said, his eyes a question.

"Oh, yes. I guess I need to put it down by the car. Silly me, I brought it up along with the groceries."

"But *antifreeze?*" He looked at her as if she had told him she was taking up big-game hunting with some girlfriends.

She looked into his eyes, her mouth turned up into a small, calm smile. "Winter is coming. I heard it's good to keep on hand."

"Would you even know when you needed it? And if you even knew that, would you know where to put it?"

She nodded. "I think so. I asked the guy at the store."

Eric wasn't letting it slide. It had been a mistake to leave the container out where he could see it. He let out a short, cheerless laugh, one syllable. "Oh, 'the guy at the store.' That explains it." He was using air quotes, something he did when he was angry.

Victoria lowered her eyes and wiped down the already immaculate counter. Quietly, she said, "Explains what?"

"You're so clueless. He was obviously some loser trying to make a move. Antifreeze."

"Oh no, it wasn't like that, Eric. I stopped him and asked him, he wasn't trying to sell it to me."

But Eric was no longer reachable. He got like this sometimes. His first marriage had left him a very unimaginative man. Victoria had learned never to give him a reason to be jealous, by eliminating male pronouns when telling him about her day. This was a dangerous line she was walking. Her heart was beating erratically, like an off-kilter metronome. She felt terrified, but alive.

He moved away from her, slapping the mail on the counter with a whap. He went over to the television and got the remote, scanning rapidly through his queued shows, clicking the buttons on the remote hard enough to make his thumbnail white with the pressure.

She stood silently a moment before quietly making her way over to him and tentatively putting a hand on his shoulder. "Eric," she said, her eyes pleading silently.

He wouldn't look at her, but his scanning slowed a bit.

He didn't respond to her hand but allowed it to rest there, so she kept it where it was. "A drink?" she suggested at last.

His eyes flicked to hers just briefly, and he nodded.

She exhaled and allowed a very small smile to pull up the corners of her mouth as she went back to the kitchen, reaching over the antifreeze jug to the cupboard where the wineglasses were kept.

She filled them both generously with pinot gris. He took his with an icy word of thanks and, much to her delight, no sommelier commentary.

They sipped, quietly, avoiding the Day-Glo-green plastic jug that screamed from the counter.

"You have a busy day tomorrow?" she asked, needing to break the silence.

"I'm always 'busy,'" he said, once again with the air quotes. "It's not like the spa where you can gossip and drink tea all day."

She ignored the dig. "Oh, I know," she said. "I just wondered if you wanted to meet for lunch or something tomorrow. Sometimes you have meetings at lunch, I just wanted to see if—"

"Lunch would be fine. I can meet you," he answered quickly.

"Oh, good." She felt a relief at being on steadier ground. "Maybe we can try that tapas place near your office that you mentioned." She hoped she didn't sound too simpering.

He looked at her sharply. "Wait. Don't you normally meet Holly for lunch on Fridays?"

She dropped open her mouth in mock dismay. Of course. Her cheeks burned at the way he looked at her. Eric hated disorganization. Her finger went to her mouth, a tooth hooking under a ragged nail, and then quickly out again when she saw his double disgust.

"Shit, that's right. But, I could cancel with her, or . . . or, we could both meet you! How about that, it would be great to have something other than salad bar for lunch, and you know how much Holly likes you. She really does."

Eric scoffed, rolling his eyes, but Victoria could tell this pleased him. He always mocked Holly behind her back (so much that Victoria needed to stop him occasionally), but he seemed to tolerate her more than Victoria's other friends. Probably because Holly preened and clucked around him so approvingly. It was good for his ego.

"Or, as I said, I could just cancel. She'll understand. It's not like our lunch was something special."

Eric took a sip of his wine, and said, "Oh, I don't care, bring her along."

This settled things. He walked a haughty walk to the sectional, settling in for some quality time with his television. While his back was turned, Victoria silently moved the jug of antifreeze, sliding it up against the white backsplash, where it fit snugly against the wooden knife block. She texted Holly.

VICTORIA: Is it ok if Eric joins us for lunch tomorrow?

HOLLY: Of course!!! 😊

VICTORIA: Can you meet us at that tapas place on St. Laurent that he likes? I'll send you the address.

HOLLY: PERFECT! 🖤 😊 💅

VICTORIA: Great. He's so happy you can be there. You're his favorite of my friends.

HOLLY: OMG, looking forward to it!!!!!

THAT NIGHT, IT TOOK ERIC A LITTLE LONGER TO FALL ASLEEP. MAYBE it was the intensity of the *Game of Thrones* episodes he had been watching, or maybe he had something else on his mind. He looked a little "off" and showed it by bumping his toe into the corner of the bathroom vanity, something he never did. She heard him curse, and he had a storm-cloud expression on his face when he emerged, ready for bed.

She fretted that he was going to try to talk to her as they lay in the dark. She counted down from five hundred, and still his wakeful breathing persisted. This nonsleeping silence of his was heavy and she felt it pressing and closing in, though he said nothing. She lay as still as possible, noticing a scratch in the white varnish of one of the legs of her bedside table that she had never seen before. Eventually, after what seemed an eternity, and the night had fallen into its deepest darkness, he moved further to his side and was asleep.

Victoria hadn't made a visit to Luke (she thought his name so often now it was the default word she came to as soon as her mind had a quiet moment) in some days. She had tried a few times, but she hadn't been able to concentrate. Random thoughts kept intruding: ones about book plots; silly things she had said during the day; and, her favorite, graphic visions of Eric, with his body in ribbons, dark red ones, a grotesque expression on his face that was part grin, part gore. These thoughts interrupted her normally blanked-out mind and made it impossible to lift from the bed, let alone make the flight to Luke's bedside. It was beyond frustrating. Eventually she gave up. The previous night, to relax herself, she masturbated almost ferociously to a rapid climax, and a heavy throbbing sleep claimed her before the vexation had a chance to build an angry fire bed on which she would have had to lay all night. It was only the next morning that she wondered if Eric had noticed her heavy breathing and jerky movements.

She felt more at ease tonight, for some reason. Maybe it was the antifreeze's comforting presence by the knife block. The knowledge that it was *there* even though she was doing nothing with it, for the time being at least. It had made her mind much clearer, made her heart return to a healthy gait, her voice gain its hypnotic, even tone.

Now, she found herself floating above her body more quickly than usual. The weightlessness was so pleasurable she felt an overarching well-being, and a smile stretched across her face, in a radiating line that continued past the boundaries of her body in a warm, luxuriating bliss. She didn't linger long.

She floated again over treetops and telephone poles, over the basilica's green dome, hearing his heartbeat clearly. She thought of Gatsby's Daisy, her green light, and felt herself to be a ghostly spirit of that sort. It was an uncomplicated journey that lasted no time but also much of the night.

He was asleep in his bed, facing the window.

When she found herself hovering by his bed, she noticed that her presence was less delicate than the last time. Before, she had felt as precarious as a bubble on a child's fingertip, ready to pop at the slightest movement. There was something more grounded in her body tonight that made her slightly freer. She knew she still needed to move slowly, with care, but also felt a little more power, more presence, which renewed her confidence.

His sleeping form was very masculine. He was shirtless, exposed to his waist. His breath was not a snore, but it was heavy and deep, suggesting strength. His face was serious, with lips only slightly parted.

She moved carefully to his side, bringing the strum of her heart up to his, until the sound entered fully into her body and was engulfed there. She found she was able to lay her body parallel to his, feeling the cool rustle of the sheet below. She lay there for minutes, feeling his warm breath brush her face. Eric never allowed her to lie facing him—he said he couldn't stand the feeling of her breathing into his face. It made him claustrophobic, he had said in the beginning, and then later, he said her breathing felt like a hot exhaust pipe. So they had always faced apart.

She pushed thoughts of Eric away and focused on keeping her breaths in sync with Luke's. Part of her was determined not to disturb him in even the most minute way, knowing instinctively that was the right thing. But part of her felt naughty, as she had as a child in day care, when she snuck into the nursery one day and purposefully woke a few of the napping babies. It had satisfied a childlike curiosity but also was strangely empowering to rouse them from unconsciousness into wailing cries. It had been worth whatever disapproval and punishment she got. But she had only done it the one time. She wondered what Luke would do if she woke him. Would his face crumple in fear and dismay at being brought into the reality of waking life? Or would he see her and sleepily pull her closer to his half-naked body, as though she had belonged there all along. She wanted desperately to know. An inner voice told her it was too soon for that.

The temptation passed, and she moved toward him. Their faces were very close now. She was so close that if she opened her eyes he looked like a slumbering cyclops, both closed eyes blurring and crossing into one. She closed her eyes and felt his heat, the movement of his breath.

He moved. His right leg, the one higher up as he lay on his left side, crossed over her, locking her in tight to him. She gasped, fully expecting to snap back to her bed at home, but was elated to find this not to be the case, and remained pressed against him. The calm of his breathing was not altered. Their groins were pressed up against each other. Instinctively, her mouth was on his, matching the pressure of their bodies. His mouth, at first warm and slack, started to respond, slowly parting, making room for her lips, gently pressing and then releasing, searching and pressing again, the warmth, the slight stubble on his upper lip, each movement of his sleep-kiss a revelation to Victoria.

The kiss became deeper when she felt his tongue touch hers. She pushed herself against him, recalling how sluglike Eric's tongue was to her. How she would avoid it at all costs, keeping their kisses as antiseptic as possible. "I despise sputum," he had once declared early on in their courtship. At the beginning, this had insulted her. But as time went on, she found the less sputum exchanged the better.

She doggedly pushed Eric out of her mind again (why was he *here*, NOW, for goodness' sake?) and focused again on the somnambulant tongue-tag she was playing with Luke. Her hand, which had been soldier-like at her side, reached up hungrily to graze his upper chest, where graying hairs declared his maleness to her. The slight cleft between his pectoral muscles beckoned.

The sheets on her side of the bed felt cold, as if she had just gotten in. Her heart hammered in her head and her chest, her breath coming in jags, her hand still reaching in front of her, but only touching air now. Eric's back faced her, a sullen but familiar sight.

She had hit a wall again. Songbirds fluttered in her heart, though, and a triumphant aria streamed through her veins in rich, thick, bloody chords.

TWELVE

SHE CHOSE A CLASSIC BUT SHAPELESS BLACK DRESS TO WEAR TO lunch. It was a shift-style dress made of a thick, good-quality wool fabric, destined to be paired with pearls and intended to make her look like Jackie O. It was a gift from her mother-in-law last Christmas and surely cost a fortune, considering the oversize designer box in which it had arrived. But somehow Victoria looked frumpy in it. It would have suited a smaller-breasted woman better, one with longer legs.

After deliberation, she paired it with a scarf, not pearls. The result was somewhat aging, but she didn't have time to choose something different. Her intent was not to look wonderful for Eric anyway.

She could see a block away from the restaurant, which sported an amateur painter's rendering of Frida Kahlo beside the front door, that Eric and Holly were outside waiting for her, heads bobbing and nodding. Her feet tapped more quickly along the pavement. Eric would probably be irritated that he had been "put in a position" to entertain Holly by himself. Such things irked him, and Victoria knew she would have to pay for her carelessness later. Never put Eric in a "position." As she neared them, she searched worriedly for his polite, tight smile that indicated displeasure. But it wasn't there.

In fact, Eric was absorbed in whatever Holly was saying. His eyes were crinkled at the corners with something approaching amusement and warmth. He didn't notice Victoria standing there at first, so attentive was he to Holly's chatter.

"I kept staring at him, the dentist guy, I knew him from somewhere, and it was really annoying me, you know? I couldn't place him. And suddenly at the end part, it just clicked! I mean, OMG, it's the freaking *Breaking Bad* guy! On *Seinfeld*!!" she all but bubbled.

Eric's smile erupted. "Bryan Cranston before anyone knew who he was," he said, as though it were some revelation.

"Yes, Bryan Crampton. That's his name. Walter White. I felt SO stupid, you know? When I realized who it was?"

Eric hadn't stopped smiling. He was in his element. "Well, I've always felt that actor has a sort of chameleonic quality. I barely recognized him when I saw him in *Contagion*."

Holly clearly had not seen the movie, as evidenced by her three blinks, but she nodded encouragingly.

There was a synchronicity in their conversation that Victoria had not noticed before. It did not appear to be inspired by Holly's "assets" either, which were framed enticingly in a soft-pink silk blouse and fitted charcoal suit jacket. Eric was looking into her eyes and seemed to be genuinely enjoying her.

"Well, so many great stars were on *Seinfeld*," she gushed. "That's part of the fun of watching the episodes again. The other day I saw that chick from *Friends* . . . and then wasn't JFK junior on there once?"

"John-John was never actually on *Seinfeld*," interjected Victoria, sidling up between them, giving air kisses to her husband, then her friend.

Eric gave her a look. His gaze lingered a moment on her scarf before returning to her face. "You know *Seinfeld*?"

"My face isn't *always* in a book," she said, enjoying his surprised expression. "Anyway, John F. Kennedy Jr. is a member at Elaine's gym in one episode, and they almost go out, but then he ends up going out with 'the Virgin' instead. But he's not actually on the show. Everything he does is implied, off-camera."

"Yes, well," Eric said impatiently, "it's a pretty famous episode. The whole world knows what happens in that one."

Holly nodded. Most of the sparkle has dimmed from her small blue eyes, but she smiled at Victoria. "Should we go in, then?"

"If you like tapas, you will really like the food here," said Eric, gallantly opening the restaurant's heavy wooden door, to Holly's widening eyes. "The chef is well known for catering to the creative palate."

"I don't really know what tapas are—do they have salads?"

Eric paused. Little muscles at the sides of his mouth constricted slightly. The moment was interrupted by a buxom, goth-faced waitress who was ready with a scowl and menus. She seated them opposite the bar at a tiny table that offered zero legroom, so Victoria was forced to sit at an unnatural angle in order to avoid touching legs.

"Water all around, and a bottle of the Chablis," said Eric, like a tour guide, to the now expressionless waitress. The restaurant was a long, skinny rectangle. Everything was wooden—floors, tables, walls, bar. A pleasant din of conversation balanced with the kitchen noise.

"The chicken sliders are my favorite," Eric said, somewhat conspiratorially to Holly, when he noticed her deep concentration on the menu.

"It's hard to pick, right, Holly? No salad bar here," Victoria said. "The options look very good, though. I can see why you go here a lot, Eric."

He nodded, behind his menu. His tour-guide persona was not for her.

"Do we order a bunch of things and then share?" Victoria asked after a few minutes. She knew once she had said it that she had mis-stepped. Eric didn't share food, even at a tapas restaurant.

His reaction was tempered by Holly's presence. "I find the plates are pretty small for sharing. It works if you pick two things. Maybe a meat thing and a vegetable thing, you know, and then you have your own meal."

When it was time to order, both Eric and Holly had the same thing—chicken sliders and a tomato salad. Holly had shyly asked him to order for her and he was only too pleased to do so. Victoria's order of octopus carpaccio and yam fries with garlic mayo was an act of bold rebellion. She didn't even want the octopus, only wanted to see his face when she ordered it. And it was worth it, seeing that look of disapproval and disgust, mixed with bewilderment. He hated to be caught unawares. *Yes*, Seinfeld *AND octopus*, she thought. *Aren't I a surprising creature?*

It threw him off, that was clear. Eric purposefully did not look at her after the food was brought to the table. He hated seafood. The tentacles and pale flesh surely turned his stomach and mortified him as though she had turned cannibal. Also, garlic was a no-no (one time after eating tzatziki, she smelled like a Greek in bed, Eric had com-plained), and she knew she was wounding him with every dip of her fries. She knew there would be punishment, in the chilly cruelties that normally she took pains to avoid. She was emboldened today, she was daring, she was burning with the heat of last night's secret embrace. Her husband's culinary sensibilities were ridiculous now, something to mock, not enable.

If he felt mocked, Eric didn't show it. He and Holly played a won-derful game of lunchtime conversation, almost as if Victoria were not there. He would open with a piece of intelligentsia (did she know Shirley Temple had been the first choice for Dorothy in *The Wizard of O₇?*), she would return an inquisitive query, he would volley back an amusing little-known fact, which she served back with delight, but not quite far enough, so that his point was scored. Eric was having a good time. His eyes weren't sullen, his face opened into a smile a few times. Victoria saw how, from a distance, most anyone could find him handsome.

She sat with her octopus and garlicky fries, a spectator with court-side seats. For a moment she felt as silent and grotesque as the cephalopod she was ingesting. Suddenly, a memory surfaced of a long-ago school field trip to the aquarium. She remembered the guide, a man with bulging eyes, explaining to her class that the octopus is a very intelligent creature and can hatch ingenious escape plans. It was hard to believe of the silent creature suction-cupped to the walls of its glass box. But the aquarium man had been emphatic. He said they had to be very careful not to give the octopus any way of getting out, no matter how small. "Because they have no bones," he said, "they can fit their bodies into surprisingly small spaces. One was filmed squeezing through gaps the size of a quarter." The man described a story of an octopus from Australia who was so determined and curious about the world that he broke out of his tank, slid across a few meters of the floor, slithered down a fifty-meter drainpipe, and disappeared into the sea, never to be found again.

That she could be so lucky!

Victoria chewed thoughtfully on her octopus. "This is delicious," she murmured.

THIRTEEN

VICTORIA HADN'T NOTICED THAT SHE HAD MADE A NOISE, BUT Eric had turned in her direction to look at her. He was on the sectional watching television.

"Didn't like it?" he asked, momentarily pulled out of *Game of Thrones*. He had already watched this episode, but it was one of his favorites.

"What?"

"Your book," he gestured. "Sounded like you didn't like it. You . . . huffed."

It was the one with the crying man on the cover. She had finally finished it, all 721 pages.

"I did? Sorry. I didn't realize. It was just so awful."

He looked interested. "That bad? Why?"

Victoria wasn't used to discussing the books she read with Eric. It felt too intimate, somehow. He didn't exist in her world of books. If he had wanted to know her at any point in their marriage, all he would have had to do was ask her about what she was reading. This might be the first time he had done so, and it was too late for such chitchat.

But the book had her blood boiling, so she answered him without thinking. "I just hate it when a character learns nothing throughout an entire book. Like, *nothing*. This guy was miserable at the beginning, and miserable at the end. He just went . . . nowhere. And we had to watch the whole entire train wreck. The guy didn't accept any help to improve his life, he didn't learn any important truth, nothing. We just had to sit there and read page after page of useless suffering."

Someone was being decapitated on the television screen behind Eric. He instinctively paused the show.

"Did the guy do anything to deserve all the bad things that happened?" he wanted to know.

"No. He didn't. He was just a victim, this guy with a huge target on his chest, a big bull's-eye. 'HURT ME.'"

Eric nodded. "So what was he supposed to learn then?"

A good question, which irritated Victoria and brought her voice up to an adolescent whine. "I don't know, how to live, how to deal with pain so that it doesn't engulf his entire life? So it doesn't end up completely destroying him? To stop being a victim and accept the love offered to him by people around him who genuinely care?"

She flushed deeply after this strange oration that came out like vomit in its uneven, gulping cadence. She focused on the back cover of her book now, hoping the conversation was over.

Eric was mildly entertained by her unusual display of emotion. Then he pressed his lips together sagely and paused before saying, "I mean, I'm not the reader here, but the character can't always learn the lesson. Otherwise all books would end up happily ever after, right? It's the same in TV. I mean, Tony Soprano never figured it out, never turned into an upstanding citizen and family man. That would have been . . . boring."

Victoria had the awful feeling of being trapped in a nightmare that she couldn't wake from. What *was* this conversation, anyway? And since when did Eric have opinions on literature?

She got up quickly and strode into the kitchen. "Would you like a tea?" she said, rummaging through the cupboard.

He watched her carefully a moment before turning back to the television. "Chamomile," he said predictably, and the battle scene continued.

She grappled to regain emotional control, experiencing a breathless, sick sensation as her heart raced quickly in no particular rhythm as she prepared the tea, feeling disdain for his flowery, caffeine-free choice. A man shouldn't drink chamomile, for fuck's sake.

She dropped silky tea bags in perfectly white mugs. Spa face replaced the indignant, annoyed-teenager expression that had crusted over her features during their short, unusual exchange. He didn't know anything about that book, or any other book. Why pretend now?

She knew Luke wouldn't have tried to defend that horrendous book. She knew what he would have said: "What was the point of THAT? Did the author delight in making us suffer along with that sad sack? What a sadist. This was a genuine waste of time."

And she would then throw her arms around him and say, "YES! YES! YES!" in a rapture that bordered on the sexual, which wasn't all that appropriate, given that she had only just been widowed the week before and needed to maintain a certain somber tone because her husband had been a decent person and she wouldn't have wished that kind of death on anyone.

Not on anyone. Even though he had kept her locked up in their ivory tower, without a hair out of place, bound and gagged in a white-on-white predictability, with joy and power on mute—and he held the remote control.

She couldn't imagine the fear he must have felt in his final minutes, after he put his empty travel mug into the holder next to the gear shift. Highway driving, midway through changing lanes. When that pain hit his gut, he knew with all the deep forest knowledge that comes with being an animal, that something was very, very wrong. In an attempt to maintain control of the vehicle, he gripped the wheel, determined. His eyes closed involuntarily, his entire body cold and wet at the same time. Did he shit himself? The pain. He tried to open his eyelids, but they were impossible to lift, broken garage doors unresponsive to the clicker. All he could see behind his red, veined eyelids was Victoria. She was smiling, she was handing him his travel mug, she was serenely kissing his cheek, she was softly turning and walking back down the hallway, she was—

"You're scaring me. Hello!! I said, I'll take my tea." Eric was in front of her, snapping his fingers at the bridge of her nose. She had been standing, statue-like, each hand holding out a steaming cup of tea, fingers tightened and whitening as they gripped the cup handles. At his words, she jumped a little, an involuntary spasm that resulted in her fingers losing purchase on one of the cups. She watched in horror, slow motion, as the cup dropped and hit the edge of the quartz countertop, splashing tea to the tiled floor, a precursor to the inevitable smash. The other overfull mug jerked but remained in her grip, spilling tea on her hand. She could see the skin turn pink and tighten where the water had lapped over it with its hot tongue.

She felt the disappointment that comes when being woken out of a delicious dream. Her voice found itself, as though underwater.

"I'm sorry, Eric. Gosh. I'll clean it up. Don't come near, you'll get your socks wet."

She expected him to lecture her, demand to know what planet she was on, to be disgusted with her carelessness. She knew he would hate that the set of mugs that had come with him before their marriage would be now incomplete. But he just stared at her as though she were a stranger and took the remaining cup from her wordlessly, gently uncurling her finger from the mug's loop—so gently, like he was handling something dangerously explosive. His eyes held her with a wariness she had not seen before.

He opened his mouth to speak, and she was paralyzed by the anticipation of his somehow knowing everything, terrified by the prospect of having to explain herself and having absolutely no idea where or how to start. But he eventually just closed his mouth, lowered his eyes, and returned to his place on the sectional. The way he clicked the show back on seemed delicate, like he was only on the surface of his actions and was really back in the kitchen with her, staring at her with eyes that had turned black and accusing.

The noise of the television should have brought a release to the tension, but all the sounds were violent ones that acted like fertilizer for her thoughts, germinating images of squeezing intestines and internal bleeding, blood pooling around organs, bathing the organs and drowning them in the rich, black liquid. She heard metal against metal, rubber painting lines on concrete, feet that were rigid yet ineffectual, a faint horn blast, the twisted silence accompanying death. And then, lightness.

She stood rooted in place until she heard his voice again. He hadn't turned around, not a millimeter. The back of his head (complete with the bald spot he tried to hide, with the veil of a comb-over) addressed her. "You better go to bed, Victoria. That book upset you. You're not yourself tonight."

"Who might I be then, exactly?" she said, squeezing a hot tea bag in one fist.

FOURTEEN

I T WAS A COLD DAY. EVEN THOUGH THE SUN WAS OUT AND IT WAS HER
day off, Victoria didn't feel like going out, not even to the café. She
had been restless all morning, ever since Eric left for work, with the
announcement that it was a perfect day for a walk. He often walked
if the weather was nice, and even though it was October, it was still
pleasant enough. He had left early so as to give himself enough "time
to arrive on time," listen to a podcast, and perhaps avoid a shared
breakfast with his wife.

Victoria didn't usually turn the television on. It took some digging about for her to find where Eric kept his collection of recorded
movies. She got it started, but her mind wandered. She was experiencing a "book hangover" after finishing the one with the crying
man. Nothing appealed to her, and her guts were churning in acidic
fury at her reading experience. She had the urge to stop random people on the street, asking them "How many times can a person actually
be raped in one lifetime?!" but knew that was totally cuckoo, so she
just kept it to herself.

The beauty of reading, the solitary gift of it, could sometimes be
turned on itself at times like these, when she desperately needed to

share her thoughts with others. Victoria had few friends and none of them would have read such a book. Holly read the occasional cozy mystery, but certainly not anything like this.

Eric hadn't come out and said anything about her mug-dropping incident the other night, but he had been acting differently. He was watching her closely, as though he were suspicious of something. He was quieter than usual, if that was possible. And he had been working more late nights at the office, as though by design. The promotion to partner was coming up soon, he told her, and he was making sure he had a "presence" at the office for those who were watching. Victoria found the nights without Eric to be both a relief and a curse. For once, the apartment didn't stink of chicken. She was glad to have the place to herself, to be free of dinner-making duties and precise timing deadlines. But when alone, she had nothing to tame her thoughts, which had the tendency to run wild.

She was scrolling through the movie list, in search of something light and fluffy, so she stopped at *Throw Momma from the Train*. She got bored pretty quickly, though—it was even worse than she remembered, and how was Danny DeVito ever a thing? She scrolled the titles again in the hopes of finding something starring Jeremy Irons, but accidentally clicked on *Dolores Claiborne*. Victoria had read the novel years ago but didn't remember much except a pivotal scene involving an eclipse (or was it something with an axe?). She decided rather than fighting with the controller to go ahead and watch the movie. She was grateful for any distraction.

Bleak and slow moving, *Dolores Claiborne* didn't provide much entertainment value either. Slumped on the couch, Victoria dozed to the drone of Jennifer Jason Leigh's bitter voice. When she awoke, it was to a closeup of the aging face of Judy Parfitt, all dolled up for a party, with eyes that glittered with emotion and teeth that looked gothic in decay. *Husbands die every day, Dolores. Why . . . one is probably dying right now while you're sitting here weeping. They die . . . and leave their wives their money. I should know, shouldn't I? Sometimes they're driving home from their mistress's apartment and their brakes suddenly fail. An accident, Dolores, can be an unhappy woman's best friend."*

She sat forward, no longer sleepy, transfixed by Judy Parfitt's face and sharp sibilance that sometimes comes with age. It was as though this crone were not just separated from her by the screen, but that she was on the other side of something far more momentous. She was living the dream, she was the high-riding bitch that Victoria needed to be, and she was free. Though frightening in her too-bright lipstick and jaunty hat, she had a message that Victoria found enticing, mesmerizing.

The rest of the movie didn't hold much interest. Not the husband thrown down the well, not the old lady's trip down the stairs, or the mother-daughter accusations. Victoria could only think about failing brakes. She envisioned oily metal parts, with bolts that could be loosened with a Phillips-head screwdriver. If postmenopausal Judy Parfitt could do it, how hard could it be?

The movie over, she turned off the television, then sat for some time on the couch, not moving. Then she rose, as though in a trance, and went to the kitchen junk drawer, which in spite of its name was still meticulously organized. She knew she could find tape, twine, flashlights, a spare doorstop, twist ties, and a socket and ratchet set, among other things that were sometimes called into use. The set was ensconced in a plastic case that was still virginally sealed shut with a sticker. Neither Eric nor Victoria was handy. Any work that had ever been done in their apartment had been seen to by a professional.

Victoria shoved the socket set into her purse and grabbed the car key. She took the elevator to the level where Eric's gray Audi sedan was parked. She disarmed it and sat in the driver's seat for the very first time—Eric was very proprietary about his car—and searched for a button that would release the hood. She found it after a few minutes. The hood sprung open like the door to Ali Baba's cave. She almost expected to see glittering jewels when she went out to look.

She couldn't help but laugh at herself as she glanced over the engine. What had she expected to see? A sign saying "these are the brakes, unscrew here"? She had absolutely no idea what to do in order to make brakes fail. She didn't know what they looked like or whether they had screws at all, and whether those screws would be movable by her tiny little unused ratchet. It was pathetic.

She used her phone to Google images of car brakes, and even Audi brakes, but still wasn't able to see anything helpful. The brakes must be underneath all this other stuff, close to the wheels.

Victoria had never used a ratchet before. Expecting it to work like a screwdriver, she struggled at first, and applied the ratchet to a bolt with very little success. Then, she pushed with her whole weight several times with the effect of tightening the bolt further, and completely lost purchase, dropping the ratchet into the car engine with a loud clatter. Her palms were bruising by the time she decided to use a socket in conjunction with the 9-mm ratchet. Eventually, the bolt moved. She turned and turned until the bolt came out. She held it thoughtfully, letting its twists leave zebra marks in oil on her fingertips. She saw another one, and did the same thing. Whatever bolts she could find, she tried and removed. At the end, she had five. Her hands were oily. When she touched the pieces that she had removed the bolts from, nothing seemed to move, not much, at least. It was hard to say whether what she had done would affect the car in a meaningful way. Though, she mused, the bolts must be put there for a reason.

She carefully closed the hood and put the bolts and tools into her purse, feeling a tingle of fear, finding herself looking belatedly for security cameras in the garage. She didn't see any. She heard footsteps approaching, though. Her neighbor Jacques, a Francophone man who lived on the same floor, appeared. He had a flat, clownish face and a large gap between his front teeth. He was, however, always dressed in expensive suits. Jacques "did the best with what he had," as Holly would say. He acknowledged her with an annoying twinkle in his eye. Had he seen her earlier?

"Wrong floor?" he said in a playful tone. Her car was one floor down, and he knew well enough that she never drove Eric's car.

She smiled and flushed. "Yeah, I wasn't thinking."

"You just wanted to drive zee Audi," he returned, his voice a smile as he unlocked his black Volvo. She could almost hear the "naughty girl" in his tone, though the words were unsaid. She had always found Jacques a little bit creepy and self-satisfied.

She laughed in reply, finding it false and unpleasant to her ear.

Back in the apartment, Victoria congratulated herself on originality—brake tampering was so cliché. Her change of plans was much better. No one would look for a few missing bolts.

Buoyed and lighthearted, Victoria felt more in the mood to go to the café. She put the tools back in the junk drawer, careful to wipe everything down first. The sticker would no longer adhere so it would have to go, but who would notice that? The bolt, those beloved bolts, went into a sunglasses case that she never used, a gaudy, gold-plated one that her mother-in-law had brought back for her from a trip to Paris last year. It was the perfect size to house the incriminating bits that she couldn't bring herself to throw out. Not yet.

Just as she had finished tidying up, the entryway buzzer rang. Her heart sank, as it did every time the buzzer rang unexpectedly. She knew with almost 100 percent certainty who it would be. She and Eric only knew one person who liked to drop by—her mother.

"Victoria? I'm between meetings and thought we could have lunch."

Deirdre's voice was tinny through the intercom.

"Oh, hi Mother."

The voice was sharper. "It is your day off, isn't it? This isn't a bad time?"

Victoria couldn't be bothered to answer. She buzzed Deirdre in and left the front door open as she quickly cleansed the living room of any evidence of life, turned off the television, and put the kettle on.

She heard Deirdre come in with the sound of stiletto on marble.

"You really shouldn't do that—leave the door open like that," Deirdre said, lightly kissing her daughter on both cheeks. "You never know who might waltz in."

"I know," Victoria answered sullenly.

Deirdre reminded Victoria of the Snow Queen in a book she used to read as a child. She wore an ivory wool coat with wide bell sleeves and large buttons, and a matching ivory wool cap adorned with a sparkling brooch in the shape of a snowflake. She was immensely tall and dignified and her stiletto-heeled Ferragamos added to her already impressive height. Her pale hair was pulled up into a severe French twist, and her lips were flawlessly lipsticked in a rather brash red.

She was more imposing because she had not removed her coat. Her formality dwarfed Victoria. She scrutinized her daughter, tilting her head to one side like a crane, ready to harpoon at any moment with her long, sharp beak.

"Would you like tea, Mother?" Victoria's voice sounded so meek to her own ears. She hated it. She changed her tone as she rummaged through her tea cupboard for her mother's usual: Moroccan mint. "I don't have anything prepared—I really wasn't expecting company."

"Well, I thought we might go out. But you don't look like you've gotten yourself ready for the day yet."

Victoria pulled her cardigan around her defensively.

"You could have called first, you know. It's my day off."

"I'm aware," Deirdre commented drily. "But you do look like

you need a change of scenery. Eric says you haven't been getting out enough."

"When did Eric say that?"

Deirdre drummed her fingers on the countertop. "Oh, we chatted recently. He called your father for some advice with—well, work matters. You wouldn't be interested. Anyway, I could hardly resist a chance to say hello to my favorite son-in-law."

It was a stupid joke that her mother liked to use almost every time she saw Eric. It was supposed to be hilarious that he was her favorite, because he was also her only.

Deirdre looked her over again and unbuttoned her coat. She sighed. "Never mind. We will stay in. I don't have time for you to do a wardrobe overhaul right now." She peeled off a suede glove, then the other, and opened the fridge door. "How old is that prosciutto?"

Deirdre would have loved a daughter who looked like Audrey Tatou, who, showered, coiffed, and smartly chic in her beret, was seen in line at the *boulangerie* for fresh baguette each morning. That daughter would never have a refrigerator full of even remotely old-looking meats.

"I don't know—not old."

Her mother bent forward and sniffed the meat. Satisfied, she put the slices on a plate. She rummaged more in the fridge and found a few cheeses and some sweet pickles. She also took out a few cans of Perrier that Victoria always kept on hand just for Deirdre. It was the only water her mother drank.

The kettle was starting to boil. Deirdre snapped the element off in an efficient and presumptuous twist of the wrist that irritated Victoria.

"Crackers? I doubt you've been out for baguette today."

Victoria ignored the comment and indicated the cupboard with the crackers. "These rosemary ones are nice," she suggested.

Deirdre must have agreed. She arranged the crackers on the plate with the rest of the food and set it on the table. "Voila, a picnic!" She drew her garish lips into a determined smile.

She indicated to Victoria to sit, as though she, Deirdre, were the gallant hostess. Her eyes lowered and fixed on Victoria's hands. "Goodness, you'll want to wash your hands first though. What in the world is that—oil?"

Victoria cringed, felt a flutter of panic. "Oh, um, I was just checking my car—looking under the hood, and the latch was all greasy. Then I realized"—her eyes trailed to the antifreeze on the counter—"That I'd left everything upstairs. So I came up. That's when you buzzed."

Deirdre was staring at her the whole time, shaking her head in tiny movements of disbelief. "Eric mentioned that you were interested in *automotive* things recently, but I just didn't believe it. Really, Victoria. How about you leave all that to your mechanic."

Victoria turned the tap on full force, hoping to drown out her mother's voice. It didn't work. The thick stream splashed all over the counter as she rubbed the blackness on her hands into gray smears.

She returned to the table.

"If I had more time, I'd boil a few eggs," Deirdre commented, as she helped herself to a cracker with cheese and took a bite. Victoria grabbed a pickle. She wasn't feeling hungry.

They chewed together, in a familiar, adversarial silence.

"Well, what are your plans for the rest of the day, then?"

Every time her mother asked her a question, Victoria felt she had been caught unawares. It was annoying for both asker and answerer. She stammered. "Oh, I guess, I was thinking of—well, I've got my book."

Deirdre's expression darkened. "Yes. Your book. Well, be sure you get out a bit at least. Maybe go for a walk, get some exercise. I find that always helps. You can go to the club for a swim, or take a spin class. You look a bit pale. I think you might be reading too much. It isn't good for one, to be in an imaginary world all the time."

"I'm not in an *imaginary world*, Mother."

Deirdre did not look convinced. "You look tired. You used to go out, with Holly or at least to that little café of yours. Now look at you. If you're not cooped up in the apartment, you're playing mechanic." She shook her head at her daughter, who was beginning to protest. "It isn't good for you, whatever it is, and it isn't good for Eric."

"Did Eric say something?"

"He's far too gentlemanly to do such a thing. Of course not. But I could hear concern in his voice. And I can see why." Her eyes raked over her daughter in accusation.

"It's not always that easy, Mother," Victoria found herself saying, her voice cracking. She cleared her throat, too loudly. There was a bit of unchewed pickle in her mouth that felt rubbery and disgusting. She wondered if she would be able to swallow it.

"He's a good husband to you, Victoria," Deirdre's voice rang out in warning. Victoria could hear it bouncing off all the hard white surfaces in the apartment in remonstrative pings. "Look at this place! He's doing very well, but that's because he has a lot of ambition. Life isn't supposed to be 'easy,' at least for most of us. It could be a lot worse for you, and I think you know it."

Victoria lifted her eyes to meet her mother's. "Oh, I know," she said, an edge in her voice.

"I don't think I need to remind you that you could have just as easily ended up in . . . what, that 'ashram' place with that horrible greasy sleazeball you were following around."

Victoria knew it was coming, but she winced anyway. Deirdre loved alluding to Damien. One of her little punishments.

Her mother opened her can of Perrier, the shush of carbonation escaping. She took a swig of it, leaving a carnivorous smudge of red lipstick on the side of the can.

"Your father and I haven't always understood your choices, but Eric was the best direction your life could go. You're an adult now, Victoria. Don't think you can run back to us for a financial safety net should you lose your senses and ruin a perfectly good match."

There was a weighty silence, a boom had been lowered, and in it a threat. Deirdre's chilly blue eyes were serious and didn't hold an ounce of sway. There wasn't the smallest bit of warmth in the room.

"Don't forget how lucky you were to meet him. More importantly, don't make him forget how lucky *he* is."

Victoria pondered how lucky Eric might be the next time he drove his car, and needed to stifle a giggle. Her mother's expression became even more severe.

"Did I say something funny?"

"No, not funny, Mother. It's just that I don't understand what this is all about. I buy antifreeze and Eric summons the artillery to remind me to stay in line. It's ridiculous."

She had tried to keep her voice light, amused, but even to her own ears, she sounded unconvincing.

Deirdre was not a woman to waste words, nor one to get the last word in. Her often too-sharp silence was far more devastating to her daughter anyway. She didn't bother responding to being referred to as "artillery." She maintained her cold expression and bit into a cracker.

Victoria, depleted by her little defensive speech, couldn't meet her mother's gaze. She realized, with dismay, that she had said the word "antifreeze." Her mother hadn't mentioned it, she had. The word stained not only their conversation, but history—theirs. Deirdre had uncanny powers of recollection. Victoria decided to dispose of the beloved plastic bottle next to the knife block as soon as possible, emoting silent apologies to Ian McEwan.

FIFTEEN

IT WAS A RAINY THURSDAY EVENING, ABOUT TEN O'CLOCK. THE apartment was quiet, with only the occasional sound of a page being turned. Victoria was in her corner of the sectional. She held a book in one hand, and with the other picked at her baby toenail on her right foot. It was down to a tiny, bleeding nub. This was a compulsion that had been with her since childhood and had gotten particularly bad in recent days.

The past week had been exciting. Every time Eric left the apartment, Victoria's heart had leapt with the possibility of his taking the car. It wasn't a given; they lived in a central location downtown close to both their places of work and virtually everything else. Grocery stores, the racket club, and restaurants were all nearby. Even the library was within walking distance. The two cars were a luxury for their urban life, but Eric wouldn't entertain the idea of going without. He used his car to visit friends, or for work if he had offsite meetings. He also drove to badminton tournaments that sometimes took place in Laval, and even as far away as the South Shore.

Victoria hadn't dared to ask him about his plans with his car. She couldn't trust her voice to sound neutral, her eyes to withhold an eager gleam. The last thing she wanted was to alert more suspicions, since he already seemed to have them. Eric's call to Deirdre had been a dire warning. Ever since dropping Eric's mug, Victoria knew she was being watched.

No, it wouldn't do to ask him about his car. Instead, every morning she had waited a good five minutes after he left the apartment for work and she heard the ding of the elevator and swish of doors fully closed. A good five minutes after that, she raced down the staircase to the parking garage, once again only to be disappointed by the sight of the Audi, smug and spotless. After four days of this, she stopped checking. She decided it was better not knowing. It was comforting just to know that it *could* happen, that it likely *would*, and the *when* was less important.

Now she realized she had read two pages without taking in a single word. Henry Miller had that effect on her. He tended to ramble, and reading him, her mind did too. She checked her phone again, to see if Eric had texted her. He should have been home at least an hour ago from his badminton game, which had come up last minute, unusual for a Thursday. There was nothing. But he didn't often message her. They weren't "phone people," Eric always said, which meant that they actually spent a fair time on their phones, but just didn't call each other much.

Her toe ached. The suspense was too much; she wasn't this strong. She wasn't this zen. She had to know.

It was stupid. She'd waited all day, and checking to see if he'd taken his car now would be like giving in to an addiction or breaking a strict diet. It wasn't healthy.

But in the midst of these thoughts she rose from her place on the sectional. Her bookmark in place, she dug in the hall closet for her flip-flops (she needed open footwear tonight). She threw caution to the wind and left the front door unlocked. She'd only be gone a minute or two.

Victoria's stomach gurgled as she waited for the elevator. Out of habit, she covered it with her hand, in apology for her body's unseemly noise. She hadn't eaten dinner. Without the duty of preparing a meal for Eric, she had taken the night off from the kitchen. This small fast felt good to Victoria. It was like a cleansing, a ridding, the vacancy inexplicably beneficial to her health.

Ever since performing amateur surgery on Eric's car, she experienced a general feeling of well-being. The out-of-control thoughts had ceased, and her mind was much more at ease. She felt more positive than she had in a long time, with the promise of something good coloring her world in vivid appeal.

Restless, she decided to take the stairs. It would take longer, but there was less chance of running into Eric or anyone else.

As she clipped down the first set of stairs, hearing her foam sandals flapping and echoing, she had to laugh. If her mother could see her now, running down the fire escape with an urgency pushing her along—only to ascertain whether her husband was driving his tampered-with car.

She recalled how, five years ago, her parents had been traumatized by her foray into what they called the "yoga world" with Damien, and triumphant when she had returned, devastated. Their attitude was *you had your chance, enough nonsense now*, and they took the reins of her personal life so quickly she hardly knew what had happened.

She had returned from the ashram like a dog that knew it had been disobedient. It had taken all her defiance to go in the first place; now she had none left. When her parents orchestrated a dinner party in which there were three couples (her parents, his parents, and then Victoria and some stuffed shirt she had never met before) she meekly went along, wearing whatever getup her mother laid out for her on her bed.

She'd been on at least a half dozen of these humiliating, nonstarter excursions before Eric, all of which had left her if not broken, in a state of brittle humor at her parents for trying to pawn her off on an unsuspecting suitor. But Deirdre had been particularly excited about this evening. "You must have heard us talk about Dick and Joan before. They're lovely people. Their son is an up-and-comer. And he's been through a nasty divorce." She dropped her voice even though they were the only ones in the room. "She left him for her *trainer*, poor thing. They're just looking for someone simple and good for their son." She smiled as though that should be encouraging to her daughter.

Victoria inwardly winced. "Simple and good." It sounded like the opposite of what she thought of herself. Anything but simple. And good? Her parents didn't know her at all. If her mother knew then what Victoria thought of when she turned out her light, she would have given up on her matchmaking efforts.

The evening had been similar to the others. The parents got on like a house on fire, but the two singletons, overshadowed, were very quiet. If he spoke, Eric talked mostly with Victoria's father. The Cavanaghs didn't see this as a problem. They all ate their à la carte steak voraciously and congratulated each other at the end of the night on a successful evening. And hadn't it been? There'd been no political outbursts like there had been with Damien. No metaphorical stabbings or shootings either.

Victoria had been shocked a week later when her phone rang and it was Eric, asking her to lunch at his club. She was almost happy about it, until later that day when her mother brought it up before Victoria had a chance to mention it. Deirdre had learned from Joan that Eric was going to ask Victoria. It seemed puppeteered, the parents with their fingers in everything. Joan had even suggested the location and timing of the first date. The club at lunch was a perfect place. A casual way for "the kids" to get to know each other better.

She'd never discussed it with Eric, not even after they were married. It would have angered him to acknowledge how parented he still was. Though he never really tried to convince Victoria that he had picked her. Eric wasn't exactly a swarthy gardener, hunting for the perfect flower and deciding he must have her when he spied her delicate petals. No, it was more as if his parents had bought her at a store and presented her to him in a good, simple bouquet. How could he refuse?

And she, having failed so utterly at her one attempt at independence, her one dalliance with rebellion, could hardly argue with her parents when they encouraged the union. He seemed perfectly acceptable, even attractive. He didn't require much from her in the way of conversation. And he accepted her rather lowly job at the spa.

It wasn't until they were wearing their rings and had installed the TV and determined whose bathroom was whose that she realized his body repelled her. That his smiles were starched and unnatural. That he saw her more as a piece of the furniture, and the more she blended in the better.

She finally reached the parking level. The fluorescent lights were garishly bright and it took a moment for her eyes to adjust. Her heart hammered, from exertion and also anticipation. She opened the door with the excitement of a child opening a cupboard in search of hidden Christmas presents. Her eyes registered the sight of the Audi with disappointment.

So, it would not be tonight. Wishing she had just stuck to her guns and her place in *Tropic of Cancer*, she took a depressing elevator ride back up to the apartment, where she reassumed her position.

The demure click of the front door alerted Victoria to Eric's arrival. She quickly scampered to the bathroom with her nail bits and bloody tissues. She hid the wounded toe with a bandage and some large fluffy socks. She flushed the toilet to further camouflage her activity.

She found him hanging up his coat in the front closet.

"How did it go?"

He grunted as he bent over to unlace his shoes. "We won. Meyers finally stepped up his game."

"Oh, that's good."

"I *told* him the short game isn't everything. He finally listened. He was holding the entire team back."

"Did it stop raining?"

He stood up and looked at her for the first time. "No, it's pouring."

"Oh. It's just—you don't look like you've been in the rain."

He ran a hand through his dry, thinning hair. "I got a ride home. I, uh, ran into Holly outside the club."

Victoria's surprise was impossible to hide. "Holly? How weird." Holly commuted from Laval, a less-than-chic suburb in the north.

He shrugged. "She was stopped at the light on Sherbrooke, right by the club. She waved me over and insisted on driving me home."

"That was nice of her. What was she doing out here, do you know?" Victoria's voice sounded loud and artificial to her ears.

"I don't know, Victoria." Eric sounded annoyed. "Trolling for men, maybe? It wouldn't be her first time. I didn't exactly *ask*. Why don't you ask her yourself if you think it's that interesting?"

Now it was his turn to sound unnatural. Humming, he pushed past her toward his bathroom, pulling his shirt off. She caught an eyeful of nipple and turned away. Within seconds she heard the sound of the shower.

For some reason, Holly had always admired Eric, like he was some unattainable prince waving from his perch on a distant balcony. Victoria imagined it a likely scenario that earlier tonight Holly spotted Eric with her sharp side vision and rolled down the window of her Civic, inviting him out of the rain. It would have been almost an honor for her to do this.

However, Victoria felt a sense of subterfuge as she texted Holly.

VICTORIA: Thanks for driving Eric home—you rescued him!

She saw the bubbles appear almost immediately, indicating that Holly was replying. The bubbles stopped, started, stopped again. Finally:

HOLLY: What do you mean? Rescued? From what?
VICTORIA: The rain, silly.

A pause.

HOLLY: 😊 LOL! NP! It was such a coincidence running into him like that! And he insisted on buying my drink. Such a gentleman!

Victoria's eyebrows arched as she let Holly's text sink in. So. There was something secret at work between Holly and Eric. Well, Victoria could have her own secrets too.

VICTORIA: I'm glad you found each other.

This was true.

VICTORIA: Thanks again.
HOLLY: Mon plaisir! He's a gem!

Gem, that word was rather synonymous with Eric, for Holly. She thought Eric was SUCH a GEM. That's exactly how she would say it, emphasizing the words in hushed tones. If only she could find someone like him.

Eric was far less kind about Holly. He was known to make disparaging remarks about her from time to time. Her "headlights" were especially low class in his eyes and thus something that colored his entire perception of her. Victoria was surprised by the callousness of his tone tonight though. Especially given their recent lunch, when he seemed to enjoy Holly's company so much.

She heard the shower turn off. She put Henry Miller down and went to the bedroom. Her toe pulsed painfully as she climbed into bed and swung her legs under the covers. She shouldn't have picked at her nail so much. Oh well. The journey she was going to make this evening wouldn't involve any walking.

Eric did not pop his head in to ascertain her whereabouts. He did not enter the room to find pajamas either. This was strange. He wasn't the type to walk around in a robe. He found it effeminate, men in robes, sort of like kilts or togas. She had to agree that it was obscene, really, the potential for his flaccid member to peek out between flaps of terrycloth. Eric was not a fan of nudity. His robe served a very utilitarian role, right after his shower, and she rarely saw him leave the bathroom still wearing it.

At any rate, he must have gone to the kitchen robed, because she heard his footsteps going in that direction, and then after a minute or so, the television provided its usual murmur of background noise.

He had been avoiding her, ever since her . . . episode? incident? accident? in the kitchen. He clearly didn't know what to do with her, sicced Deirdre on her, and was waiting for things to "get back to normal."

Well, she thought now, settling herself in the bed, she had done her best to assure him of normality. She had assumed her previously acceptable demeanor, but hadn't had much chance to display that for him. He just hadn't been around. She wasn't all that worried though. She had a trump card, or at least hoped she did, and he would soon drive away with it, with any luck, into the great beyond. She imagined it now, his final journey something like Thelma and Louise's flight into the canyon—brave, joyful, maybe even in silent slow motion, with no frames indicating the implied end. Like a song that just fades into eventual silence, Eric and his car floating into a heavenly repose.

While using this image to relax, she adjusted the pillow under her head. The image on repeat, floating Eric and his car, sometimes accompanied by Geena Davis, her impossibly wide smile and perfectly dusted, tanned face, was as effective a meditation as any "Om."

Soon, she was the one floating, hovering above the bed for the first time in quite a few nights. She felt a shiver of delight that began in her tailbone and moved up her spine in a snaking chill.

The way was familiar, after the two earlier pilgrimages to Luke's bedside. Now it was easier, as though she were following a path set out for her.

After scanning the room, she found Him, but not in bed this time. He was shirtless, sitting in a large, stuffed chair—it might have been gray but it was hard to tell in the darkness. He had fallen asleep while reading. He held the crying-man book tenuously in one hand. His head was slumped a little unattractively onto one shoulder, and a slight hint of snore whistled through his nostrils. His stomach, in full relaxation, pooled a little to form a small gut she had not previously noticed. She felt in her heart a beat of disgust. She chastised herself immediately, blaming the book for boring him to sleep. She focused on his manly size, the way he filled up the chair: his legs, open; his lap, inviting.

She moved to the chair and gently rested her knees on either side of his legs, straddling his lap, feeling his warmth impart warmth to her groin. She pressed against him without thinking and felt a thump on the carpeted floor, as the book fell from his delicate grasp. His arms were finding her, encircling her back, pulling her even closer. He smelled like wood and sweat. His eyes were closed, as ever, but his head lifted and his mouth searched until he found her neck. Her body erupted in a prickly shiver as his lips leisurely traversed from ear to collarbone, pleasure infusing his exhales in the form of faint moans.

A pleasant rocking was taking place between their hips. His lips left her neck, and he blindly pressed his face on her shirt, his nose between her breasts, while the thickened friction below became warmer and closer.

Victoria gripped his arms as she felt herself lifting away. "No . . . no!" she heard herself protest as she was hit with being back in her bed, her words reverberating off the mirrored sliding doors of her closet. She felt her veins vibrating, she was pulsing, her core was hot to the touch, and then with this small touch she was shuddering, with a choked cry that she tried to swallow, unsuccessfully.

SIXTEEN

VICTORIA WASN'T FOCUSED TODAY. SHE WAS DISTRACTED, THOR-oughly distracted, by the previous night's erotic romp. She lost herself, over and over, replaying the events in her mind, reexperiencing the thrills and perhaps inventing new ones that she imagined and was now uncovering like hidden treasures. Walking through the aisles without really seeing, she missed all of *P* in her reverie.

Victoria loved the library and routinely spent many hours wandering through the stacks. She often had to fight annoyance at the paltry selection—it was a lot to ask to have a full complement of French *and* English books, she supposed, but why such disparity? There were so many more French than English. Her library had a French copy of William Gay's *Provinces of Night*, but not an English one. She wondered how many French Canadians were on the lookout for a Southern gothic novel. Not many, she supposed. The softcover spine was in pristine condition.

She got to a shelf that featured titles recommended by various library staff. Not all were winners, of course. She stayed away from the "Mary-Lynn" shelf, which was full of earnest, politically correct new releases. "Vikram" preferred science fiction. "Genevieve" only read YA. In the past, Victoria had had good luck with the picks from someone named "Luce." *Of Mice and Men* was the first one that caught her eye, but she'd already read that in high school. A dead rabbit. A dead girl. A mercy killing. *Crime and Punishment*, an intellectual murder in which the fittest decides who lives or dies, for the greater good. *The Secret History*—she'd read that too, a deadly walk in the woods for that Bunny character, with his best friends. These books contained something she wasn't sure she had—killing hands. Could she push? Bludgeon? Suffocate? It seemed impossible.

Victoria pulled out a book to have a look at the cover. *L'Étranger*, by Camus. Gosh, this Luce person had dark taste in literature. But all good literature dealt with death, didn't it? It was impossible to escape it, either in life or in books. She was tempted, and searched the shelf fruitlessly for an English translation.

Camus's Meursault didn't touch his victim. He pulled a trigger though. She knew she couldn't do that. It all came down to the hands. It was that squeezing she would have to do, and it would be too much of an exertion in the moment. She would lose her resolve. There couldn't even be a "moment." It had to just happen, like the spilled milk of the universe. Eric had to be milk, all over the table. Spilled milk, so harmless. And it was no one's fault. You couldn't even cry over it.

As she returned *L'Étranger* to the shelf, she had a sudden flash of recollection—the sound Luke made as he kissed her, his upper leg muscles moving and flexing as he moved under her. She closed her eyes involuntarily, emitting a sigh.

Although short-lived, it had been the most intense of their encounters. It had been such a relief to see him, after days of failed attempts, whether at the café or in her nighttime flights. She couldn't help but wonder if by loosening the bolts she also somehow loosened the chains that had been keeping her from making nocturnal visits. She recalled that after buying the antifreeze (now in the basement garbage bin, unopened) she had experienced a similar increase in her and Luke's ability to interact, if that was the word, before being banished back to her bed. The rewards were increasing but so were her actions. That was a little scary. But she was determined to follow whatever signs she was getting (from Luke? the universe? both?) to bring her closer to where she needed to be.

As Victoria absently flipped through a battered volume of *Madame Bovary*, she hoped against hope that the five bolts were all it was going to take. It would just be an accident. She could almost make herself believe it. Every day that went by stretched the link between her actions of removing the bolts and the results of those actions. One day it would be as though the two things were completely unrelated. It would be as though one had absolutely nothing to do with the other, like Eric and Victoria. They would peel apart from each other's lives so effortlessly, with nothing sticking them together to begin with. It was deceptive. If an octopus could fit through a two-inch tube, without harm, her exit could be just as slippery. She had to wait a little longer, stretch herself to the needs of time and place.

SEVENTEEN

THE CAFÉ WAS QUIET IN THE TIME FOLLOWING THE LUNCH RUSH, before classes let out and the students poured in, many grabbing complicated caffeinated concoctions before a bus ride home, and others who paid a few dollars to sit with a steaming mug and their laptops writing assignments or preparing for exams. Victoria liked this quieter time, and usually parked herself at the café for a couple of hours—as long as her bladder would allow, because she hated to use the public toilet—in the hopes of seeing Luke in the flesh again.

She had eventually picked out a slim, dark volume at the library— *Eileen* by Ottessa Moshfegh. She hadn't heard of this author before, but liked both the slimness and the darkness of the novel. Surely Luke had finished the crying-man book by now.

She positioned herself at her favorite spot—in the far corner, facing the door. She wouldn't miss anything from this ideal vantage point, aside from the people sitting on the other side of the fireplace, which was right in the middle of the room, with seats all around it in a square. If he happened to sit there, she would move.

She had treated herself to a nonfat pumpkin-spice latte, which was made with less love than usual. It wasn't very hot. The foam was thin and flat, and the milky brown liquid had an oily sheen to it she didn't much like.

A chic-looking man wearing a leather jacket and neck beard made a bit of a show of offering Victoria his seat, which she took politely without returning his flirtatious smile.

She had taken extra care with her appearance today. Her wavy hair never really did what she wanted, which led to a nervous habit of flipping it with her hand, to liven it up. Eric didn't like this ("You're making your hair greasy by touching it so much, Victoria. . . ."), so she had taken to tying it back in a simple ponytail or pulling it up in a French twist. Today, though, it cooperated, falling pleasantly onto her shoulders. She had picked clothes that she hadn't worn in a long time. They were pre-Eric. A fitted gray minidress with soft black leggings underneath, and a thick gray leather belt with two prongs cinching her waist. Knee-high boots, crossed legs. Her makeup was an amateur attempt at "smokey eye." Her lipstick was Come Hither, a daring red that did not suit her. But she couldn't resist the name—it was the perfect incantation.

She hoped he would come in today. She felt that he might. She was beginning to believe in her intuition more, also in her power over the universe. She was making things *happen*. She had started to see herself as a witch, a weird sister, with secrets and spells and potions, even the ability to fly through the night sky to meet her sleeping lover. She delighted in such private thoughts, inwardly cackling, laser-beaming people with her perceptive and magical gaze, seeing into their hearts, gleefully intruding from her perch.

As she sipped her lukewarm latte, she spotted a man standing at the counter wearing an expensive-looking camel coat. He ordered a coffee and brownie to go. He looked harried and spilled some of his drink onto his coat, his thick black brows tented in irritation. He dabbed fussily, blotting the liquid away. Victoria saw he had his impending divorce on his mind and suspected his soon to be ex-wife of dating someone he vaguely knew through friends. He'd always hated that guy and his smug, athletic healthfulness. He'd better not try to get all sporty with little Jack. It was so typical of his ex. The man's heart beat with hatred. He longed to punch her in her mouth, to split the lips he used to kiss.

An older woman wearing turquoise earrings and a matching chunky necklace came in with a girl who looked about ten and ordered a hot chocolate. The girl was carrying a Harry Potter book. Victoria could see the woman was thinking about the lump that she had found in the shower that morning, though her animated smiles and chatter convinced the girl that it was a day like any other. She had time to make up for, and now maybe more than ever.

A middle-aged man with a long, drooping nose waited behind them, texting a woman he had met online. It was the fourth message he had sent this morning. They hadn't met yet, but he was already imagining their lives together. He was mentally clearing out half his closet and thinking that he'd better get rid of the stuff in the basement. He was going to look for a full-time job and stop playing that stupid PlayStation all the time. He wondered if she'd send him another picture. He hoped she liked electronic music, would at least listen to it with him.

Victoria played this game of clairvoyance with everyone who came in, "seeing" with more and more ease each time, feeling pity for the souls she peeked in on, and a self-satisfaction grew in her belly. When she tired of it, she turned to her book and soon became pulled into the story, which was littered with empty whisky bottles, dead rodents, peanut shells, and laxatives. It was a thing of beauty.

"Is this seat taken?"

Startled, in the small moment between hearing this and her eyes flicking up, she hoped a desperate hope that it was Luke, and saw her whole life as it unfolded from there. But when her eyes looked up from the page, she saw it was her husband.

"Eric?" she could only sputter his name ineloquently.

He sat down. "I had a bit of time between meetings and thought I'd see if you might be here," he explained. "And here you are."

She didn't put her book down. "Here I am." This was not what was supposed to happen.

"I thought—maybe I should get a drink. They have other things—not coffee?" He was arching his neck around to see what was offered in the glass case at the front of the store. He got up, hands in his coat pockets. Hunched, he surveyed for a while before selecting a bottle of water. Her mind-reading powers had halted. When she looked at him, all she saw was the back of his head, a head that looked suddenly very young and vulnerable.

When he returned, her book was still open, held in both hands.

"Well, this is a surprise."

"Yeah, well, I took a chance," he said, his eyes taking on a hurtable quality that made her feel uncomfortable. "We haven't seen much of each other lately."

"No, we haven't."

"It won't be like this forever. It's just—intense right now, and I can feel I'm this close—MacPhearson is making up his mind soon, and this just isn't the time to make a mistake. People say I'm the first on his list, and I can't let that change, not now."

"No, of course not. I understand."

He opened the bottle and took a swig, then looked out the window of the café.

"I . . . I appreciate that, Victoria. Your—your understanding." He dragged his eyes to meet hers then, with a softness she wasn't used to seeing. She didn't like it. She was used to their unforgiving, unbending, almost black color. He wasn't allowed to change now.

She nodded, letting the book she was holding rest on the table.

"We've got the Christmas dinner coming up in December. You'll be there, right?"

She willed her jaw to stay where it was. This entreating, almost pleading tone was foreign to her. Eric never asked her to attend things like this; her presence was assumed, the event marked on the Ansel Adams calendar in black ink, capital letters.

"I'll be there," she managed, hoping her face didn't look as frightened as she felt inside. His being vulnerable right now made her feel trapped all over again.

He looked visibly relieved. "Thanks. I know Bill's wife likes you. Well, she will when you make a little effort. And I promise it won't be like this forever. I mean, of course I'll be busy. That's a given. But I'll be able to take time off next year. I was thinking, we could go somewhere. Maybe Paris?"

Paris, she scoffed in her head. Such an unimaginative place to suggest. Luke wouldn't have suggested Paris. He would have said, *I hear Reykjavik is beautiful this time of year. Or what about Rio? Let's make love under a waterfall in Antigua!*

Still, there was something childlike in his manner now that made her feel bad for him. He was trying. It was pathetic, but he was trying. It was funny that he thought going to Paris with him would make her happy—that spending more time with him would be a good thing. It was funny, and sad.

She smiled faintly, the best she could do. "Maybe."

He took another long drag from the bottle.

"I do want you to be—you know—happy," he said, looking down at the table. "It's important, you know. Whatever it takes, to keep it together. There's a lot at stake here. For both of us."

"Oh, I'm happy," she said, in her best reassuring spa voice. She thought about his drink last night with Holly, the drink he never mentioned.

He looked up, clueless. "You are?"

"Yes." It was a coo of calm, a balm on his seeking eyes. It's what he had come for, reassurance that his wife wasn't cracking up and capable of sabotaging his blossoming career, and at a most critical juncture.

He nodded to himself as he cradled the plastic bottle with both hands. "Good. Good. Well. I guess I better let you get back to your reading."

He stood up, and bending at the waist, kissed her cheek. It was just a peck, but it made her heart feel too big for its cage, fluttering in a hot panic.

"Bye, Eric," she said, unable to keep the nervous laugh out of her voice.

"See you later. . . . I'm having dinner out again tonight. The partners invited me to join them. Some place in Mile End."

And he was gone. She didn't know what the front of him looked like, whether he had assumed his usual harried, serious expression. But the back of him still was looking young, and hopeful, and sad, and not knowing he was going to die soon.

After the door closed and she watched him disappear into the crowd on the sidewalk, getting smaller as he walked away, she slumped in her chair and dropped her book carelessly onto the table, losing her place. She felt ill, like her intestines might betray her. Her breath felt raw. Suddenly her outfit and all the care for her appearance seemed terribly wrong and wasted, all at the same time.

A deep self-loathing washed over her, and she buried her face in her hands as she thought about his car, what she had done to it. Had she been completely mad? She hadn't taken in the fact of his vulnerable, soft neck. It was all she could think about now.

Panicked, she reached into her bag and scrabbled around until she found the case that contained the collection of bolts. She felt as though she'd just woken from a very bad dream.

She gathered up her things quickly, slinging her purse over her shoulder, her hand inside, fingering the bolts feverishly. She knew what she needed to do. She needed to get home and put the bolts back before he drove his car again.

When she got home, she grabbed the ratchet and the bolts and took the elevator down to the parking garage with a do-gooder determination to put things right. But the car was gone.

EIGHTEEN

VICTORIA WAS BACK IN THE APARTMENT. SHE HAD STARED AT the empty parking space a long time, agape, squeezing her fingers tighter and tighter around the bolts that had no business being in her hand. She hoped the flesh of her palm would engulf them, and that when she opened her hand they would no longer be there. It would be just one of her fantasies. But they were there. They had printed lines on her skin, painfully and almost puncturing, but they were still there.

Sitting dazedly on the couch in front of a black television screen, she recalled Eric telling her dinner was at a place in Mile End. That was why he took the car. He must have taken it right after saying goodbye at the café. She imagined with a start that he might be driving it right that moment.

She rushed to the window, looking down twelve stories to the street below, but saw no puff of smoke over a flaming, combusted vehicle housing her husband's charred remains. She saw nothing, heard nothing.

A quick glance at her phone, but there were no texts or emails. She tried his phone, but it just rang and went to voice mail. Then she tried it again. What was she going to say to him anyway? "Stop driving your car—I tampered with it!" Or maybe it was too late already—perhaps he wasn't able to answer the phone because his body no longer worked.

Another call to Eric. Still no answer. There was nothing left for her to do but what she did best. Wait.

THERE WASN'T MUCH IN THE HOUSE TO EAT. SHE WALKED TO THE store, phone gripped tightly, where she bought a large bag of caramel popcorn, something she hadn't eaten since her pre-Eric days and something she would never eat in the presence of another person. The enjoyment was always fuller if she could indulge by herself. Maybe this was the beginning of many caramel popcorn dinners, she mused.

Fueled by anxiety, tainted with guilt, boosted by adrenaline and anticipation, the walk to and from the apartment did her some good. She focused on people on the street and in the store. The people all looked blameless, like they couldn't possibly know or imagine what was going on in her mind. All were earnest and single-minded, hardworking, well-intentioned people. None able to harbor the sickness of duality. She wanted to soak up their goodness. She longed to be knowable and single layered, like they were, in their heavy coats, hurrying home to their families. But how could she, with her bag of caramel corn, rushing home to a house that was empty, with the hopes that it would remain so? She felt like a stain, a black cancer among the wholesome.

She was trying to keep the thought of Eric's neck out of her mind, his uncharacteristic kind words that caught her off guard. She was also trying to rein in her imagination, her witch's second sight that was seeing all kinds of automotive atrocities. She was somewhat successful, but the thoughts that replaced the ones she had banished were ones of self-loathing, mixed with a twisted feeling that resembled hope.

At home, she read *Eileen*, phone in one hand, the book's spine broken enough so that it could sit open on her lap, and her other hand free to bring the popcorn to her mouth. She felt a kinship with this very strange protagonist. She felt no repulsion, only an understanding of otherness. As for Eileen's personal hygiene and odd eating habits, Victoria recognized them for what they were: the secret underbelly, the no-one's-looking parts everyone had. They may look a little different depending on the person. One person might pick their nose and eat the mucus while breastfeeding their new baby. One might eat so much that she threw up, and then have seconds for dessert. Another might imagine the naked bodies of his friend's adolescent children. And another might only enjoy an evening tea if the packet was stolen from work. It comforted her to be reminded of this normality. It made her realize that she had been wrong about the people in the grocery store. They weren't all sweet little hobbits. They had their secrets too.

It was 11:30 when she heard the key turn in the lock. She had fallen asleep with her book in her lap, phone still clutched in a claw-grasp.

She jumped up guiltily, the popcorn bag tumbling to the floor, with the small messy remains of the bottom of the bag spilling out on the couch.

Hastily, Victoria tried to clean up the evidence, but Eric was in the room too quickly.

Her head snapped up.

He was looking at her, coldly observing her scrabbling to pick up tiny husks and pieces from the surface of the sectional and the shaggy soft rug.

"I—I fell asleep," she explained clumsily.

"I see."

"How was the dinner? Looks like it went late."

"No, it didn't. It was over at nine." He walked over to the fridge, found the pinot gris, and poured himself a generous glass.

She continued to pick up the mess. It seemed like a thousand tiny husks were wedged in the rug's fibers.

"Did you stop at the office on your way home?"

He took a pensive sip from his glass. "No, no I did not. But I did—I did make a stop."

The sound of his voice made her look up. Her heart had ceased its regular rhythm. Now it was jogging and jagging all over the place. He had an exaggerated storytelling tone to his voice that she wasn't used to hearing.

"Yes, I made a stop. An unplanned one. On the side of the highway near the Jean Talon exit. I'd heard it was really beautiful there at night, and gee, it really was. I just couldn't get enough. I stayed there for about two hours."

She didn't like the way he was looking at her. She saw him touch the knife block, near where the antifreeze used to sit.

"Eric, what are you talking about? Two hours?" her voice shrilled. "On the side of the road?

"Why yes, Victoria. In this lovely November weather. It was just wonderful."

She rose from the couch carefully. She didn't want to ask. Asking meant she knew. "I don't understand."

"No? You don't? Well, let me tell you. My fucking car started making noises when I was driving home. Weird grinding noises. Then a bunch of warning lights went off, and my steering wheel got really stiff and I could barely pull over. I thought I was going to have an accident."

"Oh!" It came out in a tiny soft puff of air.

He drank the rest of his glass in an angry gulp.

"I opened the hood, and the engine was a mess. There was oil all over the place. I opened one of the things and I burned the side of my hand when it basically exploded with steam." She noticed then the angry red and white of an oblong blister on the hand holding the now-empty glass.

"Oh!" she puffed again, reaching forward in futility. He had turned from her, and was refilling his glass.

"It took ages for CAA to get there, and it was fucking freezing too."

"How awful! Why didn't you call me? I would have come and got you."

He surveyed her with a cat's suspicion. "Where's the antifreeze? Did you put the antifreeze in my car?" he asked, eyes narrowed. "Put it somewhere it wasn't supposed to go? I told you, you don't know anything about cars."

Her eyes widened in genuine surprise. "No! No, I didn't use the antifreeze, I didn't. I looked at my car and didn't even know where to put it. You were right. It was silly of me to buy it in the first place. Where is the car now?"

He took a more measured, pensive sip, but his eyes didn't leave hers in their black intensity. "The CAA guy had no idea what was wrong with it, but said it shouldn't be driven. I had it towed to the shop."

She got a cloth from the drawer and poured cold water on it. She moved toward him, offering it. "For your hand. It's clean." He waved her away, refusing her help.

She stood there with the cloth, dripping a little. "You should have called me, Eric. I would have helped. I could have picked you up. I was just here, I wasn't doing anything. What an awful night you've had."

He glowered at her. His eyes were accusing and angry. "Oh, I don't know. Sometimes it's good to think," he said, emphasizing the word "think" with an extra sharp "k." "I didn't want to interrupt your . . . evening. You had a nice night, from the looks of it."

She knew he was mocking her popcorn mess, but she was caught now and felt like she couldn't move. The cloth kept dripping. She felt the air on her eyeballs, she must have been opening them widely. She lowered the lids a little.

"Just a quiet night with my book."

He placed his wineglass on the counter. "Was it? I missed three or four calls from you earlier on. While I was at dinner."

"Oh!" the third puff escaped her, and she was unprepared to explain.

He didn't give her the time. "I'm going to take a shower," he announced. He looked at her again, then turned to go down the hall. "Mop up that mess on the floor before you go to bed." She heard the bathroom door close and then lock before the water turned on.

She cleaned up, even used the vacuum to make sure no evidence of her gluttony was left behind. She used the Swiffer on the kitchen floor, though that too was overkill for a few drops of water. Surprised he had not emerged from the bathroom—usually she could time his showers to the minute—she did her nighttime rituals and got into bed. It was then that she heard him leave the bathroom, and again (robed? this was such a strange trend) walk toward the living room. He was on his phone. She could hear him, low-toned, words indistinguishable.

Knowing he wasn't coming to bed any time soon, she was able to relax a little. She blinked in the darkness, let air pass between her lips in long deep breaths. She stifled a sob, the first of many, as she turned on her side.

NINETEEN

A S SHE HUDDLED UNDER THE DUVET, A FEELING OF FRAGILITY pervaded her body the next morning. It was as if she had undergone some kind of metamorphosis overnight, had turned into a wintered branch, all life and vitality frozen out of her, only a husk remaining, and the weight of a tiny bird would cause her to crack in a dry, clean break. Wood falling lightly to the cold ground, unknown and unnoticed, and the bird finding another place to perch.

She rolled from one side to the next in bed. She hadn't slept well. Her stomach bothered her—that bag of caramel popcorn, maybe. Maybe her intestines were now part of her internal turmoil? Sick in body as well as in mind. She wondered why her love was so . . . Surely there must be a living, breathing love stuck in a crevasse somewhere in her heart. But she couldn't seem to bring it out. She could love the back of Eric's neck, but was that all? If she could convince him to walk backward from now on, would she be content? Better still, what if she twisted his neck 180 degrees? She snorted derisively at the thought. What a miser she was. She was so stingy, Eric had to reverse his entire being to receive her scraps.

These feelings of guilt and self-reproach lasted several minutes while her stomach pinched and bloated.

She decided it was probably time to put herself together for the day. As she stretched, she noticed sounds coming from the television. Unusual. Eric never watched television in the morning. She quietly opened the bedroom door a few inches and peered down the length of the hallway, where she could see Eric's profile on the couch. He wasn't looking at the television screen. He was still wearing his bathrobe, his head cast downward. He was writing something on his phone.

It looked as though he had spent the whole night there. A blanket was bunched at his feet. She saw with a glance back at their bed that his side was undisturbed.

She closed the door with a velvet hush, and tiptoed back to bed. She somehow knew instinctively that he wouldn't want to be seen there, on his phone. And she didn't want him to see her seeing him, either.

Thinking of him sleeping on the couch in his robe, she was uneasy. Was he afraid to come to bed with her now? She should be elated at this new development, but she felt instead a clutch of anxiety. She remembered the accusing look on his face last night with a chill. For a moment, it was as if *he knew*.

Soft footsteps passed by the bedroom down the hall. He was heading to his shower. It was a Saturday, but they both tended to work that day. Soon, he would have to come into the bedroom to peruse the walk-in closet for his suit, shirt, and tie. They wouldn't be able to avoid each other.

She hated this silent game they were playing in their flawless white coffin of an apartment. The predictability, the timers, the carefully drawn parameters. The scripts, the stage directions. Say this, don't say that, smile here, ding! Make the chicken. Oh, and above all, *be grateful*. Deirdre was right, she "had it good." But Victoria was suffocated by those satin pillows. She was muted in this soundproof box. If she dared to climb over the mountains of money and respectability, dig out of her living grave, would there be any true life on the other side?

She got up quickly in a sudden determination to leave the house before Eric was out of the shower. She couldn't stand the thought of running into him. "Good morning" seemed an impossibility, words she wouldn't be able to force out.

At her dresser, she slipped into work clothes and ran a brush through her hair. She'd have to go without makeup today. She sprinted to the kitchen to grab a granola bar for breakfast.

Snatching up her bag and keys, she felt relief, and went to the front door. She stepped into the hallway. She was out! As she briefly gazed back at the apartment, it was almost like she was seeing it for the first time. White as paper, as a hospital ward, as a snow drift. As a mausoleum in white marble. Walls, floor, fixtures, furniture. The apartment looked like it belonged to someone else, or to no one at all. The black-and-white art on the walls had a generic, unapproachable quality, like in a hotel. The ivory tray on the glass table under the mirror. She could not recall ever touching it. Who bought it? Only one personal item indicated that two people, a man and a woman, lived here—it was a small photo of their justice-of-the-peace wedding housed in a silver frame. But those people, bent over their signatures with serious expressions, could have been anyone.

BERNADETTE WAS VICTORIA'S FIRST CLIENT THAT DAY. BERNADETTE always arrived well before her appointments, even though Victoria made a point of never taking her a minute early. The mad dash from the apartment had given Victoria more than enough time to prepare her room. She turned on the blanket heater, the oil diffuser, and the ocean music. She stocked her cupboard full of clean, white towels. She checked her hair and washed her hands. Sighed. Bernadette wouldn't be here for at least ten more minutes. It was only eight thirty.

Restless, Victoria went up to the front desk. Mercedes, the receptionist who was apprenticing to be a makeup artist, was leaning against her desk, examining her nails. Today they were acrylic, shocking pink, and bejeweled. They were ridiculously long and a source of great pride.

"No one here yet?" Victoria asked. It was an obvious question. The room was empty.

Mercedes checked the appointment book using one of her talons, then scanned the waiting area. "Not yet. It's going to be a long day. *Tabernacle!*"

When Mercedes saw that Victoria hadn't retreated back to her room like usual, she glanced up from the tall counter with mild curiosity. "You're here early."

Victoria flushed and touched her hair self-consciously. "Yeah. I left in a bit of a hurry today."

Mercedes gave her a knowing nod. "Will you let me do you? I need practice any chance I can get. We have time till your little lady gets here."

Victoria's face burned. Was it so obvious she hadn't properly put on her face? She let Mercedes lead her by the hand to the makeup counter, where she perched on a tall, swiveling stool.

"I'll just do an everyday look," said Mercedes, scanning colors and manipulating brushes and palettes in a way that seemed miraculous, given those claws.

She was gentle—one could almost say loving—the way she drew the brushes across Victoria's face, studying her. Victoria felt an undivided attention that she rarely experienced, and was warmed by it. Being touched almost put her in a swoon.

"You have such nice skin," Mercedes murmured as she applied a final coat of mascara, wiggling the black wand slowly through Victoria's eyelashes. Her perfectly powdered face, fragrant with whatever moisturizer she used, was inches from Victoria's, close enough to kiss. Her breasts softly pressed against Victoria's arm.

"You think?" whispered Victoria, not wanting to move, to break the spell of this unexpected intimacy.

The chime of the door sounded and Mercedes's concentration immediately dissolved. She put away the mascara and stepped back, wearing a professional, welcoming expression. She gave Victoria a small nod of dismissal.

"Thanks," Victoria said, though too quietly for anyone to hear.

It was Bernadette who had interrupted them with her presence. She was mousy as ever, wearing a pilled polyester jacket with racing stripes down the sleeves that looked decades old. She appeared to be particularly swamped by the weight of her life today. Victoria felt a distinct impatience with Bernadette's disheveled state. When she greeted her, she noticed there was a ski hill of dandruff in the part of her hair.

Victoria fought a momentary disgust, flashing her teeth in a smile of welcome. It was time to be spa girl again.

TWENTY

VICTORIA CLOSED THE CAFÉ DOOR BEHIND HER, FEELING A PAV-lovian reaction to the smells and sounds there. She needed a coffee badly after her workday, a little break to regroup before the dread of facing Eric at home.

There was one barista at Café au Lait who knew her order and always put extra care into the latte. She had a matronly vibe to her, as opposed to most of the student-aged people who worked there. She had a huge uniboob under the green apron she wore, and a double chin. Her hair was very curly, the top part held with a barrette that fixed a bouffant mound in place. She had probably been doing her hair like that since the 1990s. Victoria liked her because she made the foam extra dense, usually with a dainty leaf on top. Today, it was a heart.

"You have a new book today, I see," she said, eyeing *Eileen*.

"Oh, yes, well, it's from the library," Victoria stammered, surprised to find herself caught off guard. It was disturbing to her that the barista noticed that she had started a new book. She wondered if the staff at the café talked about her. Laughed at her for spending so much time there alone. It was embarrassing, almost.

"A good place to find books," said the barista with a smile. She gave Victoria a conspiratorial wink as she pushed the mug toward her. "My son reads a lot too. He loves anything fantasy. Can't get enough of it!"

Victoria imagined the barista's son, a sadly overweight kid with fungus on his back who was always gobbling a big pile of Kraft Macaroni and Cheese. His avatar in online chat groups was Ekoltin (anagram of Tolkein, of course), where he spent many nights arguing the finer plot points of Elfin spells with people in other time zones. He was fluent in the language of Klingon, and his only real-life social activity was to attend Comic-Con, where he wore the handmade costumes his mother made for him. Ka-Plah!

Victoria snatched her mug in an attempt to remove herself from what was becoming an awkward exchange. The coffee slopped a bit and the heart stretched out on one side, warping it to look more like a big nose.

"Thanks," she said before turning away.

She was about to take her usual place in the corner when she decided, in a perverse impulse, to sit somewhere else. She imagined if the barista knew what book she was reading, she had probably also noted that Victoria always sat in the same place. Well, now she'd show her that it didn't much matter where she sat. She flounced on a chair by the fireplace, which put her back to the front door. Immediately she regretted it. It thwarted her purpose. Luke could come in, order, pay, take his drink, and she would easily miss the whole thing. Her need to teach the barista a lesson made it impossible for her to move though.

She decided, through gritted teeth, that today would be a wash. She would finish her coffee and then just leave. She hadn't seen Luke here in weeks anyway. Maybe he didn't even come here anymore.

She would read a chapter of *Eileen* and head home. Eileen was busy stalking the prison guard she had a crush on. After following the guy home, she touched herself in her truck while watching his silhouette in the window. What a fabulous creep Eileen was! Victoria was enjoying it. It was nasty but also oddly alluring, like a beautiful woman with rotted teeth behind a close-lipped smile.

Then He was there. Eileen was touching herself in her horrible old truck, and Luke was there sitting in an overstuffed armchair across from her, by the fireplace, only the table that Victoria had set her mug on between them. Victoria couldn't believe her luck.

Then more luck came her way, when he spilled his tea on the table. His eyes flicked up to hers, and he grimaced in embarrassment. "I'm so sorry," he said, and went to get napkins. When he returned, he mopped up the liquid. She watched the muscles in his forearm twitch and work as he did this. He was wearing a plaid work shirt with the sleeves pushed up to the elbows.

"No problem," she said almost ebulliently.

He looked at her and smiled briefly as he sank back into his chair.

"You're still reading that," she said, indicating his book.

He looked at the cover, as though for the first time.

"Maybe you don't remember. We had the same book the other day," she reminded him.

A look of dim recognition lit his eyes. "Oh, right. I thought I recognized you. Yeah. It's taking me awhile to get through it. I'm slow."

"Well, I don't blame you. I couldn't take it, all that . . ." She was searching for another word for "rape," "rape" being such a horrible first-real-conversation word.

He smiled again. He had a dimple that appeared in his left cheek each time he smiled. Did he have the slightest idea how adorable he was? "I know. It's pretty brutal. You finished it?"

"Yeah. I didn't want to . . . but I kept hoping it'd get better. I hung on to the bitter end."

He looked amused. "You didn't like it, I take it?"

"Well, I—are *you* enjoying it?"

"Enjoy—no, that would be the wrong word for this book. It was highly recommended to me by a friend who reads a lot. She said this book changed her life, so I figure it must be worth taking a look."

She. "Changed her life? Wow. That's quite a statement. What do you think about it? Has it changed your life?"

A harried woman trying to lasso her wild toddler tripped over Luke's bag, which was sitting at his feet. The toddler sat in front of them and screamed like a feral beast. Luke smiled in relief when the woman scooped the child up and marched out of the café. Order restored.

"I don't think it's changed my life, no. Mainly, it's really just sad. I can't believe how much the guy has been through."

Victoria wanted to be more cool, but couldn't contain her excitement. The words just bubbled out before she had a chance to restrain herself. "Exactly! That's why I hated it. Even just picking up the book is painful, having to look at that guy's face. Seriously, if I had to see that crying face one more time . . ."

Now Luke was laughing. She loved the happy creases by his eyes. He leaned back. "Tell me what you really think."

She smiled coyly. "Okay. It's torture porn. Don't add to the torture by finishing it."

He nodded, took a sip of his tea, what was left of it. "Got it. By the way, you know that the guy on the cover isn't crying, right?"

She gestured to his book. "What do you mean? Of course he's crying."

He cleared his throat. "Ah, well, I have it on some authority that it's a picture of a guy . . . er, *not crying*." He fiddled with the lid on his travel mug.

"He sure looks like he's crying—I don't get it." Victoria had tilted her head to the side in what she hoped was a becoming angle. "I mean, look, his face is all scrunched up, he looks like he's in pain."

"Yeah, well, from what I heard, his expression is less emotional, and more, er, you know . . . physical." He made a vague hand gesture.

Victoria raised her eyebrows and crossed her legs. *Tell me more about the physical*, a little voice in her wanted to say.

"That's just what I heard," he said with a laugh. She saw a ghost of a blush emerge on his face. She was feeling warm too. "I didn't think it up myself, don't worry. I listened to a podcast, they interviewed the author and she explained the cover."

"Oh," she said, and their eyes locked a moment. "Well, now I think I hate it even more. I wish he *was* crying now."

He laughed generously, clasping his worn hands together. She was both elated and simultaneously worried that her comment made her sound too prudish. She amended, "I mean, there's a time and there's a place." *Like now*, the little voice chimed. She felt her cheeks flame.

He gestured at *Eileen*. "So, is that any better?"

"Oh, yes. No contest. So much more realistic, if you can handle it. Plus, it's shorter!"

"You don't like long books?"

"I mean, of course I like long books, and there are great ones. But the best book length is two hundred and fifty to three hundred pages. If authors can say what they need to in those pages . . . well, they have my respect. I think it's more difficult in many ways to keep it succinct."

He was nodding. "Sounds like you read a lot. Maybe you can recommend my next book."

"You're really going to finish that thing?" she asked playfully.

It was so easy, talking to him. She felt herself unravel from her usual coil of muscles. She heard her voice undulate, up and down, her laugh bubbling and spontaneous. It felt marvelous. She didn't recall the last time she had felt so natural.

They were interrupted when his phone rang. "Excuse me," he said, before picking it up. "I have to take this."

He turned away to take the call. She watched him as he spoke. The edges of everything around him went fuzzy, and all she saw was his figure, his mouth as it moved, his hands as he made slight gestures—he couldn't be more perfect. All that was missing was the romantic violin music in the background.

He hung up, shaking his head. "Duty calls," he said, standing and pulling on his coat. "I'd like to stay and chat, but I have to get back to work."

Her heart fell. She couldn't think of what to say.

"Too bad," she managed.

He pulled his bag onto his shoulder and shoved the book in. His eyes lingered on her, and she felt a buzz of electricity between them. "You know, you do seem familiar. I feel like we might have met before. Maybe you browsed my store recently? I make wood furniture. I have a store on Notre Dame."

"You do? What's your store called?"

"It's called DuBois, my last name and a wordplay on the materials I use." He fished in his bag and handed her a card. It was simple, on thick white stock. HANDCRAFTED HARDWOOD, LUKE DUBOIS, DESIGNER, then his phone number.

"Maybe one day I'll come by," she said.

"I'd like that."

"I don't have a card," she stammered. What a stupid thing to say!

"That's okay," he laughed, slinging his bag over his shoulder. "You know where to find me."

LONG AFTER LUKE HAD LEFT THE CAFÉ, SHE STARED AT THE STIFF rectangle of paper in front of her. The universe had unlocked something crucial, bestowed a key of sorts. With minimal effort, she had found herself sitting opposite him today, talking. Without asking, he had given her his card. Not so that she could visit his store. But so that she could "know where to find him."

She already knew where to find him, at night. But now the fantasy was bleeding into the day, seeping from sleep to wakefulness, from psychic to physical.

It was what she wanted, but she hadn't been prepared for this. The ease of it, the lack of planning. No wheedling or manipulation needed on her part. No stalking around in a truck, like Eileen. She felt exhilarated but also a little knocked off balance.

She started the walk back home. She wondered, had he noticed her wedding ring? She usually thought to remove it, but she hadn't really had the presence of mind to do so today. If he had, did he care?

Then the thought jumped into her mind, had anyone seen them talking? Montreal was a big city, but there was always the chance of bumping into people who knew her, or her parents, or Eric. Most of the time, though, it was such a lonely place. The city rumbled along, indifferent to her, buzzing with the slight acrimony of bilingual conversations. The city crumbling with its cracked pavement and crooked politicians. The city colored with the daily scruff of immigrant struggle, and the universal fight against the rough elements. It was difficult to feel part of Montreal.

But today, it seemed that the city had eyes, eyes seeking her instead of looking past her. The world around her suddenly seemed curious, as though she were spilling light and music as she walked. Her gait had purpose, her hips swung as though they were worth looking at.

When she walked the street with Eric, she took smaller steps, looked out of her eyes as through the slits of venetian blinds. She felt shrouded in an invisible burka. She was part of the 1 percent, she wore designer clothing, ate organic produce, her hair was washed with salon products, and she was out on display for the world to see. These things weren't a pleasure, though. They were an expensive bark, a costly covering-up. Both she and Eric were constantly covered up—from the world, and from each other.

What would he do, she thought, if on impulse, she linked arms with him and pushed him playfully into the mailbox and kissed him as they walked? He would be mortified, that was certain, and angry that she'd made him look so undignified, checking to see if the grimy mailbox had smeared his coat, jerking his arm away from her with the smallest movement possible, keeping his expression neutral but not able to hide the tightness in his jaw, worrying she'd left unseemly lipstick on his mouth.

She imagined if she did that with Luke, it would be the beginning of a sidewalk wrestling match, wet jeans and leaf fragments in the hair, bursts of laughter and expletives, ending with a breathless, smiling kiss that had all the optimistic charge of a Maybelline advertisement.

A couple of young men, each with a stocky pit bull type of dog straining at the leash, passed each other warily. The one with a shaved head spat something out of the side of his mouth. The one with the leather jacket hesitated before jaywalking across the street, prompting a few honks.

Turning the corner, she imagined again the scenario with Eric, but this time she pushed his head into the corner of the mailbox, not just once but a dozen or so times. A sexual rhythm, bang, bang, bang, *yes*, bang, bang, bang, *oh*! Until the corner, a sharp corner indeed, opened the skin, then cracked the skull, and Eric's body lay slumped on the ground by the mailbox with a little brain pulp and a lot of blood on the pavement underneath him.

In this scenario, he put up little resistance and did just as Victoria wanted. She barely noticed touching him, actually. She was standing close to him, she could hear him panting, could see his hair follicles at the back of his neck—time for a haircut—but it was almost as though someone else were doing the deed, and she was nothing more than a very proximate witness.

However gratifying the thought of it all was, she had to let the fantasy slide because she realized that she would never be able to do it. It was too hands-on. No, her crime belonged in a Miss Marple novel, where, through some brilliant planning, the murdered isn't actually touched by the murderer. The most personal thing—taking a life—was best done in the most passive, detached manner. She reflected that if Eric was given a choice, he would prefer that anyway. No messy grappling about or sharing last choking epithets for him. He would hate for someone to watch him die—he needed privacy to trim his nose hairs, for goodness' sake. To have someone watch life drain from his face, to see his frightened tears collect, to smell the effects of his loosened bowels, that would be unbearable. Murder from afar. There was much more dignity in that.

As she turned off Sherbrooke Street in the direction of the kosher butcher shop, Victoria took comfort in remembering there was no such thing as Miss Marple. There was no brilliant, deducting granny waiting in the wings to figure out how a promising young lawyer suddenly died. That only happened in books. The thought pleased her.

SHE RETURNED HOME AFTER PICKING UP GROCERIES FOR DINNER. Her mind was swirling happily with thoughts of bloodied mailboxes and her meeting with Luke. The universe had expanded further, had opened its hand. Humming a jaunty "Mack the Knife," she breezed past the front closet without noticing that Eric's coat was hanging there.

Eric was sitting at the kitchen counter on one of the white stools. He wasn't watching television, or looking at his phone, or reading a piece of mail—all usual activities for Eric. He was just sitting. Victoria recoiled, nearly dropping her shopping bags.

"Eric! You scared me! I wasn't expecting you until later!" She put down the bags and held a hand over her throat.

"I'm sure you weren't," he said accusingly.

"But, why . . . ?"

"I got a call from the mechanic. To come pick up my car."

Victoria could feel the room's stillness and the chugging of her heart in her ears.

"Did they fix it already?" She reached into her bag unconsciously, shaking the sunglasses case to feel the weight of the bolts.

"Well, there wasn't a lot to fix. The alternator went, that's why I lost power on the highway."

"The alternator? Well, at least they found out what went wrong."

He was looking at her strangely. "Yes . . . well, that's not all that went wrong."

"What else? I hope they aren't trying to rip you off. Remember how they were with your last car."

"No, I don't think so," he said, thoughtful. "Jake was really nice. He was concerned, took me to the office to chat."

"Concerned? Why, isn't the car safe to drive now?"

"Yeah, concerned. He said that the alternator failed because 'someone had messed with it.' Like, on purpose."

Victoria felt her mouth go dry. Her lips felt cold and thin. And dry. She licked them. "No . . . but who? How does he know?"

"Well, obviously he doesn't know one hundred percent for sure, but he said it looked to him like someone had just opened the hood and removed a bunch of bolts. Which is weird. He said bolts don't just suddenly all unscrew themselves."

"Well, no they don't, but isn't it possible . . ."

"And you can't just pop the hood unless you unlatch it from the inside the car. So someone had to either unlock my car or break into it to open it up."

"But—I don't understand," she stammered.

He looked at her peevishly. "What is there not to understand? Someone fucked with my car, Victoria. Jake said thankfully they didn't seem to know what they were doing. Otherwise they could have cut my brake lines or something, and I would have really been in trouble."

"I'm sorry, Eric. You must be upset." She knew better than to lay a hand on his shoulder. She knew better than to ask why anyone would do this.

His eyes flashed. "That's a bit of an understatement, Victoria. Someone," he said, moving toward her, his enunciation exaggerated and slow, "fucked. With. My. Car."

"I know," she whispered.

He was in her face now. His breath had a hot, acidic coffee smell to it. She could see he hadn't shaved today. His hair looked puffier than usual. Unwashed? Or had he been running his hands through it, something he did when he was fretful?

He held his glare for a few moments before just letting it go, in the spirit of "what's the point." He sat back down on the stool and winced.

"Could it be someone at your work? Isn't that Grant guy competing with you for partner?"

He shook his head, leaned forward, head in hands. "No. No one at work." He heaved a deep sigh. "I keep going over it in my mind. It doesn't make any sense. It's like a nightmare. I can't remember. I keep racking my brains." He looked up at her, looking tired and worn. He was almost likable, like this.

"What can't you remember?" she asked, hushed and sympathetic.

"Keys."

"What?"

"My *keys*, Victoria. I've been going through my mind who all have keys to my car."

She knew she looked like Bambi with eyes too large for her face, but couldn't change a thing.

"Jake," she prompted, mouth still dry.

"Yes, Jake. I had keys made for him two years ago when I got the car."

"The guys at your work, who park the cars at the garage."

"Yeah, they have the keys too. I thought of them."

The silence stretched.

"That's it?" she finally said, when it was clear he wasn't going further.

"No," he said, looking at her, more directly it seemed, than he ever had.

His phone buzzed on the counter, breaking the tension of the moment. He answered it. It was work.

"I have to get back," he said. "This is the absolute worst time for me to deal with this shit. I have to be at the office."

"Maybe whoever did it didn't use keys," Victoria offered. "Maybe they used one of those"—she searched for the word—"A slim jim?"

He looked back at her. His eyes looked tired but hopeful.

"You're right, it must have been a slim jim," he said, turning to put on his coat. "I don't think Jake or Leigh had anything to do with this. Especially when they know about cars. They would have done it properly."

"Of course. And if he had done it, Jake wouldn't have told you he thought the car had been tampered with."

He turned back to look at her, with palpable relief on his face. Bull's-eye. She was on his side with this comment.

"That's what I was thinking," he said in a confiding tone. "That's exactly what I was thinking. It was probably punks. Vandals."

She nodded gravely. "I'm so sorry, Eric."

"Anyway, I'm going to get the keys back from the guys at the garage, just to be on the safe side. Jake gave his copy to me without my even asking for it."

Neither of them had mentioned her key.

"I have to get back. See you tonight." He kissed her lightly on the lips, hovering for a brief, decisive moment before leaving.

TWENTY-ONE

THEY MET AT THE SUSHI BAR IN THE FOOD COURT AT EATON CEN-
tre. Holly was there first, always on time. She smiled brightly,
though her eyes looked smaller, more careworn than usual, puffy too.
Always good about observing Remembrance Day, Holly wore her
poppy perfectly placed on the lapel of her black winter coat, with her
rose-colored mouth to match.

It had been a while since Victoria had heard from her, which was
unusual. Holly's texting habits were fairly easy to predict: Victoria had
learned to expect at least an emoji most days when Holly was about
to begin her commute home from work. Often, the exasperated face,
followed by a wine bottle, or an LOL. Most weekends there was a para-
graph about the man in Holly's current dating life. Then there were the
checking in texts—How r u honey?—which Victoria hadn't thought she
would miss until they stopped coming. Same with the Friday lunches.
They hadn't happened the last few weeks, so Victoria suggested they
meet today, a Wednesday. Victoria happened to have the day off and
she knew Holly had ways of explaining hours away from her desk.

She had asked Holly if she wanted to go shopping—something

she knew Holly wouldn't be able to resist. And Victoria wanted a new outfit, for when she saw Luke next. Nothing she had was right.

"Should we get sushi before we shop?" Victoria asked, stopping in front of a little Japanese restaurant that sold pretty plastic boxes of premade rolls. She scanned the options. "Do you want to share a combo with me? I'm not that hungry."

Holly looked doubtful. "Okay, but I don't like anything with roe. No eggs."

Victoria knew that already. She picked the safest thing she could see, not that there was much the mall could offer that wouldn't offend Holly's narrow palate. "California rolls are always a good bet," she said.

"I don't know how you can even care about food right now. I just can't get over it. I can't believe someone tried to *kill* Eric."

"Oh, I don't know if I'd say that." Victoria's face was now creased in irritation. She moved to the counter to pay for the food. She lowered her voice. "Let's not be melodramatic."

Holly waited for the transaction to be over and indicated an empty table, where they sat and separated their wooden chopsticks. "I'm hardly melodramatic!" she hissed. "I know you're really good at keeping calm all the time, but this time you're allowed to freak out. I'm freaking out! I know Eric is!"

Victoria remembered Eric texting on his phone in his robe the night his car malfunctioned. She stirred a healthy chunk of wasabi into her soy sauce.

"I guess he told you about it. Yes, of course he's upset."

Holly flushed a little. "Oh, he texted me. I'd sent him a *Seinfeld* joke that I thought he might find funny—you know, we were talking about Seinfeld at lunch the other week? Anyway, I guess I sent it soon after he'd had his accident. So he told me about it. I can't even . . . It's so *crazy* someone would actually *tamper* with his car! I thought that only happened in movies."

Victoria thought about *Dolores Claiborne*. "It was probably some kids fooling around. Thankfully they didn't know what they were doing."

"Honestly, Victoria, I don't get it. I actually *cried* when I found out. You don't seem to be upset at all."

Victoria raised her eyebrows. "Would you prefer that I freak out? Some car thieves fooled around with his car, and thankfully he is okay. He got his spare keys back from the parking guys. Moving on."

"Oh my God, I just thought of something. He's up for that big promotion. Do you think anyone at his office might have done this?"

"But they're all so stuffy and professional there. I just can't imagine it, to be honest. And I mentioned it to Eric, and he couldn't think of anyone."

"I know. But isn't that always the way? Aren't murderers—you know, the ones in movies and books—aren't they all . . . normal looking on the outside, but as soon as they're alone, in their heads, aren't they just twisted psychopaths? That's the scary thing, isn't it. They *look* normal, but they're not."

"Yeah, sure. But don't forget, those are books and movies."

"Okay, and real life too! Wasn't that killer Ted Bundy supposedly really cute? Someone you'd never expect to go around eating people?"

Victoria bit into one of the California rolls. They used too much mayo here for her liking. "I don't think Ted Bundy ate people. I think you're mixing him up with someone else. I think he just raped and murdered his victims."

"'Just.' Nice. I could have sworn he ate them too. Well anyway, he was like a monster in disguise."

"You think there's some cannibal out there, tampering with Eric's car?"

Holly rolled her eyes. "No, geez. I'm just saying it's possible that someone who doesn't *seem* like they'd do something like that, might. Because it's always someone who doesn't seem like it."

"Is it? I always thought it was the simplest solution."

"What's the simplest solution?"

"That some idiot kids broke into Eric's car and decided to play what they thought was a prank. Thankfully, it turned out to be pretty harmless. End of story. Oh, don't look at me like you think I'm heartless. I know he's upset. I suggested we go for drinks and steak at his favorite restaurant Friday night. I was hoping you could join us. It would cheer him up."

Holly approved, and brightened considerably. "Oh, so that's why you wanted to go shopping. You want an outfit for Friday night? Well, so do I, I guess. Are you sure you want me to come along? Third wheel and all."

"You can bring someone if you like," offered Victoria, though she knew Holly had just ended a fruitless dalliance with a bartender known jokingly as "the Cocktail Shaker" and hadn't mentioned anyone taking his place. "You wouldn't be a third wheel. I know Eric had a great time at lunch last week. You have a lot in common. And who else knows *Seinfeld* like you do?"

Holly beamed. She nibbled at a roll. "I had a great time too. Well, if you're sure. I don't think I'll be able to rustle up a date with only a few days' notice."

Holly helped Victoria find something at Fascination, a store Victoria had never set foot in before, full of items totally different from the rest of her Eric-approved wardrobe. It was a little humiliating at first, trying on hideous spandex tops with keyhole necks intended for women who had a far larger bosom than Victoria's, things with large plastic beading to draw attention to one's décolletage. But if not for Holly, Victoria would never have found the simple, sexy black cocktail dress with leather inserts. Then she would never have gone next door to Exit 69 and found the pair of high-waisted, Saran-Wrapped black jeans paired with a pale-pink angora sweater that the sales girl described as "touchable."

The cocktail dress was for their threesome steak dinner. The jeans and "touchable" sweater were for Luke. Holly was encouraging, as always, enjoying the thoughtless consumerism, the way her friend could spend money as though it didn't matter. Holly, too, splurged on a deep-green velvet dress that most people wouldn't have had the nerve to so much as try on. In addition to being dangerously short, the dress had shameless cutouts at the sides that made wearing a bra impossible. She also bought some rather cheap-looking costume jewelry that lessened the effect of the outfit but that sparkled. Eric, being something of a magpie, would have no choice but to notice.

"You've found some good basics," purred the salesgirl, bringing their things to the register. She talked Victoria into a wide black patent-leather belt at the last minute. "This will go with so many things. Do you have tall boots?"

TWENTY-TWO

V ICTORIA STOOD IN THE KITCHEN CHOPPING CARROTS, THINK-ing of Lorena Bobbitt as she sliced the root vegetables from finger size to nubs. Poor John Wayne Bobbitt losing his . . . "unit," as Eric called his. She held on to a carrot about Eric's size. The shopping trip had put Victoria in a positive mood—an unexpected result. There was so much to look forward to, and on top of it, she would look good. She was going to wear her new clothes in a future that was so close she could almost step inside it.

Eric wasn't home yet, but would be soon, barring any unforeseen circumstances. Victoria was chopping, dicing, and slicing to David Bowie's "Fame" playing through her earbuds. It was a rare moment. Music was a solitary affair in their home. Eric didn't like much in the way of music, and this was the compromise she had reached with him early on. It was a tragic waste of his top-of-the-line Bose sound system.

Eric had told Victoria that morning that he would be meeting a client in West Island. Given his reluctance to drive after the recent incident on the highway, he would have to take the metro. This amused her. He never took the metro. It was too much of a congregation of the "great unwashed masses" for Eric. The crowds, the smells, it was his personal hell.

While she hacked the chicken into strips, she imagined him now, standing proper and stiff in his suit and long wool coat, his laptop bag slung over his left shoulder. She saw him looking up at the dot-matrix television screen, reading the alert that the next train would arrive in three minutes. He sniffed the air, an unpleasant expression clouding his face. He consulted his phone, reading notes on a client's file. He didn't notice a wiry man in a black puffer coat behind him, who checked over his shoulder before making a quick grab for Eric's laptop bag.

Suddenly, the men were in a lurching, to-and-fro dance as each struggled for a grip on the bag. Eric looked wildly around him for an ally but couldn't afford to divert his attention from the man. Eric's shiny shoes backed closer to the edge of the platform, over the track bed, where two rats scampered in terrifying randomness.

Forward, back, gritted teeth, clenched ass. Grunts, yells, the dirty wind and howl of the approaching train. Both men refusing to release their grasp, their hands contorted to painful claws. Fury and fatigue battling until—Eric's back foot found no ground underneath and he plunged down, bringing his laptop with him. His mouth an O as he fell, thinking of rats, as the train mashed him underneath, legs first.

Victoria fed long stalks of celery into the Cuisinart, taking pleasure in the fibrous whir of the machine, watching the green mush accumulate in the clear plastic container.

She remembered how she'd been told years ago that puppies got worms because they all had worm eggs in them that were waiting for the chance to hatch, and usually did, with the stress of being born. She imagined with the impact of the train Eric's worm eggs blossoming and blossoming, his dead body erupting in a bouquet of worms. Worms wiggling under his still-warm skin, their blind heads seeking release through wounds, stray worms leaking from his mouth and eyes, disgusting the paramedics.

Suddenly, her reverie was interrupted, and so was Bowie's song. One of her earbuds was ripped out, and Eric's face loomed inches from hers.

"What's so funny?" he asked, his forehead creased in irritation at the tiny, miniature tin band sounds coming from the earbud.

She glanced at the knife clenched in her hand as though she didn't know where it had come from. There was blood on her other hand. She had cut herself.

"Eric, you can't surprise me like that." She couldn't think of anything more intelligent to say, stripped of the rhythm of the music and her thoughts.

He narrowed his eyes at her. "You were . . . laughing to yourself." His face contorted in disgust. "And put a Band-Aid on that."

LATER THAT EVENING, AFTER SHE HAD SERVED A DINNER THAT WAS eaten in uncomfortable silence, Victoria was aware of Eric watching her. She tried to pretend she didn't notice this. When they moved into the living room, she hoped he would do his usual thing in front of the television, and the tension could dissipate.

She was about to recline on the sectional with a book by Herman Koch, when Eric stopped her, grabbing her wrist. First he met her eyes, then his gaze traveled down to the book in her hand. He raised his eyebrows in a "May I?" expression before taking the book between two fingers in the manner of someone picking up something dirty.

Reluctantly, Victoria allowed him the book. He rose and read the back cover, his lips moving slightly, a habit that Victoria found worse than annoying.

"This sounds pretty . . . sick . . . Victoria," he said.

Victoria willed herself to maintain calm in her voice, but she felt panic threatening. Eric taking interest in her book like this was un-familiar territory. "Oh, it's not so bad. It's really quite literary. He's a Dutch writer."

"Oh I know all these 'literary' types," he said, rolling his eyes. "People who want to see phallic symbols in everything. People who write about incest, like it's a good thing! And all kinds of other sick shit, in the name of being intellectually superior." He held up his hand to stop her protest. "You know exactly what I'm talking about too. There's that one everyone raves about, the Russian one, about the pervert who fancies himself in love with a twelve-year-old? Oh yeah, and there's the one about the guy who . . . jerks off in the bathroom while his mother is right on the other side of the door, and then com-plains about her to his shrink? Really intellectual, high-brow stuff. There's that 'feminist' crap too, the one by the woman with the Asian last name who everyone thinks is so wonderful for leaving her hus-band and having sex with gross guys. Or that French filth you were reading. 'Erotica' my ass. I picked up that book of short stories once. I just had to look at the first few pages and I found myself reading about a guy, a freak show actually, who was diddling little girls and then his own son, while he slept! And that other writer, the one you love so much, who is famous for that awful book of his about a guy who leaves his wife and son—correction, *pregnant* wife and son, to go live with a prostitute?"

"John Updike is a lovely writer, and he won a Pulitzer Prize for that 'awful book,'" was all Victoria could utter in defense. But it didn't make a difference. Eric was orating, not listening. He was on a roll, as though he were in a courtroom.

He shook the Koch book in her face. "What can you possibly be getting out of a book like this, Victoria?"

She rose also, reaching to take the book back, but he held it away in a petty game of keep away so that she quickly abdicated. He had an unfair height advantage. She forced her arms to lay at her side in submission, her cut hand still throbbing.

"The last one you told me about sounded dreadful. Even you admitted it. And this one—" He waved the book again. "An evil doctor vacationing with deviants? I shouldn't be surprised that you act the way you've been acting, reading this type of trash."

"The way I've been acting?"

"You haven't been yourself lately. For a while now. And it's not just me who's noticed, either. I think"—he paused, for dramatic effect—"I think you've been reading too much."

She laughed, desperately trying to sound natural. "Reading too much? Eric, I had a little accident in the kitchen tonight. I hardly think—"

"Normal people just don't read this much," he decided, more to himself. "And they don't read *this*." He tossed the book. It landed on the floor in front of the television.

"Eric, that book belongs to the library."

"I'll tell you what I think about *the library*. I think you need a break from the library. You need to do something normal. Watch a movie, for god's sake."

"Like what?"

"Well, how about *Sleepless in Seattle*?" He looked triumphant, like he had just performed a slam dunk. "Tom Hanks."

"This is really silly, there's nothing wrong with reading," she said, anger rising in her voice. She took a few steps, with the intention of picking up the discarded book. He stopped her by stepping in front of it. It felt like they were in a chess game. She was a lowly pawn, and he was a bishop, tall and pompous. She looked into his face. All she could focus on were the prominent pores on his large nose.

"Well, you might not think so, but I did a little research on it, and you may be interested to know that statistics link reading with depression."

"Oh, please. Where did you find that?"

"Hear me out, hear me out. They did a big study at one of the American Ivy League universities. They say it's all the alone time, the ruminating. It's the solitary process, the unshared experience. It's unhealthy. When your nose is in a book, you're not getting enough fresh air and sun."

She scoffed. "Next thing you're going to tell me reading is the leading cause of scurvy! Please, Eric, this is ridiculous."

"I don't think so. Do you know anyone who reads as much as you do? Face it, you're . . . extreme. And I think it's taking a toll. You're acting weird, talking to yourself, in your own little world all the time. Laughing like a—a hyena!" He indicated her bandaged hand. "It's like an addiction. It's not healthy."

He put on a very earnest expression, one an actor would use. Say, Tom Hanks.

"I'm not *addicted* to books, Eric. I can't believe we are even having this conversation."

"Okay, then if you're not addicted, why can't you stop, just for a little while? Prove me wrong. If you don't feel better after . . . two weeks? That sounds reasonable—yes, two weeks, no books, and I propose you will feel a lot better."

She stared at him with an inky black hatred in her heart. She felt herself losing. "I don't need to feel better," she said. "I'm fine."

"Nonsense! Who doesn't want to feel better? Think of it as an experiment," he persisted. "If you aren't convinced, then fine, by all means, you can go back to your little corner and huddle up with another morally bankrupt story. But I predict you'll notice a difference. Think you can do it?"

"Of course I can do it," she snapped. *But I won't.* . . . .

"Great," he said, smiling, ending the sales pitch by picking up the remote. "I am going to introduce you to the world of cinema, Victoria. I've got a ton of movies that I think you'll like."

She sat limply on the couch, the Koch book's aquamarine cover bright in mocking cheerfulness on the floor. He seemed satisfied, but slightly uncomfortable. He had won the battle, which had him feeling superior, but he wasn't used to her attention on the screen. He took a long time to find *Sleepless*, scrolling through the options with a new self-consciousness. He needn't have worried, though, she wasn't watching the television. She obstinately focused on a dot on the wall just below the screen. She refused to look at a single moment of the movie.

TWENTY-THREE

Baths were overrated. Victoria had only been in two minutes, and she already felt hot and claustrophobic. The water had a weird, slimy texture from the salts she had poured in. She lifted one foot out to rest on the bathtub's ledge, feeling relief at the sensation of the cool air.

She thought about people who died in the bathtub. She thought about red bathwater. She allowed her head to slide down, her body shifting so more of her legs came out and her head was submerged.

Eric had been rather jubilant this morning. "Why don't I return your books to the library for you? I don't mind—I pass that old place every day on my way to work!" Milk had dribbled from his mouth as he talked.

She had returned his helpful offer with an icy smile, and even supplied him with a green, reusable cloth bag in which to carry the books.

It was ridiculous, *he* was ridiculous. Stupid man—how could anyone see something wrong with reading?

After he left for the morning, she Googled "reading leads to depression" and did not find the study he quoted the night before. She found articles that described how depression leads to less reading. She found books about depression. She found chat boards in which people talked about how reading actually *helped* their depression.

Eric was full of shit.

She came up out of the water. The heat was suffocating. She stepped out of the tub and let the water run off her body onto the bath mat. She clenched her fists at her sides. The thought of the days and evenings stretching in front of her, bookless, was intolerable. The hours, those wasted hours "improving" herself and her marriage, no doubt, according to Eric's special project. After enduring *Sleepless in Seattle*, she was dreading Eric's next selection. *Top Gun*, maybe? "Take me to bed or lose me forever." She couldn't stomach another scene with the all-too-perky Meg Ryan. Aw, shucks!

She wrapped a towel around herself, tucking in the corner tightly between her breasts. She went to her room and opened her bedroom closet. Inside, at the very back, she found a white Tupperware bin that Eric had labeled VICTORIA—TO BE DONATED in very neat black printing years ago, when they had first moved in together. She opened it and went through items of her past. Essays she had written in university, a few diaries, other things she hadn't wanted to leave in her parents' home. She nearly squealed with delight when she saw the battered cover that she knew she would find here: it was a vintage copy of *Strangers on a Train*. She had bought it at the Strand bookstore on a trip to New York with her parents as a teenager. It wasn't until she was in the hotel room that she noticed that it was a first edition, signed and numbered by Patricia Highsmith herself.

She knew it would be useless in those hours when she and Eric were in the apartment together, but the very presence of this slim volume with old, small-type pages gave her solace.

TWENTY-FOUR

VICTORIA GAZED AT HER REFLECTION IN THE FULL-LENGTH MIR-ror. The outfit was an outrage when worn in the apartment. It rebelled against the whiteness, the respectability, the agreed-upon level on which they lived. She looked a little bit like she was playing dress-up. But she liked it. The sweater was *touchable*, the salesgirl was right. The fluffy, pink aura of softness was a flirty invitation.

The clothes she'd worn this morning—expensive but ugly turquoise sweats with white piping down the legs—were now in an abandoned heap in the bathroom. They had been worn for Eric's benefit, though he had barely looked at her. He had been in a rush to get to an early meeting and barely acknowledged her in the kitchen when she handed him coffee in his stainless-steel travel mug.

Not that she had been keen to see him either. They had been living far too closely for her liking the last few days, ever since he coerced her into that stupid two-week reading ban. He'd made her watch *Steel Magnolias* last night. She'd wanted to cry, but not because a young, diabetic Julia Roberts insisted on living a full life fearlessly and then paid the ultimate price. Not because Dolly Parton was so good, kind, and wise. It was the thought that there were twelve more days ahead like this, and she didn't have any way out. But she didn't give Eric the satisfaction of misinterpreting her misery.

She had also wanted to cry because, after the film, he surprised her with a gift—a box wrapped with a red ribbon, from (and this amused Eric to no end) Victoria's Secret. With a deep reluctance, she had opened the box. In it was a blindingly bright lime-green push-up bra and the tiniest matching panties. The bra had large gel inserts, almost aggressive in size, designed to "lift and separate," according to the informative tag.

The obvious implication was that she would give him a fashion show, and then they could get down to business, even though it was a Thursday night.

"You . . . like this look?" she had asked him, after a long and awkward silence.

In the bathroom, it was apparent that the brassiere was too big for Victoria's ample curves. The cups gaped unattractively, even with the inserts.

"Never mind," he had said, when she informed him from behind the bathroom door she'd need to exchange for a different size. To her relief, she heard his bedside table drawer open then shut. The earplugs were in. The night was over before it had started.

Still staring at herself in the neon costume, Victoria had realized with a jolt that this was the exact kind of thing Holly would buy. Maybe even the right size. The color would set off Holly's tanned skin. The push-up feature unnecessary, but still a tool she much employed.

They never mentioned it again. When Eric was home, she filled much of her time by taking long baths, afterward lying naked on the white tiles as her too-hot body radiated away waves of heat. The previous evening, after staring at the same spot just below the television screen for an hour, she busied herself with painstakingly polishing the already spotless crystal glasses they never used. She fantasized about the copy of *Blood Meridian* she had seen in the window of the charity shop close to her work. She mentally flicked through titles on her to-read list, numbering them in priority order in her mind. They were all immensely appealing. Even the almost impenetrable *The Golden Notebook* seemed worthy of a reread now.

Eric was his usual self, though an unspoken self-satisfaction gleamed in his eyes. "You seem so much happier now!" he had crooned in her ear, almost seductively, while she stood polishing the crystal.

He had no idea, of course, that she was reading on the sly at every opportunity, that any time he was in the office was her chance to extricate her precious *Strangers on a Train* from the depths of the closet.

She had been forced to acknowledge Eric this morning when he called out, "Don't forget dinner tonight," before he left the apartment.

"Dinner?"

"Yes, it was your idea, remember? With Holly? I made a reservation at Mezzo's."

Of course. Dinner with Holly. She had actually forgotten, in her stunned state.

"I'll meet you there," she'd said, providing him a turquoise vision before he turned to leave the apartment.

Now, in front of the mirror, she pulled her hair out of the ponytail, gave it a shake, and felt less ill at ease in her new clothing. She was going to do something today.

She found parking a few blocks from DuBois. Perfect not to be parked too close, as it would give the impression that she was walking along the street, stopping in casually. It was a cold day that required a down jacket, and a scarf too, though after deliberation, she'd worn her silk scarf, a shocking tumescent pink, thrown over her shoulder. She kept her coat unzipped—it would be a shame to hide her new "touchable" self. This allowed the wind to knife through the sweater's delicate knit without mercy. Still, it created its desired effect.

It hadn't snowed yet, and wouldn't today. It was too cold. But it was coming, it was in the smell of the air and the gray cloud cover. The tree skeletons would soon be blanketed for the winter.

The store was small and had old-fashioned writing stenciled on the main front window in gold and black. The dark-green door was a peeling, chipped mess that tinkled a bell when she opened it.

She fixed her face as though she were marching a runway, maintaining her "I don't know how beautiful I am" expression while surreptitiously searching the small space for Luke.

She didn't see him. Not in the rows of tables topped with rustic, reclaimed wood, or in the corner where office pieces were displayed, adorned with an occasional plant or area rug, or what she would best describe as "the chair section."

She heard a few footsteps that she recognized as feminine in the clicks they made as well as the quickness of gait. A brunette appeared from behind a door. She had long dark hair and a thick fringe above her large eyes. She smiled at Victoria with dazzling and sexy red lips. Victoria wished she had worn lipstick.

"Hi there," she said, a little breathless. She brushed her hair off her shoulders. She was wearing a silky, low-cut blouse, also "touchable" looking.

"Hi," said Victoria, a little coolly.

"Let me know if you have any questions," the woman offered, accustomed to people needing space to look around.

Victoria touched a low coffee table. Its legs were a metal U shape, upside down, and the top was an unevenly shaped but smooth slab. The dark wood had an oil-finished surface that was so impossibly smooth and warm, it felt like skin. It was asking to be touched. She ran her hand along the length of the piece, imagining how Luke's hands had also worked at it. Now they had both touched it.

"Thank you, I will," she replied.

She wondered who this woman was, who she was to Luke. An employee, a girlfriend? She wondered what she had been doing in the back room. Was Luke there also? Had she interrupted a private moment? The thought distressed and excited her.

She ran her fingers along the top of a dresser that appeared to be made of the same type of warm wood. Opened and closed a few drawers.

"That's a lovely piece," said the woman, crossing her arms as she came a few steps toward Victoria. "Very midcentury. A really lovely piece."

"Yes, it's gorgeous," agreed Victoria. "Was it made in Montreal?"

"Yes, designed and made here. The designer, Luke DuBois, made all the pieces in this showroom," she gestured in Vanna White–style with both hands, displaying glossy red fingernails to match her lips. "He's just fantastic."

She said the word "fantastic" as though it had never been said before, like she invented it. She made the word a sensual experience, when her tongue met her teeth on the *t*, the roof of her mouth on the *c*.

"It is. I love this wood."

"Yes, black walnut is a beautiful wood. Very stylish, the color is warm. It's a piece that could be at home in pretty much any room of the house." At this point, the woman ran her hand over it and let it stop there, possessively. "Are you looking for something in particular?"

I sure am, Victoria thought. "Oh, I was walking in the neighborhood, saw the store, and thought I'd have a peek at what you've got here."

The saleswoman nodded, still friendly, though detached, as though she knew she wasn't going to sell anything. "No problem, take your time, enjoy."

Victoria slowly took in each piece, touching the wood Luke had touched, seeing the flawless corners joined together, admiring the size and structure. She imagined the time they took to make. She envisioned Luke's strong, sensitive hands crafting the wood, each knowing touch bringing it closer to its intended destiny.

Each piece was so pleasing to her. Even if she had not known him, she would have felt this way. They were just her style, the warmth and artistry of the transformed wood contrasting painfully with the bright, soulless white of pretty much everything in her apartment.

The salesgirl was flipping through a large home decor magazine on the counter. Her air was that of babysitter. She was here because Victoria was here. If Victoria were to leave, the salesgirl too would leave, back through the door she had come from, to the workshop, where Luke surely was, bending over the wood, sweating, concentrated.

Victoria realized that this is where he'd been every time she had waited for him in the café. He had been here.

The phone rang a few times, and the girl answered it. Victoria heard more footsteps come from the back of the store, and then the door opened and He appeared, in a smart, hipster flannel shirt with black and blue checks. He smiled, and then the smile broadened in recognition.

"Well hey there," he said, greeting her with kisses on each cheek. He looked her in the eyes while doing this, which lent an intimacy to the act that it usually lacked. "Fancy seeing you here, in my little shop!"

She shrugged her coat off and slung it over one arm. "Hey yourself. Well, I was in the neighborhood."

His smile was open and charming. "Great." He seemed to be looking her all over. She felt herself respond in kind to his warm gaze.

"I have been admiring your work. You're very talented. Really."

"Well, thank you, I appreciate it."

The girl had hung up the phone. "That was Bra-ad," she called to Luke in a singsong voice that intimated a backstory.

"Oh good. He's alive!" laughed Luke.

"So it would seem," and the bombshell sauntered over to join them. She smiled. "Find anything?" she addressed Victoria. Her black silk blouse was open to the third button, with a push-up bra making more of what didn't need making more of. Her question sounded like a dare.

"Yes, I mean, I'm definitely going to get this." Victoria gestured to a suede leather pouf that had tassels and subtle beadwork.

Luke nodded. "Those are great," he said. "I have a Native friend who makes those in Oka. They always sell really well."

She flushed. She hadn't picked something of his. "And this," she pointed to a bookcase on the wall, a large piece with substantial shelving.

Both Luke and the girl had a look of faint surprise on their faces. "Oh, you shouldn't feel like you have to buy anything," Luke said, a little embarrassed. "I mean, I'd love to make the sale, but there's really no pressure."

"You know each other?" the girl asked, smile still wide, lipstick still glossy.

"No, no, I want to," Victoria said, deliberately ignoring the girl and her question. "I've been looking for something exactly like this. How could I leave without bringing it home?"

She noticed the pouf was $579. She didn't dare look at the price of the bookcase. She wasn't worried that they couldn't afford it; it was how she would explain the purchases to Eric.

"Well, you must need a shelf for all the books you read. Victoria is a real bookworm," he added, for the girl's benefit, who just continued to smile and nod, not really impressed. Victoria guessed, with all the feminine cattiness she could summon, that this girl was likely of the ilk who read vampire romance books. You could have all the elegance money could buy, but it usually didn't come with intellectual discernment. Though right now Victoria would have liked to pick her brain about makeup application and brow shaping.

"Luke, you're a reader too, don't sell yourself short." She used his name on purpose in a proprietary way. Not a small retribution in it. It made the girl blink and look at her, knocked off balance a little. Slightly irked at this familiarity. Just a moment ago she'd been explaining to Victoria about "the designer."

The girl fetched the pouf, sat it by the register, then went behind the counter to write an invoice for the two items, bent over for all to see. Now really, wasn't that a bit gauche?

"Give her the special friends and family discount," said Luke, which necessitated her starting again.

Victoria didn't even try to feign protest, just smiled. Special friends, huh?

When the transaction was completed and arrangements for delivery were discussed, the girl faded back with discretion, just another beautiful article in the room.

"Well, that was the easiest sale I've made all month," said Luke, exuding warmth. "It's not every day I sell a bookcase. That one's been there so long I'm surprised it hasn't put down roots."

Victoria laughed, though she wasn't surprised. It had cost over three thousand dollars. "I'll probably be back tomorrow to buy the rest of the store. You're so talented."

He put his hands together in prayer stance and bowed to her, Buddhist style. "Wow, well, thank you. What's on your schedule for the rest of the day?"

Victoria stepped back, surprised at this turnabout. This was actually happening. "Oh, not a lot. It's my day off."

"I've got a few calls to return, things to take care of here, but what do you think of a drink at, say," he glanced at his watch, "five thirty? My treat, to thank you for being my favorite customer this month."

He didn't take all his customers out for a drink, did he? Or was this more of the special friends business? Smiling, she said, "Sounds great."

"All right. Do you know where Gros Luxe is, a few blocks down? They've got a great drink list, cocktails, whiskey, wine, and comfort food if we get hungry."

She did. It was a cozy restaurant in the lobby of a boutique B&B that she had passed many times.

"Perfect. Thanks again, Victoria. See you later," he kissed her cheeks again, maintaining eye contact as he did. She slipped her coat on, this time doing the zipper.

Outside on the street, the world seemed like new to her as she walked. The cold washed over her with a refreshing newness, a cleansing, exhilarating kiss of life. She had been in his presence. They had touched, he had watched her as he kissed her. And they would see each other in a few hours, by themselves, without watchful eyes.

She walked with great vigor, and soon she didn't feel the cold at all. It wasn't until she saw the signs for a funeral home that she realized she was in unknown territory, and that she had walked blocks past where she'd parked her car. It didn't matter. She had lots of time before she was to meet Luke.

Drinks with Luke at five thirty and then dinner with Holly and Eric across town at seven thirty. It was doable. When he asked, there had been no hesitation or question in her mind. The path was cleared for her, and who was she not to step onto it?

TWENTY-FIVE

S HE WAS THANKFUL THAT SHE HAD BOUGHT THE NEW COCKTAIL
dress. She felt svelte and mysterious, like a 1940s passenger on
Murder on the Orient Express, like a Bond girl, all rolled up into one.
She hoped that he would be there waiting for her, so she could make
an appearance, but she arrived first to a quiet scene. The *cinq à sept*
crowd hadn't filled in yet.

The bar was cozy, though. She was seated at a low table, with a
velvet cushioned armchair and loveseat. Old-fashioned chandeliers
twinkled in the dim light.

She didn't wait long. He arrived, huffing, like he'd been running.
He stood in the still-open doorway, bringing a rush of wintery chill
into the restaurant.

She stood up to greet him. His eyes lingered on her and the effects of the cold air through her dress.

"So sorry. I got held up at the end of the day."

"No problem," she chimed.

"I hate being late."

"It's not, really. Five minutes? Who's counting."

He unraveled his scarf and hooped it on the back of the loveseat. She could see the top of his chest, just where his shirt was a little open. The skin there was tanned and looked weathered. She liked that. It wasn't fair that men become more attractive with each passing year, she thought.

He took an appreciative glance that made her think of the expression "elevator eyes." "You look amazing."

"Oh, gosh, thanks," she said. "I feel a little overdressed. I might have dinner plans later tonight."

"Might?"

"Well, nothing set in stone." She thought of the wedding ring she had left at home, in the Birks box it had come in. She would have to drop by the house before heading to the restaurant later. Or not.

He looked pleased with her answer.

"What is your poison?" he asked, picking up the drinks menu.

"Oh, I don't know . . . a glass of white?"

He looked disapproving. "Oh, now, you need to be more creative than that. You are celebrating a bookcase, for goodness' sake!" He made overly grand gestures with his arm, lowering his voice for dramatic effect.

She smiled. "Okay, let's see. I'll have a vodka martini, then. It was my drink, back in the days when I had a drink."

"When were those days, may I ask?"

"I dunno. I'm dating myself. The nineties?"

"Oh, very stylish. Most girls back then drank horrible milky sweet drinks, awful things, like paralyzers, and you were ordering vodka martinis?"

She knew just the girls he referred to. Holly used to drink paralyzers. They were totally passé now, so she drank Bellinis wherever they were available, or slushy margaritas. "Yes, with a twist, please. Not an olive. This is an important distinction."

When he ordered a pale ale, she was a little disappointed. She didn't like the smell of beer on the breath. She thought of burps and gas and yeast when she thought of beer. She thought of bellies and butt cracks and hairy backs. She had been sure he was a scotch drinker. It disappointed her to be wrong this time.

The door creaked open many times, and soon the room was full and animated, and the music was turned up. Michael Bublé was crooning a Christmas song. By the time she was finishing her second martini, they decided to order food, and for the occasion, poutine. It was a good idea, because she could feel the alcohol moving through her brain. She was used to sipping on one glass of wine, and almost never finishing it.

She was talking about misogyny and even referred to the works of John Updike and Philip Roth as "dick lit"—which might have gotten her points with someone who had actually read Updike and Roth. She got the distinct impression that Luke was more than delighted to hear a woman in a fancy dress say "dick" so casually. But she was pleased to entertain him, and, more importantly, impress him.

"Okay, well, it looks like I have a lot of catching up to do in the reading world," he said, which she took as a gentle signal for her to ramp down the book talk.

"I've done the math, and I think I started reading about seventy-three years too late," Victoria said, nodding to the waitress who had gestured a wordless "another?" when picking up her empty glass. "I've got major catching up to do."

Luke shook his head in amusement and leaned forward, elbows and forearms on the table. "What's your story, miss? I mean, I feel like I know you, but I don't really."

"I know exactly what you mean—exactly!" She blushed at her exuberance. Hopefully the poutine would come before drink number three. "I want to know your story too."

"Well, I'm divorced," he began.

"Me too! Me too, I'm divorced! Oh, sorry, I interrupted you. Sorry."

His eyes were merry. "No problem. Keep going—isn't being divorced the best thing ever?"

"Well, I'm *almost* divorced. In the process of," she said, willing her words to come out slower, hoping her hand gestures weren't too large.

"I see."

"It's very civilized," she explained. "No throwing vases or fighting over the cat's collar or anything like that."

"Well, that's good."

"And we are still living together, but not for much longer."

"That's good, too. So, may I ask, what prompted it, the breakup?"

"Frankly, Luke," she said confidentially, "I shouldn't have married him to begin with. I married him thinking I should feel so grateful that he wanted me. That I would grow into being worthy of him. So I lived like a guest in someone else's life."

Her third drink had arrived, and she took a large gulp. Were martinis always such a revelation?

"It was like being dead. For four years." She held up her martini. "I've been like the walking dead."

She wondered if she had gone too far, but it felt so good, opening her mouth and letting the truth spill out. He didn't look bothered; he looked like he knew just what she was talking about.

"Then I should congratulate you on starting your life again," he said, covering her hand with his. In leaning over the table like that, his leg leaned against hers, and stayed there.

"Thank you, thank you," she said, pressing her leg back against him. "I can feel the best part of my life is about to begin."

They remained like this for several seconds before the spell was broken by the arrival of the poutine. His laughter punctuated the air.

"The best part of your life IS about to begin. Fries, cheese, gravy, what can be better than that?"

"Nothing—not even sex," she joked, and their legs remained together.

SHE WASN'T DRUNK. NOT REALLY. SHE WASN'T SLOPPY, FALLING over, an undignified, slurring mess. But she had drink number four, and was moving more deliberately, her cheeks flamed. Her laughter was louder, and she was more prone to punctuated bursts, a big, round "HAH!" whenever he said something that she found amusing. She let her laughter tinkle all down her body, down the length of her arms to her fingertips, and then, touching him on the arm lightly, into his body. Her smile had come to stay for the evening.

The poutine was now cleared away and a plate of deep-fried pickles and a mayonnaise-based dip was in front of them.

Luke excused himself to go to the bathroom, and she checked her phone. She was shocked when she saw the time: 7:05. If she ran, she just might be able to get to the restaurant in time. No time to pick up her rings. She could say they were being cleaned. She'd have to take a cab though, no way she could drive like this.

She looked at the pickles. She couldn't just leave Luke with a plate of pickles to eat all by himself.

And she was having the best night she could remember. Tears pricked behind her eyes as she saw Luke approach the table. When had she felt this happy? Why should she leave?

"Ah, she's on her phone," he said. "Are you late for dinner?"

"Oh, they aren't really expecting me. I said I'd drop by if I was in the area."

"And?" he looked at her, raising his eyebrows hopefully.

"And . . . I'm not in the area, apparently. I'm in another area, apparently."

"Yes, aren't you." He looked pleased.

Giggling, she said, "I know, I'm being rude, just give me a second. I'll let them know I won't be joining them."

She hesitated, the excuses blurring. She texted both Holly and Eric.

VICTORIA: Feeling sick. Can't make it tonight. So sorry.

She knew they'd both be en route to the restaurant now. They would be furious with her for spoiling their Friday night. She didn't care that Eric might return home to see how she was doing, and how explaining that she had been out would be difficult later.

She couldn't worry about that now. She felt like a slippery fish, with an equally slippery memory. After the text was sent, she dropped her phone into her purse, uninterested in whatever response she might get.

Her vision was slower than the movement of her head. It could no longer keep up. The small white Christmas lights around the restaurant windows streaked pleasantly, and then she met his eyes. They were warm and held the promise of happiness in them. He took her hand in one of his, and covered it with the other.

The evening passed in a beautiful blur, like a dream. She learned about the demise of his two-year marriage, or at least as much as she wanted to learn. She learned about his travels through Asia. By the time he asked for the bill, she'd had five martinis and was feeling a little numb around the mouth.

"It almost seems a shame to leave a place like this," he said, as they put on their coats and were passing through the lobby, where a few people with luggage were checking into their rooms at the B&B.

She met his eyes and knew exactly what they were suggesting. Her eyes wanted to cross a bit. She felt a clutch of fear in her stomach (or was it nausea?) that it was all happening a bit too fast, so fast that it might just fly by her, missing her completely.

She giggled and grabbed his hand as though it were the most natural thing in the world, and pulled him through the doors to the safety of the public sidewalk.

He called her a cab. They stood in the cold together. He put his arm around her shoulders and smiled. "You know," he said, "you didn't have to buy the bookcase. I would have asked you out anyway."

"Oh, was this a date?" she asked with a coy look.

He answered by leaning close, pressing her against the brick wall as he kissed her, his lips warm, his tongue wet. She felt like she was in a movie, like she could see herself from high above. She didn't mind that his mouth tasted like beer. All she could see was two happy people, together at last.

TWENTY-SIX

THE RIDE HOME IN THE TAXI WAS AN INFERNO OF THOUGHTS AND scenarios and excuses that piled on top of each other in Victoria's brain. She imagined Eric waiting for her, arms crossed, icy demands harpooning her, one after the other. She imagined her parents listening to the whole thing from the closet, revealing themselves to her in dramatic, stony disapproval while she made herself smaller and smaller in the corner of the room.

She imagined telling Eric that she had been kept at a work function, that they wouldn't take no for an answer, that her career was important too, that she was sorry and that she would make it up to him. Or maybe she would say it was time for them to talk, and ask him if he had been happy. The thought of that conversation made her physically sick. She was nauseated. She closed her eyes and prayed that the driver would stop lurching every time he took off from a stop, tapping the brake senselessly when there was no one ahead.

At home, she paid the driver and stepped out, vomiting into the bald hydrangea bush.

Her stomach quivered and squeezed on the ride up the elevator. She was pale and her mouth tasted bitter and she had no plan except to face what there was to face when she opened the door.

TWENTY-SEVEN

❦

THE APARTMENT WAS EMPTY. THERE WAS NO SIGN OF ERIC. SHE checked everywhere, even his sanctum, his bathroom. She realized that she hadn't looked at her phone since she had sent the text saying she wouldn't be coming for dinner.

Holly had sent several.

> HOLLY: OMG, are you serious?
>
> HOLLY: I'm at the restaurant—got here early, what am I supposed to do now?
>
> HOLLY: Are you okay?
>
> HOLLY: Does Eric know?

Eric had written one.

> ERIC: Whatever.

The singular word was meant to singe.

She undressed, showered, and brushed the bad taste from her mouth. She tried to drink water, knowing its restorative effects would be felt in the morning. It only caused her to retch what was left of the poutine and the strange nubs that she identified as the deep-fried pickles she had helped to consume.

She spent much of the night on the shower mat, not wanting to be far from the toilet, not eager to lay down in her bed, even if Eric wasn't in it.

IT WASN'T UNTIL THE NEXT MORNING, ABOUT FOUR OR SO, HER BODY sore from hours on the floor, that she lifted her head from the mat and shuffled out of the bathroom. Eric was home. He was lying on the bed on his back, arms by his sides, in a strange formal way that she associated with corpses.

She tried to slide quietly into the bed without disturbing him, though she suspected he wasn't asleep. Gingerly, she turned on her side, away from his coffin-ready pose, and fell into a very troubled sleep.

SHE HEARD THE ESPRESSO MAKER WORKING A FEW HOURS LATER. IT was still dark, not quite seven o'clock. Strange for Eric to be up so early on a Saturday morning. She came out of the bedroom, her eyes pounding and her mouth watering, as though she needed to be sick again. She looked at her hand and remembered her rings. They were still in the box in her bathroom, and she plunged her hands in the pockets of her pajama pants.

He was on his phone, stirring sugar into his coffee, when he noticed her. He looked back at his phone.

"I'm sorry, Eric," she began.

"No need to apologize," he said, his curt tone cutting her off. "You were sick."

Her foggy brain took a few seconds to register.

"I was sick," she repeated as though she had never heard the words before.

"I heard you, all night," he said, sipping his coffee, with distaste on his face.

"I'm sorry," she repeated.

"You could try closing the bathroom door next time," he said, but his voice wasn't as cutting as she had expected.

She nodded mutely.

"Can you manage a coffee?" he asked, reaching up tentatively for a cup.

She nodded again.

"Really sorry I . . . I ruined your night," she said, as he went through the motions with the coffee machine.

His back to her, he shrugged. "You didn't. We had a good time."

"You . . ."

"Well, you didn't give us any notice, did you? I kept the reservation because Holly was already there, waiting."

Ah, Holly. Thank goodness for her.

"Oh, good," she uttered weakly. "How's Holly?"

"Holly was Holly. We ate, we drank, we went our separate ways."

He put the mug in front of her.

"Well, I'm going to get ready now," he announced, walking down the hall.

"It's Saturday."

"You know how busy I am. I have to get to the office."

The lack of questions, the lack of recrimination, didn't bring the relief she thought it should. She felt edgy, and edged out. At least when he was angry, when he was shaming her into silence, she knew what to expect. She knew how to curl up into submission, and then everything, painfully, would go back to normal.

With a still-nauseous, nervous energy, she got up and went to the front closet to get his coat and scarf ready for him, a servile thing she did sometimes to assess Eric's mood as he was leaving for the day. Shrugging the camel coat from its hanger, something seemed off to her. Victoria's sluggish brain took a moment to put it together. The coat had a smell to it. Dog. It also had black hair on it. Lots of it. Brando.

Eric had been to Holly's last night. Not quite "separate ways."

She lay listless on the bed after Eric left. She looked at her phone. No messages. She knew now why she hadn't heard more from Holly. Usually Holly would have written to her to find out if she was feeling all right, send a picture of what she had eaten for dinner, or something.

Oddly numb, Victoria decided that maybe this wasn't so bad. Eric, distracted, and Holly finally getting what she had wanted.

Eventually she made herself some toast and smeared the lightest layer of peanut butter on it. She knew if she didn't eat, she would feel even worse than she did now.

It wasn't until she was halfway through the second load of laundry that her phone buzzed. Her heart fluttered in anxiety, and then she saw the text was from Luke. It was almost noon.

LUKE: Morning, bookworm 💀

TWENTY-EIGHT

DEIRDRE WAS WEARING A WOOL SUIT IN A SICKENING PUCE COLOR that brought to Victoria's mind indigestion medicine. She wore matching pumps that gave her a formidable height advantage over her daughter. Her mouth was covered in a matte lip color that resembled dry paint.

"Well, daughter," she said, as though waiting for an important answer. She held her wineglass pensively.

It was parental dinner night again. Victoria, uninspired to do anything culinary, and still feeling the remnants of her hangover, decided to have the evening catered. She hoped this would make everything a little less daunting, but without the pressure and activity of pulling the meal together, it had left her prey to more focused attention from her mother.

The men were in the other room. Eric was showing Mick and Dick his new badminton racket. It looked exactly the same as his old one, which hadn't been that old.

"Yes, Mother? How is the wine?"

Deirdre disregarded the question, giving Victoria a "What am I going to do with you?" kind of look.

"I hear you've been ill."

Victoria sighed. "Yes, I had a stomach bug. Nothing too serious, though."

"You were vomiting." She made the statement distastefully.

"Yes, if you must know. Was it in the newspapers?"

Deirdre pursed her lips. "All night, and into the morning."

"I'm feeling fine now, thanks for asking, and please inform the president," Victoria said, arranging crackers and cheese on a board. She wondered if Eric was now providing her mother with daily updates.

"I don't think I need to tell you, Victoria, but a pregnancy at this stage in Eric's career would *not* be prudent. I *hope* you're thinking of him at this time."

Victoria's face snapped up from the tray. Her mouth was agape. "Excuse me?"

Deirdre stepped toward her. "I know you're not getting any younger. But you can't be making selfish decisions at this delicate juncture. I hope you realize this."

"You think I'm . . . pregnant?" Victoria was horrified.

Her mother's thin eyebrows arched. "Am I to take it that you aren't?"

Victoria didn't answer right away. Her temples were pounding. "What if I were?"

"I shouldn't have to remind you about these things, Victoria. I shouldn't have to explain to you the strain Eric is under, trying to make partner. He doesn't have time for distractions now. There will be plenty of time for you to play mommy later on. Or not. It should be something you discuss with him."

"I actually cannot believe this," Victoria said. She wanted to tell her mother that Eric had had enough time to watch *Steel Magnolias* and the like, almost every evening that week. "Does Eric think I'm pregnant too?"

"I know you don't believe that I understand anything about you," Deirdre said coldly. "But I can see more than you think. And I know a great deal about life. I know that women who don't have much ambition tend to gravitate toward motherhood. Good for them and society, I've always said, God knows we need the population to continue, the world must have more nannies and concierges and valet drivers and kindergarten teachers and so forth, those kinds of people. But you cannot take this decision lightly. I know I didn't." She took a regretful sip of her wine.

"I hardly think it's your business, Mother." Victoria's words came out clipped and hot.

"Oh, maybe not. Maybe this isn't a mother's place. Maybe we don't have that kind of relationship."

Flushed and unwilling to look her mother in the eye, Victoria wordlessly busied herself with arranging the appetizers.

Deirdre pursed her lips. "Let this just be some advice from your legal representative, then. The lawyer who read your prenuptial agreement." She laughed drily. "Who am I kidding. I practically wrote it. I know just how much you stand to lose. I'd watch my step if I were you."

Joan appeared in the kitchen. She had been in the bathroom, and had evidently reapplied her coral lipstick, which was smeared on her front two teeth as she beamed at the two women in front of her. She was wearing a bright-green brooch in the shape of a frog, with glittering rhinestone eyes and an obscenely long tongue.

"What'd I miss?" she said brightly, oblivious to the hateful glare Deirdre was receiving.

"Oh, just some girl talk," Deirdre replied, with a wide, forced grin. "Victoria was just saying how proud she is of your son."

Joan tittered, pleased. "Oh, yes. It's so much fun just to be in his cheering section, am I right, Victoria?"

But Victoria had stalked out of the kitchen, cheese tray in hand. The men eyed the food immediately and began loading up crackers with jellies and brie, not interrupting their conversation on stock trading for a moment, giving her as much attention as they would the waitstaff at a wedding.

She was having a hard time catching her breath. The anger in her belly was churning. Her mouth felt dry. She placed the tray on the table when the men had finished and went to the bathroom for a short escape.

She closed the toilet lid and sat on it, her head in her hands. She couldn't even vomit without the information being reported to her parents. She had thought that being married would mean independence from them, but it was obvious Eric was just a conduit to them, and they were his reinforcements if she ever stepped out of line.

She knew she was not pregnant—she had made a big show of taking tampons out of the grocery bag yesterday so that Eric would know not to make his weekly Saturday-night advances on her—but what if she was?

She closed her eyes, imagining what it would be like to be a mother, to hold her newborn baby to her chest, kissing the top of its soft head, smelling the impossible perfection of its newness, seeing her own features in miniature mirrored back to her, feeling her heart open, rapturously in love. She would lean forward and promise undying devotion to this little being. "I'll love you always, my darling," she'd murmur. "I'm so sorry that your father couldn't be here today, but he just couldn't stay a moment longer. But don't worry, I'll love you enough for two. You'll never feel like you don't belong."

And she'd tell her little baby the story of its father, how, on one beautiful fall morning he had been walking down the street on the way to work (he was such a hard worker, little baby) and was passing by a construction site (so many of these on the Montreal streets, my sweet). The sky had been dazzling against the last of the autumn leaves. It had been too beautiful to miss, so he had walked that day. He walked by the construction site, not knowing that it was to be his last moment. And it was such a beautiful moment, baby, I promise he didn't have an ounce of fear in his heart. He had no idea that the crane that held the bundle of reinforced steel rebar was swinging in his direction. He was thinking that morning about the freshness in the air, the possibilities the day might bring, about putting one foot in front of the other (and he had such a confident stride, dear darling).

He saw the bluest sky as the mistake happened, as the arm of the crane jerked and fell, and the operator tried to correct the error, but not before the arm swung, in an upside-down rainbow arc with your father, the treasure, harpooned at the end of it, your father's head a glorious pot of gold, held on a hook. He didn't feel a thing, beautiful baby. He didn't feel a thing.

Victoria breathed deep, cleansing breaths, cradling and rocking her arms tightly against her chest.

A knock interrupted her serene moment. It was Eric.

"Victoria? Where are the crudités? Everyone is hungry!"

TWENTY-NINE

THE BRIGHT NEON SIGN ABOVE THE FRONT DESK READ "WORK IT." An overtanned, tattooed, black-haired woman sporting a high ponytail took Victoria's payment, then resumed her blank stare toward the back of the room.

Holly had suggested they meet at her gym. The afternoon rush hour drive to Laval was a hassle for Victoria, but the guest pass was cheap. Plus, it was Monday so Eric was playing badminton and wouldn't need dinner. Ordinarily, Victoria despised the gym—stinky socks, mildew and too-bright lights—especially Holly's, which didn't have a women's-only section. But she wanted to see Holly. She had been strangely quiet since "the dinner" that Victoria had opted out of, and though Victoria thought she knew why, the idea was an abstraction to her. The feeling of disconnection from her friend, though, that felt real.

It had taken a few days for Holly to contact Victoria, but Victoria had been in the throes of a flirty text conversation with Luke, so she didn't bother to question her friend about why she hadn't been in touch after her dinner with Eric. Victoria didn't even guilt her lightly about not inquiring about her illness. Yes, it had been self-induced (if she never saw another martini again . . .), but Holly didn't know that.

Luke's texts were powerful—they could pull Victoria up out of a day that would normally have necessitated an ugly cry in the bathroom or a few screams into her pillow, pull her right up into a feeling of lightness that she could hardly define. With only stolen moments spent reading, and far too much time with Eric, Victoria should have been on suicide watch. Instead, she had a hopefulness brimming in her heart that was difficult to contain.

Of course, the texts were sporadic, and perhaps a little too fluffy for Victoria's taste. Luke was masterful at the emoji and at making a cheerful and quick exit just when Victoria had settled herself in for a stretch of witty banter. Work calls, catcha l8r, gorgeous!

She tried not to notice his spelling, which was occasionally awful (sport's bar, last rights, and, by far the worst of the bunch, auntie depressants). She blamed autocorrect and instead focused on his sense of humor and relived the heat of their first kiss.

She tried not to be the one to initiate the texting, because of the one time he took over nine hours to make a bouncy reply to her Hello, Handsome! Involuntary thoughts about his sexy work colleague had infested her brain, with graphic ideas of all the trouble he could be "up to." She also tried not to overanalyze why they bothered with the texting at all and didn't pick up their phones to just *talk* to each other. If she thought about it too much, she might have come to the conclusion that Luke's intentions with her were a tad too casual. Still, she couldn't stand to burst her balloon just yet.

This was one situation where Holly's vast knowledge would have been helpful. She knew all about this dance, the mating rituals, the etiquette of the newly attracted. But Holly didn't—and couldn't— know about Luke.

"So, who are you dating these days, anyway?" Victoria asked her, watching Holly's mirrored reflection do perfect bicep curls with a fifteen-pound weight. She tried to imitate Holly's form, but with a lighter weight.

Holly made a sound of disgust. "Men," she scoffed. "I'm swearing off them."

Victoria suppressed an eye roll. "Oh, no you're not. Why do you say that?"

Holly switched the weight to her other arm. "I'm serious, I took down my dating profile. I've done it before, it's not a big deal, I can put it up again. But I need to be off the scene for a while."

Victoria raised her brows questioningly, trying to push out the image in her mind of the black dog hair on Eric's coat.

"Remember that bouncer, Todd, from Verdun?"

"Oh, the one on all the steroids, with the little . . . ?"

"Yes, him," Holly held the weight up a moment longer, a slight grimace on her tanned face. "He's been . . . freaking me out a bit."

"Really?"

"Well, he sent me a bunch of creepy messages the other night."

"Creepy, how?"

"It's probably nothing. He was probably drunk. It was a few nights ago. He sent me like . . . five messages? About how I made a big mistake, how I'd regret it, how he'd 'show me' . . ."

"Show you what, his baby carrot?"

Holly didn't smile at Victoria's joke. "He called me names too," she said, lowering her voice dramatically. "He called me *the c-word*."

"What a freak," Victoria said, more serious now. The weight was killing her arm. "I guess it's good you took down your profile, but doesn't he still have your phone number? Does he know where you live?" She asked the question, already knowing the answer. In the past, Eric liked to refer to Holly's apartment as Hotel Holly.

"I blocked him on my phone. Of course he knows where I live. He's been there enough times."

"Oh, Holly. He doesn't have a key, does he?"

Holly paused in her lifting, the weight at waist level. "I've been trying to remember. I don't *think* so . . ."

Victoria didn't bother lecturing Holly, not earlier, and not now. She had warned her countless times about making keys for guys she was dating. It was part of Holly's innocent belief in people, and also part of her desperation, thinking the key would make the man more permanent in her life. So far it hadn't worked. There were probably a dozen men in Montreal who hadn't even bothered to return Holly's hopeful token. At least a dozen men who could enter her apartment at any time.

Victoria had told her over and over that she needed to change the locks, but Holly always brushed her off. "Nah," she'd say, "they're all too lazy to walk up the four flights to see me, and they know there's nothing worth stealing in there, unless you count size-eight shoes."

Holly was right, her building was shabby and had no elevator, and she didn't have much worth stealing (including the shoes, in Victoria's opinion), but it still didn't seem like a good idea to have the keys floating around everywhere. Victoria had one, too, in case of an emergency.

"Hmm, I can't believe that guy resurfaced like that! When was this?"

"Um, a few nights ago . . . the night you were too sick to come to dinner." Holly's voice sounded tight, but she was on her second set of reps.

"Oh, then. Really sorry I missed it, by the way. Eric says you had a good time, though?" Victoria's voice sounded shrill to her own ears.

Holly's small blue eyes flickered uneasily. "Well, we figured we were both there. You didn't give us any notice." Victoria couldn't tell if her tone was defensive or accusatory.

"Of course, I'm just glad the night wasn't wasted on my account. I hope Eric was nice to you."

Holly gave her a strange look. "Of course he was. He's always nice. Why wouldn't he be nice?"

Victoria laughed, for a moment feeling sorry for her friend, wanting to put her at ease. "Jeez, Holl, there's no reason, never mind. I just hope you had a good time, that's all."

Holly changed the topic. "Oh look, two Stairmasters are free, side by side! Time to get in some cardio."

They sweated alongside each other for the rest of the workout, Victoria unhappily feeling like some bird on a hamster wheel, and Holly bouncing healthily, her breasts bobbing in time to Bon Jovi. They didn't speak, which was normal by anyone's standards, but Holly, who was in great shape, usually liked to chat while exercising. She was quiet and serious, and afterward had to leave for an unspecified appointment, anxiously tossing her hair. Victoria wondered if Holly really was nervous about this Todd guy, or if her conscience was the real intruder.

THIRTY

After the gym, Victoria checked her phone and saw with delight a text from Luke.

> **LUKE:** Heading out of town tomorrow for the next few days. Can I take you out again when I'm back? I'd like to thank you— properly.

Her heart leapt in a joyful arrhythmia. *Properly.* She'd been waiting for this, yet feared it, too, almost content to be in the delicious limbo between the last and the next meeting, with only the anticipation to experience and none of the reality to face. For example, how to orchestrate this? What excuse could she give Eric? A visit to the library was out. A mani-pedi? That new *Also Calls the Heart* film was playing—but what torment!—that was just too much. She still hadn't figured out what to do with the two-ton bookcase that she had purchased and would soon need to have delivered.

She lingered on this thought briefly, then pondered the last word in Luke's text. *Properly.* An unbidden smile crept up her face.

THAT NIGHT, AFTER BADMINTON, ERIC WAS ALL SET UP IN FRONT OF the television. *Beaches*, starring Bette Midler, was all set to go. Victoria could not fathom what made Eric choose these movies, movies that he was convinced Victoria would love and that he proudly presented as part of her "Filmography 101 education," as he was jokingly calling it. He was pretty pleased with himself. Last night they had watched *Sleeping with the Enemy*, which, Victoria had to admit, was the best of the bunch, probably because of the ending. The asshole husband finally got what was coming to him.

But tonight, she just didn't have it in her to sit through another saccharine, poorly aged chick flick. And she definitely didn't want to get that cheeseball song stuck in her head—*Some say love, it is a river . . .*—it might turn into an earworm that would never leave.

She had picked at her dinner, leaving much of it behind, and yawned several times behind her fist before clearing the dishes.

"Gosh, I'm not feeling so well," she murmured at the sink. She hoped he didn't hear her stomach growling.

"Really?" Eric responded.

"Yeah, I feel sort of sick. Lightheaded. Tired, too."

"Maybe you overdid it at the gym. You're probably out of shape. You haven't been going regularly enough. Another effect of too much reading."

Actually, Victoria *had* felt nauseated after her workout, but resented being called "out of shape." She stacked the dishes in the dishwasher with more force than necessary, creating a clatter.

"Maybe. The workout was pretty intense. Holly is such a gym bunny. You know how important it is for her to keep fit. She needs to look good for all her guys." She hoped her last sentence, uttered casually enough, would have a stinging effect.

Eric looked back at her. "I don't know about that. I think she's one of those naturally athletic people, like me. You're just the type that has to work at it a little harder."

Victoria smiled slightly. "I guess you're right, Eric. I don't know, though. I wasn't feeling great even before the gym. Maybe I should lie down, go to bed early. I just don't feel right."

"Now that you mention it, you do look kind of pasty. I hope you haven't caught something contagious. First that awful stomach bug, and now this." Eric was a germaphobe. His nose was wrinkled up in disgust. "I told you, this is exactly what happens when working with the public, like you do, touching random people's practically naked bodies . . . honestly, I don't know how you do it."

"They aren't 'random people,' Eric. They're my clients."

Eric rolled his eyes at the word "client." Only he had clients. Victoria, on the other hand, had random naked people. They had had this conversation before, many times. It was no secret what he thought of Victoria's job.

"Maybe I'll sleep in the spare room to be safe," she suggested, pressing the back of her hand against her forehead, as though testing it for fever. "I would hate for you to catch this."

AS SHE STRETCHED OUT ON THE SPARE ROOM BED, VICTORIA FELT like she was staying in a luxurious hotel. Sure, it was a smaller, harder mattress, but it felt so removed from the rest of the apartment, so untouched by the anxiety that permeated the space between her and Eric, that it seemed like she was on vacation somewhere. For many weeks, no one but the cleaning lady had even stepped into this room.

She breathed easily, knowing that her privacy was guaranteed. Eric would treat this room as though it were quarantined. A hoot of inane laughter burst in the distance, confirming that Eric was well into *Beaches*. That would occupy him for some time.

The one disadvantage of sleeping in the spare room was that reading her book was out of the question, as it was still hidden in the back of her bedroom closet. It seemed like a minor price to pay.

She scanned her texts with Luke, ending with the most recent, his promise to thank her "properly." It was almost certainly sexual innuendo. She wondered, as she had many times before, what kind of lover Luke would be. What sex would be like with one's soul mate. It almost defied her imagination. She realized, with a start, she had never had sex with someone she was truly in love with, and who loved her in return.

Victoria remembered suddenly how Doris Lessing had gone on in *The Golden Notebook* about different types of orgasms, about how a woman could have a clitoral climax with just about anyone, but could only have a vaginal climax with a true love. At the time she read the book, Victoria had thought it a little silly. It had never occurred her to worry about this distinction—to her, an orgasm was an orgasm, and she'd never turned up her nose at one, or a few—but now the idea of experiencing something new and supposedly superior with Luke, a product of their deep love and connection, intrigued her.

She turned out the light, pulling the sheets and blanket over her, thinking of Luke's face, feeling his knowledge of and attraction to her and letting it relax her. The room was very dark, and she closed her eyes.

She imagined being next to Him in the bed, her eyes closed, feeling his nearness and the synchronization of their breathing. It was soothing and reassuring to hear his breaths, so deep, and feel the warmth of his exhale caress the back of her neck. She felt she could stay in this blind cocoon forever, but just as this thought passed through her consciousness, she felt herself lift up, and again she was on a familiar night flight across the Montreal neighborhoods. She passed by crumbling roadways and construction sites that were pep-

pered with orange cones, over the graffitied metro station entrance
that buzzed with people and reeked of urine, over the St-Viateur bak-
ery famous for bagels, over an old and decrepit Catholic graveyard
where many of the decayed gravestones were eroded to neglected
nubs in the cold earth.

She followed the sound of his breathing, his familiar rhythm,
eventually to his window, where she gazed on him in his bed, asleep,
clutching a pillow. She scanned the room, noting an overnight bag at
the foot of the bed. Presumably he had packed for the short trip he
was to take tomorrow. She also saw a pair of silver circles glinting in
the darkness, on his bedside table. They looked like earrings.

She was dressed only in a T-shirt and underwear. He was the
same. She slid under the covers and lay down next to him, spoon style.
She was the outer spoon, pressing herself against his back, smelling
his neck, cedar there, or was it vanilla, reaching around to touch the
curves of his chest. She felt his heartbeat through the cotton of his
shirt.

Instinctively, he stretched his arms and pulled his shirt off. He
turned to her, his eyes closed as though still asleep, held her close
to him, so that their legs intertwined. His left hand held her bottom
firmly against his body. His right deftly removed her shirt. His mouth
greedily found her breast before he even kissed her lips. She gasped,
her hands cradling his head against her. His head bowed to her breast
in an ancient posture of adoration.

His hand moved from her backside to the front, down her white
underwear, and soon her mind was a field of fresh flowers, perfect
stalks of grass, a bed of earthy warmth, opening and circling with
blossoming, fecund life. It was aswirl with an ascending joy, a beau-
teous pressure of crystalline waters pressing against a dam.

She saw a flower open, displaying another one inside it, opening
as well, a perfect, pink bud, rising and full of nectar.

And then the face of Doris Lessing came crashing into her mind. Not the beautiful 1950s Doris Lessing, cigarette in hand, coy intelligent smile on her face, but the withered, grumpy, Nobel Prize–winning Lessing, certainly a Lessing who slept alone and had long lost her taste for lovemaking. She was wagging her finger at Victoria with disdain.

Victoria pressed her eyes together in frustration, willing the image away. "Keep going," she whispered to Luke, who had hesitated, as though he had sensed the old crone there too. The field was losing its vividness. The stalks of grass were out of focus now, just a homogenous green blur. She felt grasping and desperate. She lifted his head from its prayerful bow, seeking his mouth in an attempt to recover what had been interrupted. But as she brought her face to his, she felt a deep dismay and awareness that she was alone again, that she had left the field and would not return any time soon.

THIRTY-ONE

ICTORIA WENT TO THE CAFÉ THE NEXT DAY, TO PASS THE TIME
between clients. She brought *Strangers on a Train* with her, willing to take the risk of Eric seeing her with it, if he decided on a whim
to drop in like he had that day. Nursing a coffee in her usual corner
spot, she couldn't imagine what she would do at the café without a
book. There would be no point.

She didn't bother to change out of her work clothes, as she knew
that Luke was gone—to Ottawa, he'd revealed in a text that morning, a "snoozefest" trade-show type of event where "a bunch of guys
talked about wood."

Victoria had considered several innuendoes she could volley back
in response, but her heart wasn't in it, not after the previous night,
contaminated by the distinctly inappropriate presence of a deceased,
disapproving author. Perhaps, she thought, smiling to herself, Eric
had a point. She might be reading too much.

But of course that wasn't true. She was just under too much
pressure, and the stress was taking its toll. She felt discouraged and
blocked. Every time she thought about her visit to Luke the night before, she thought about the wagging finger. And maybe even more, if

she were going to be honest with herself, the earrings. The earrings definitely bothered her.

There was no good reason she could think of for Luke to have a pair of silver hoops on his bedside table.

She had imagined all kinds of explanations—they were an heirloom belonging to his deceased mother; they belonged to his exwife, earrings recently found in a drawer and set aside to return to her; a gift for a platonic family friend, taken out of its box for closer inspection—but none of them rang true.

She sighed and gazed moodily at her book on the table. Negativity had now seeped into her magical connection to Luke, and she didn't like it.

She sipped her latte, destroying the leaf design in the foam. She alternated sips with bites of coconut cake, a rare midmorning indulgence and definitely something Eric would disapprove of. She had set the book down for fear of soiling its pages with cakey fingertips. Instead of reading, she looked around the room.

Across from her was a table of four students, probably college age, all bent over their laptops. One of them, a dark-haired guy with Mediterranean features, wearing black jeans daringly tight, looked up for a moment with an expression of boredom. Their eyes met briefly. She could see he was being forced to study for a vocation he wasn't interested in, a vocation that required a scientific calculator. His domineering mother didn't support his artistic endeavors. Uninspired academically, he joined study groups and pilfered notes from the prettiest girls in his class, and like today, sometimes even whole assignments. He ate his momma's baked ziti with hate in his heart, slept resentfully on sheets she had washed and ironed, and then transferred this maternal bitterness to any relationship, treating the women in his life with a casual, callous manner, despising them for his need of them. Only his true love, a pit bull cross named Rosie, got any measure of tenderness from him.

She shifted her glance to a small woman with pockmarked cheeks sitting across from a toddler who was eating cheerios from a cup, one at a time. It was plain to Victoria that this woman, giving anxious smiles every so often to the child, lived in an overflowing well of self-pity. The woman believed everyone who looked at her felt sorry for her. They could see her fatigue brought on by selfless sacrifices, apparent in her wide, saintlike eyes. If asked, she would tell them how she gave up every evening to co-sleep with the child, gave up all spare time with the commitment of "breastfeeding on demand"— really, she was a prisoner! She'd tell about the tedium of multiple visits to the park every day. She'd hint at the lack of insight and help-fulness of the baby's father, who had gained thirty-five pounds since they'd first met. She wouldn't, however, admit to anyone the three abortions she'd had before, during those dark years in Romania, the last one such a nightmare she had thought she would never be able to get pregnant again. Those stories would stay untold.

The woman sensed she was being observed and glared insolently at Victoria. Victoria dropped her gaze from the woman's piercing eyes to her book, where the text on the cover seemed to swim. "A novel of an evil man . . . and a weak one . . . and their terrible bar-gain." Victoria wondered what the woman saw when she looked at her from across the café. She wondered if her own despair was visi-ble. If her loneliness oozed from her in weighty, dark globs. Or if she simply looked like a woman with nothing better to do on a Thursday morning than sit in a café with a book, alone.

The cake was all gone, even the moist crumbs, after Victoria had dabbed at them with her finger. She'd barely been conscious of eating the cake, which was a shame. She wiped her fingers carefully on a napkin before lifting the Highsmith novel and opening it to her dog-eared page. Sacrilege! She looked around, almost guiltily, before she started to read.

"People, feelings, everything! Double! Two people in each person. There's also a person exactly the opposite of you, like the unseen part of you, somewhere in the world, and he waits in ambush."

THIRTY-TWO

WINTER WAS LOOMING. THE SHOCK OF RADIANT LEAVES HAD fallen, and they were now in rotting, homogenous heaps. The impossibly blue autumn sky was long gone, replaced by a dirty gray. There was an edge to the cold. People talked about the weather, shaking their heads, how they couldn't believe another winter was coming—it seems like the last one just ended!—and a collective depression descended. Montreal harsh and concrete. Graffiti was more pronounced, garbage and grime in clear focus. Orange detour signs due to end-of-season roadwork (undoubtedly keeping the mafia in business) added a punctuation of color, but made drivers more irritable than usual.

It had been only a few days since her mother warned (threatened?) Victoria against the perils of pregnancy, but the entire surreal episode still smarted. Despite the bitter taste she had in her mouth, Victoria reinvigorated her spa-girl persona with Eric, who she now knew to be a spy who couldn't be trusted with the most minor detail. She hid her contempt for his tattle-tale run-to-mother antics behind a distant, serene exterior.

Now spa girl, alongside Eric, exuded a cool veneer of calm as he forced her through another rom-com. A young Hugh Grant with puppy-dog floppy hair was being insipidly charming again, despite having a deep fear of commitment, but that would be resolved in about ninety minutes, never fear!

"Watch, this next scene is just fabulous," Eric said.

It was all Victoria could do not to roll her eyes. *Shoot me now*, she thought.

She hadn't heard from Luke since his last text, telling her he was in Ottawa. Would it kill him to drop her a line? Her mood had skidded down into surly sulks, as she imagined him in bars lit with flickering candles, casting warm light on other women's cleavages as they leaned toward him, open mouthed, laughing in mutual attraction. She imagined a woman running her hand along his forearm, as if it were one of his wood coffee tables, purring over it as it flexed in response. She imagined his pleased smile, infused with a bit of pride and a lot of self-satisfaction. *Isn't it great being divorced?* She was beginning to understand. He lived quite the life. She was now fairly sure that she must be only one of the beautiful moons in orbit around him, not a sun for him to revolve around.

She accidentally kicked the glass top of the coffee table as she recrossed her legs for the dozenth time. Eric's chamomile tea sloshed a little onto the *GQ* magazine he had been reading. He grimaced. "What's with you, Victoria?" he said, exasperated. He lifted the dripping magazine, the cover featuring a man dressed in nautical colors, wind in his hair. "You can't seem to sit still tonight."

It was true that she didn't seem to know how to relax this evening. She was filled with a restlessness that even spa girl couldn't conquer. She hadn't made a night flight since the last one, partly because she couldn't summon the concentration and peace of mind necessary, partly because she was afraid of bringing along Doris Lessing or some other dead, unsexy author to ruin things.

She blamed her bad mood on the reading ban, of course. It had been seven days since she agreed to Eric's stupid idea, and it was affecting her. In stolen moments she pored over the Highsmith novel, but she had to admit to herself that it wasn't enough, and her evenings were spent in painful proximity to Eric. Not only were the movies horrible, but she was forced to sit through his running commentaries (*Isn't she a doll? Watch out!*) next to him, his eyes shining at her in expectant glances. He was so keen to share his experience with her it bordered on desperation.

She made sure her hands were busy—a cup of tea, a bowl of approved organic corn chips, and once, she'd resorted to a silver-polishing project that involved a cleaning agent Eric wouldn't tolerate on the couch—thereby ensuring he didn't try something silly like holding her hand. Granted, it wasn't Eric's thing, he hated how her hand got "switty" (sweaty-sticky) after a few minutes.

"Sorry, I'll get a cloth to clean this up. You don't need to pause it," she said, rising and escaping to the kitchen for a few minutes, grateful to kill even a few seconds, all but ready to poke her eyes out.

She checked her phone to see if any texts had come in from Luke. None. One from Holly, though.

HOLLY: OMFG! That guy just called me! He's freaking me out!

Victoria shook her head as she grabbed a dishcloth and reluctantly went back into the living room. Hugh Grant was spluttering about something while a beautiful woman in a glittering evening gown glowered disapprovingly. She soaked up the tea with the cloth.

Her phone buzzed again. Holly.

HOLLY: He didn't say anything, just breathed! 😱

Victoria shook her head again. When she looked up, Eric was eyeing her with great disapproval. He didn't like Victoria to look at her phone during the movie. It showed a "lack of presence." She "might as well be reading," he once said. She wished.

"It's just Holly," Victoria explained. "One of her Prince Charmings is turning out to be a psycho."

Eric looked away, suddenly focused on adjusting the color on the set. "What? I didn't think she was dating anyone these days," he said into the remote.

"An ex, which one I wouldn't know. With Holly it's an eternal catch-and-release season," Victoria said breezily, enjoying the panicked look on his face. "One of her exes. He's freaking her out, apparently."

Eric's dark brows knotted together like two fighting caterpillars. The woman in the sparkly dress threw a glass of champagne in Hugh Grant's face. His floppy hair dripped as he glanced sheepishly about.

The remote seemed to be giving Eric some trouble. "It's these online dating sites," he said bitterly. "I've been saying it for years. Full of trash. She won't find anyone decent there."

No, you only find someone decent with the help of your parents—or through your best friend, Victoria sniped inwardly. "Well, apparently she came around to your way of thinking," she said. "She told me the other day that she took down her profile."

Eric nodded, his expression still dark. He set the remote down. He no longer seemed amused by the frantic antics on the screen inspired by a misunderstanding so banal Victoria had already forgotten what it was.

"I'm just going to tell her again to calm down and change her locks," Victoria said, in explanation for her breech of phone etiquette. "Not that she'll listen to me."

Victoria thumbed out a response.

VICTORIA: How do you know it was him? If he was just breathing?

HOLLY: It was his number, duh! Who else could it be?

VICTORIA: Do you want to come here? Are you really scared?

HOLLY: I don't want to interrupt ur movie date. LOL. I'm sure he's just drunk or something. No worries.

VICTORIA: You're not interrupting. I'm sure you're frightened!

Holly didn't reply. Victoria thought she heard Eric's phone buzz.

VICTORIA: Really Holly, you are welcome to come over. It wouldn't be a problem. . . .

A minute later, Holly replied.

HOLLY: I think he's harmless. He just creeped me out, that's all. Enjoy your night!

Victoria put her phone down, shrugging at Eric's inquiring expression.

"I told you," she said, "she doesn't listen to me."

She returned her gaze to the television with a sigh she couldn't suppress. Hugh Grant was now chasing after a woman in a waitress uniform, groveling and begging her to give him a chance to explain. Victoria had no idea what was going on and couldn't have cared less. But what did serve to amuse her was Eric's preoccupation with the remote and the skin tones being so pink.

THIRTY-THREE

S HE NEVER SHOULD HAVE ANSWERED HER PHONE, SHE THOUGHT, streaking the screen with polish. First of all, she usually screened her calls, only answering if she knew who it was. Second, she had all but finished painting her nails—Vixen was the color, a brash and slutty red—and they still needed a good five minutes more to dry. Normally she had her nails done at the spa, and she knew that her colleagues would notice the amateur job she had done, but she had been desperate for something to pass the time between the end of her work day and dinner preparations, to keep her from checking her phone like a junkie.

But when her phone rang from "DuBois" her heart skipped a beat and she didn't think before picking up. She had assumed Luke was calling first thing after returning from his trip.

"Hello, may I speak with Victoria?"

It was definitely not Luke. It was the dulcet tones of his sexy shop assistant. Victoria grimaced at her error.

"Speaking."

"This is Alexia, from DuBois. To arrange delivery of your pouf and bookcase. I've phoned a few times?"

Of course she had phoned, and Victoria had screened, wanting to avoid or at least delay the delivery. She still hadn't figured out how she would explain her purchases to Eric. She had never brought something into the house without his express agreement before. She already knew the mammoth wood bookcase was completely out of the question. And a pouf? Eric would *hate* the pouf.

"Oh, hi," Victoria said, in a deflated tone. She switched her phone to the other hand, inspecting her manicure for smudges.

Sexy Alexia wasn't aware of or wasn't bothered by Victoria's less-than-enthusiastic reply. "As I mentioned in my messages, we'd like to offer you free delivery," she said smoothly. "If you give me date and a three-hour window when you will be home to receive it . . ."

Victoria was irritated by the "we" in Alexia's sentence. As though Alexia and Luke made decisions together in an intimate huddle. *Should we offer her free delivery, dearest? Oh yes, you yummy thing, I think we should.*

"Well, I'm not sure. A three-hour window . . ." Victoria stalled, trying to think of a way out, but she'd clearly painted herself into this corner.

"I know Luke is anxious for you to be able to enjoy the piece," Alexia said. "He made me promise hand-over-heart to book the delivery first thing this morning."

Victoria was snared momentarily in her thoughts. Should she be happy that Luke was making her a priority, or should she recognize that he'd spoken with his shopgirl yesterday, but had not sent her so much as a text since he left for Ottawa? She couldn't decide.

"He made you promise?" Victoria's words sounded more biting than she had intended. She was thinking of his hand over her heart—or was it her breast?

Alexia laughed softly. "Practically *forced* me."

There was so much subtext in those three words Victoria was stunned speechless for a few seconds. So, she wasn't just being presumptuous.

"Anyway, if you can give me a day that would work for you, we'll send your items over."

"Um, okay. Tomorrow afternoon, I guess. Not too late." It was her day off, and Eric would be at work. She'd have to face this sometime; it was already charged to the credit card.

"So, between noon and three?"

"Noon and three. That works."

Alexia took her address and said "Ciao" before hanging up, which annoyed Victoria even more. She threw her phone down on the couch with a whap, wrapped her arms around a big white couch cushion. Who actually says "Ciao" anyway and can take themselves seriously? If it must be said, it should be ironic, in an old-fashioned movie-star voice, something Bogey-ish, *Ciao, dahling*.

Victoria stewed awhile, pressing the pillow tighter against herself, until she remembered her nails. Horrified, she examined the pillow. There was one red half-moon shape in the middle of the pillow, marked in bold Vixen.

THIRTY-FOUR

A FTER SHE HUNG UP THE PHONE, VICTORIA WENT THROUGH THE whole apartment. It was pretty much the only option, but after analyzing every possibility, she decided the bookcase would go in the spare room. There was a good chance Eric wouldn't see it for days, maybe even weeks. He never used the spare room. After she moved a small bedside table out of the way, there was plenty of space for it against a big, unoccupied stretch of wall.

It would look out of place, of course. The enormity of it. The organic wood of it, next to the white, white, white. The handmade one-of-a-kind-ness would appear naked, almost obscene.

She had no idea what Eric would do when he saw it. She fantasized briefly of a scenario in which his face turned purple with rage, then, in the middle of an inarticulate rant, he grabbed his arm, staring at it with angry, wide eyes, as though witnessing a betrayal. He then staggered over to a chair but didn't make it, crumpling to his knees in a prayer pose. Unable to sustain this position, grunting in pain, he collapsed against the pouf, his sweaty head pressed against the aboriginal beadwork, such an unlikely juxtaposition that Victoria had to suppress a giggle. He wouldn't have noticed, though. By that time he had let go of his arm and his eyes were sightless but pointing directly at the bookcase looming high above him.

This was just wishful thinking, she decided, not allowing herself more than a few seconds of hope. Eric was too healthy; he didn't have a heart attack in his immediate future. He would be furious, though, through the roof. There was no precedent for this act of rebellion in their relationship. It violated all the unspoken rules. There would be consequences, explanations notwithstanding.

Without Luke, the bookcase hardly seemed worth it. If he had abandoned her (which is how she felt, on day two of no texts), why risk everything now? She felt her insides churn, as she envisioned herself doing a complete reversal. Castigated by her husband, she would have to send the bookcase right back and demand a full refund. She would promise anything to Eric—a month of no reading! She'd plead temporary insanity, whatever it took to appease him. It had been book withdrawal that had her buy the piece in the first place. She had an acute case of bibliomania. It was in the DSM-5, he could look it up! She would endure whatever parental repercussions came, with the patience of a monk. She'd figure out how to erase the ideas in her mind of a different life, even if they proved to be as indelibly marked as the bloodred nail polish was on the couch cushion.

She'd just have to turn her dreams over, like the cushion. They'd be hidden, wouldn't see the light of day. Maybe one day, she would forget that they'd ever been there.

She ran herself a bath and had just lowered herself in when her phone buzzed. Her heart soared when she saw Luke's name.

LUKE: Hello there, beautiful!

It was silly how happy these three words made her. She stayed in the contentment of this text for a minute, luxuriating in the balm of his greeting. If only it were possible to live in the dimension of this moment, never replying, never moving from the delicious, sparkling potential. This perfect, unspoiled moment.

She leaned her head back against the lip of the bathtub, chastising herself for giving up on Luke so easily. She had let Doris Lessing get to her. She had made too much of the past few days' silence. She had let her imagination get the better of her, as her mother used to say, deeply disapproving, when she was a little girl.

Slowly she keyed her reply.

VICTORIA: Well, hello to you too. How was Ottawa?

Immediately after sending her reply she felt unsure again. She couldn't take more casualness, waiting hours for his response. She had been on top of the world for all of sixty seconds. All of that could be easily stripped away.

But it only took a few moments before she saw he was writing back. Her heart jumped.

LUKE: Boring! When do I get to see you again?

He didn't waste time on small talk, not even on a "How are you?" She told herself this was a good thing. She never was much into small talk. She answered coyly:

VICTORIA: Well, not tomorrow between noon and three . . .

A small pause, and then:

LUKE: ?? So specific a time?

She felt she had won a small victory. If he didn't know about the delivery, he hadn't talked with Alexia.

VICTORIA: That's when a certain bookcase is coming to my house!
LUKE: LOL. Gr8 you set that up. Thought you changed your mind about it.

Victoria propped her feet on the edge of the bath, already feeling too warm. The cool air on her feet would buy her a few more minutes. Her body shimmered before her, under the water. Before she had a chance to reply, another message buzzed.

LUKE: How about dinner, my place? Monday? Been told Im a good cook.

Monday? Monday was four days away, and not exactly a typical date night. She had been hoping to see him sooner. It would have been fun to go for a walk with him in Old Port, even though it was cold—an opportunity for mittened hand-holding, conversation, ducking into art galleries, and leaning over steaming cups of tea. But of course this would be better. She could see where he lived, not just the bedroom, but maybe that too. Their two worlds might finally converge.

VICTORIA: Okay, sounds good . . .

She wondered who else he had cooked for. Had Alexia complimented his skills in the kitchen?

He sent a flurry of emojis, each a happier face than the one before it. She couldn't bring herself to send one in return. She felt weird about using emojis, like she was speaking a different language. She could no more send an emoji than she could say "LOL." She said instead:

VICTORIA: You're cute.

LUKE: No, your the cute one in this relationship.

She ignored his second abysmal spelling and apostrophe error and burst into a happy smile, a flush on top of her already warm cheeks, pink from the heat of the bath. She sat up straight as though the change of posture would help her read his text more clearly, her breasts rising above the water level.

This relationship. This relationship. This relationship.

THIRTY-FIVE

E RIC WAS WANDERING AROUND THE APARTMENT SHIRTLESS. HE
sometimes did this after a shower if he was feeling particularly
good about himself. He had been in a good mood the last few days,
and it showed. Revved up, perky. He gave Victoria more approving
looks now and seemed to seek her out with an irritating regularity.
He often walked in on her for the sole pleasure of observing her while
she was in the midst of any number of mundane activities: reorga-
nizing her closet, folding freshly dried towels, replacing a toilet roll,
emptying the compost bin, and even staring out the window, mug in
hand, at the Montreal streets below. Oblivious to her inner desperation, he was tremendously pleased at her compliance with the reading
ban. It made him much nicer to be around, though *nicer*, Victoria
reminded herself, was a relative notion.

Victoria had risen very early this morning, unable to sleep.
Anxious about the bookcase delivery, she went to the kitchen, and,
knowing Eric's propensity for shadowing her at any inopportune moment, she decided to do some baking rather than sneak a few pages
of Highsmith.

She had been icing a simple sheet cake when he marched in,

proudly bare-chested, proclaiming his two protruding pink flesh buttons.

He raised his eyebrows. "You . . . *bake?*"

She smiled serenely at his incredulous question. "Sometimes," she answered, as she continued to spread the icing with a too-sharp knife, which stabbed the cake, mixing crumbs in with the icing and creating a slightly bumpy texture. She knew the imperfection of her technique bothered him, but he said nothing.

He leaned over the cake, inhaling the warm, sweet scent. Forced to look away from his puffy nipples, she imagined that he would leave two circular dents in the cake's surface as they dipped into the icing. When he stood up again, they would surely appear like two mountainous peaks adorned with the winter's first snowfall. Or like the pointed hats of two garden gnomes. It might be an improvement. He would look ridiculous, of course, but at least she wouldn't have to look at those pubescent, swollen . . . no, there wasn't a word for it, it was just too ghastly.

But when he stood up a moment later, his chest was icing-free. He wore a suspicious expression. "You made this . . . this morning?"

"Yes," she answered, simply. "I couldn't sleep."

"No shit. You must have been up at the crack of dawn."

"I was. I thought since I was awake, I might as well do something productive."

He seemed to approve of this explanation. "Well, okay. It does smell good. But I don't think we need to make a habit of dessert."

Victoria had made the cake with the rebellious intention of eating the whole thing for breakfast, before Eric got up for the day. But it had taken longer than she thought. "No, we mustn't pleasure ourselves too often," she returned, focusing on her task. "That wouldn't do."

She felt like Mrs. Brown from *The Hours*, as she continued to ice the homely cake. Something about her task was meditative. It also allowed her to focus on something other than Eric's face.

"I have a meeting today, I'll be home late," he said, taking a swipe of icing from the bowl with his finger. He averted his eyes from hers as he brought his finger to his mouth.

"Should I make dinner?"

"No, I'll grab something," he said.

"Oh, I haven't put it on the calendar, but I might be going out Monday."

He looked curious. "Really? What are you doing?"

"Just drinks with people from work," she explained, still not looking at him. "For Mercedes's birthday."

Victoria knew that she couldn't use Holly as an alibi now that Holly had become "friendly" with Eric. But he had zero interest in her colleagues, and his eyes flickered with boredom as soon as she mentioned Mercedes's name.

"Oh, fine. I'll be out then too. Mini tournament at the club."

This happy news sent shivers up her spine. "Great," she said. Her night with Luke was safely set aside.

"Yeah," he answered. He started running on the spot. Now she really couldn't look at him, even though she could still see the nipples bouncing up and down like dark pink balls in her blurry peripheral vision. "It'll be good to burn off some energy. It'd do you good to do the same, you know." He eyed the cake again, and turned around, jogging down the hallway.

THE BOOKCASE WAS DELIVERED THAT AFTERNOON. IT SEEMED EVEN more enormous now that it was in the apartment. It stood like an obelisk, a giant's possession mislaid in a dollhouse. It looked crude, even rustic, standing next to their possessions. A sore thumb. Something too monolithic, erect.

She giggled nervously as she recalled a Sesame Street tune she hadn't thought of since childhood: "One of these things is not like the others, one of these things just doesn't belong . . ."

She directed the movers to the spare room. They squeezed the towering piece through the doorway through expert tilting maneuvers. When at last they left, she returned to the room and was newly shocked at the cartoonish immensity of the bookcase. It stood daringly close to the ceiling, buttressed by the spare room bed and the other wall. The space that Victoria had previously thought so large was devoured by the case's extravagant width.

It garishly declared: I am WOOD. I was made to house BOOKS. Hundreds of them.

No lie could cover its unapologetic expanse. When Eric saw it, it couldn't be explained away.

She retrieved the Highsmith novel from her bedroom closet and placed it on the middle shelf. It leaned there, diminished by the grand container, a mere Tic Tac. Victoria was in awe of Luke's creation for a moment. Anything that could reduce Patricia Highsmith was something to be reckoned with.

It wasn't likely that Eric would enter this room in the next few days—it could realistically be weeks. Maybe even months. But she needed to come up with some kind of answer, on the off chance that he happened into this room.

Probably more pressing, though, she remembered, was the charge on the credit card. Eric paid the bill; Eric scrutinized the charges. He would undoubtedly question her. Maybe by that time it wouldn't matter. She could pack her few possessions and have the bookcase moved to Luke's, where she and it would have a welcome home.

Or, she imagined, as she lay back on the spare-room bed, the bookcase looming like a skyscraper, dizzyingly tall above her, she wouldn't have to move out at all. Eric, after discovering the case, would yell, "Victoria, I demand to know the meaning of this!" like a character in a bad movie—or was it just Hugh Grant again? Victoria would appear at the doorway. "Yes?" "What the hell is *this*?" "Well, it's a bookcase." "I can see that. What made you think you could bring this into my house?" "I guess I needed a change." She would smile and knock lightly on the side of the case. "Something big and . . . hard. You know, for my . . . books." "Always the goddamn books! I'll show you what I think of all your books."

And then Eric would use all his force to pull the case away from the wall, to show her that he meant business. To his credit, he demonstrated that a guy who played a lot of badminton could possess decent upper-body strength (something Victoria always doubted). The bookcase wouldn't move from where it stood, but it tilted toward him. Tilted a little, then more, so that it hovered for a second before succumbing to gravity. With the weight of ten trees, it would fall on top of him. "Timberrrrrrrrr!" she would cry with glee as it leaned, creaked, and then swallowed her husband in a massive, heavy crash.

She would feel regret at the splintery sound of the crash. The case would be damaged. But she would be grateful to it for being so large that she didn't have to see Eric's broken body. That she could say, with all honesty, as he made a few final moans, "It's too heavy, Eric, I can't budge it an inch!"

THIRTY-SIX

CROW LANDED ON THE BALCONY, THEN ANOTHER. TWIN POR-
tents of doom, they blinked glassy black eyes at Victoria through
the sliding doors. She tried to stare them down, like one might a dog.
One of the birds clicked its beak aggressively, bringing to her mind
eye pecking and grub eating. The other one lifted its tail feathers
slightly and let a gooey shit drop. Victoria looked away.

She drank the last sips of her coffee and placed her cup in the
dishwasher. She checked her appearance in the mirror. Her crisp
white work clothes were unblemished, her hair pulled back in a flawless bun. She looked like she could work in a hospital. The psych
ward, maybe. She knew that she would have to fix her hair again
once she got to the spa, and she pulled on her toque and wrapped her
scarf around her neck a few times. She sighed as she got on her heavy
boots. No getting around it—it was freezing outside.

Eric had not entered the guest room yesterday, nor had he mentioned the charge on the credit card. Last night he was his usual self.
He had cut himself a big piece of cake and parked himself in front of
Ghost, which turned Victoria's stomach because she suspected he'd
chosen it because he thought she would find it erotic. Afraid he might

attempt an unusual Thursday night move, she'd preempted the possibility by fabricating a dry, hacking cough that had him looking at her in irritated disgust by the time Demi Moore was getting felt up on the potter's wheel.

And now, the bookcase was always in Victoria's mind, its secret presence like a hidden body that would soon start to stink. She knew time was running out, and it preoccupied her thoughts almost continuously. She longed more than ever to be able to pick up a novel and lose herself in the pages, but there remained still four more days on the reading ban. Victoria looked with envy at anyone she saw with a book, be it a mass market mindless romance involving mystical creatures or a political autobiography. She wasn't so picky now. Literary merit didn't matter much at this point. She just wanted the words again—the words and lives of other people—to populate her brain. Not her own, which were on repeat. *How did I get here?*

When she arrived at work, Bernadette was already in the waiting room and gave her a timid, wide-eyed wave. This irritated Victoria, who only liked to interact with her clients when on the clock. She nodded at Bernadette, took a sweeping look at the schedule at the front desk—she had a packed day—and ducked into her room to prepare.

Whale sounds playing, essential oils diffusing, Bernadette was a foil to the serenity of the room. She was jittery. Her wide, haunted eyes conveyed an expression of continual horror. Her complexion today was particularly sallow. She wore a frilly polyester blouse two sizes too big, whose apricot hue was doing her no favors.

"Hi," she said, with a nervous smile. She began unbuttoning one of the buttons of her blouse with a hand that had a slight tremble.

"I'll give you some privacy," said Victoria. Normally her clients undressed and lay on the table while she was out of the room.

"Oh—oh, that's all right," chirped Bernadette, who seemed stymied by the button and was looking at it with great concentration. "You—stay. Please. It'll just take me a minute."

It was true that Victoria had been working with Bernadette a long time and had seen her down-to-the-underwear body through the white sheet many times, but it seemed more than awkward to watch her undress now. It added a vulgarity to the already strange intimacy Victoria shared with her clients.

Bernadette was two buttons down when Victoria turned and pretended to be busy, folding and refolding towels in her already organized closet. She tried to clear her mind of the vision of Bernadette with a gaping blouse, the large, dark mole on her sternum, prominent as a bindi dot.

"So, how has your week been?" Victoria's voice rang out louder than she'd have liked. She normally didn't make small talk with her clients. She liked to stick to professional topics—where does it hurt, is this too much, things like that.

"My week? Oh, it's been, well, oh gosh, I guess it hasn't been too good."

Victoria wondered how long it had been since someone asked Bernadette this question. Though really, what had she expected her to answer? Had Bernadette ever had a good week in her life?

"Oh, dear," murmured Victoria, "sorry to hear that." She could hear the rustling noise of Bernadette's blouse and hoped she was almost done with the buttons.

"It's my—my, well, my cousin, Archibald. He's . . . he's no good. Drugs."

"Oh, dear." Victoria wondered idly how many other people in Bernadette's family had three syllable names.

"He, he keeps bothering Mother for . . . for money, for his, you know. Habit."

"Really."

"Yes. She, she never should have given—created a monster—he keeps coming back, broke the dancing lady, Mother's favorite."

"The dancing lady?"

"Royal Doulton, porcelain, worth a fortune . . . beautiful pink skirts, very delicate, nothing I would ever be able to care for, such a klutz, but still, Mother's favorite. Such a shame. So upset."

"He—your cousin—knocked it over by mistake?"

"Oh, no. No. No mistake. Threw it, threw it against the wall. Almost hit her, almost hit Mother. Mother crying please please please Archie. After everything she did for him when he was little. Such a shame."

"Wow, that must have been . . . frightening."

"Yes, and then he took the taxi vouchers and the grocery money from the jar. I shouldn't have been so—so stupid to leave it in the cupboard like that, so stupid anyone could have found it. Mother said it was like a gift for him, I just forgot to wrap it. Wrap it with a bow and everything. Idiot I am. Idiot."

Bernadette made a choking sound as she said this last word. Victoria couldn't help but turn around in sympathy, and saw the woman was crying, her apricot blouse in hand, a dirty beige bra with no elastic left hanging loosely off her small sagging breasts that Victoria could see were more nipple than anything else. Her face was crumpled into an expression of pain.

"But Bernadette, it isn't your fault. How were you to know he was going to rob your house? What an awful thing. Did you call the police?"

Bernadette nodded, her eyes still clamped shut in shame. "Mother called. Made a fuss. I showed them the—the kitchen window—broken. They're—doing all they can. Looking for him."

"Well, I guess that's good," said Victoria lamely.

"Not very good, no, not good," said Bernadette, opening her wide eyes again. "I think—think he still comes in. I see things—missing. Mother's cookies, favorite ones, the orange creams—I don't touch—all gone. She, she was so upset. And the big knife, from the block."

"You think he's coming in when no one's home?"

Bernadette's face didn't show comprehension. "Mother—she's always home."

"So when is he coming in then?"

Bernadette's expression darkened. "N-night."

"That's really scary. I'm so sorry, Bernadette."

"I—can't sleep. I—I—listen for noise all the time."

"Yes, I'm sure."

"I—keep a bat now."

"A bat?"

"Baseball bat. Yes. Under my bed."

Victoria couldn't imagine timid Bernadette swinging a bat at an intruder. Suddenly she fought the urge to laugh—why of course, it was the perfect way for Bernadette to defend herself, looking more and more like Wendy Torrance than ever, with that weak, shaky grip, the pleading horror on her face. She might just use it, after all. She could surprise her cousin, who no doubt underestimated her. It was a powerful advantage, being underestimated. A psychotic husband, a hatchet, a blizzard, none of these things can stop the underestimated, in the end.

Victoria went up to Bernadette, who was standing by the massage bed in her ratty old underthings. She grasped Bernadette's pathetically thin shoulders and looked into her bulging eyes. "When the time comes," she said, "you swing that bat."

She might have been imagining it, but she thought she saw a steely spark flicker in Bernadette's eyes.

THIRTY-SEVEN

❧

THAT NIGHT WHILE ERIC WAS AT HIS LATE-NIGHT WORK MEETING, Victoria went to bed alone, and lying on her back and staring up into the dark, found herself imagining and reimagining a calming scene in an attempt to control her anxiety. It was the crash of the bookcase. When it fell, it was like a tower of marshmallows, making no sound, but completely engulfing Eric in its suffocating, brown bulk. Sometimes she could see Eric's feet sticking out from under, like the Wicked Witch of the East's. The feet looked small and pathetic in his gold-toed socks.

When she felt herself lift, finally, she was flooded with a feeling of euphoria. She had missed this feeling of weightlessness and well-being, and determined to soak up every moment of it, as well as share it with Luke, she followed his heartbeat again.

Outside, the winter air was biting. Her naked legs were whipped by it. It felt as though there were minute ice crystals prickling her, and she fought against the pain and approaching numbness by focusing on the reassuring beating of Luke's heart. The city below, a show of lights, was unconcerned with her journey. It was busy being fractious, swarmed below her in a mess of traffic, decay, and hurried bodies.

By the time she reached Luke's window, she was painfully cold. The calm of his room was welcome, though her skin hurt, thawing with sharp, needling sensations.

Luke was in bed, covered under a duvet, one bare arm curled outside the covers. His skin looked warm to the touch and silky, like one of the tables she had caressed in his store. Tentatively testing her feet to be sure she could feel them enough to walk, she took small, slow steps toward him. Her desire grew with every step she took.

She pulled back the duvet and slid into the bed, pulling off her shirt. She was naked now. She and Luke faced each other, and his curled arm now held her shoulder. He was so warm, bathwater warm. She felt herself melting against his skin, pressing herself close into his space.

Luke, still asleep, instinctively knew where to touch to impart more warmth. His hands moved from her shoulder to her left calf, he squeezed and held it, then slid up so that his fingers lingered in the cool and sensitive back of her knee. She shuddered involuntarily.

His mouth pressed against the place her collarbones met, heat transferring from his lips. She gasped as his mouth slowly traveled down her body, stopping at underarm, breast, bellybutton, hip, leaving behind the warmth of his kiss, which imprinted pleasurable scorch marks on her skin. She lifted her neck as he moved. She could see the moon, full, through the window, its ancient yellowed face a witness. This was really happening.

He moved lower still, kissing thigh, calf, ankle, toe, until her body was vibrating in pleasure and anticipation, a mix of cold and hot. His knees were bent under him in prayer pose, as though worshipping before her. Then his mouth was on her sex. With the pressure and the texture of each gentle tongue lap she was awash, climbing high, high, higher toward a roller-coastering plunge. She reached out and grabbed the edge of his bedside table, where something silver glittered in the moonlight. She shut the sight away, arched, offering herself up to him.

She could scream, she could weep, the heat and wet, begging, so good please don't stop, feeling love, was this love? The wild violence of climax reverberated in a thousand sparks through her body, shooting her out of his bed to solitary panting, and soon sleep, supine in the position he'd left her.

THIRTY-EIGHT

T HE SALAD BAR LOOKED PICKED OVER TODAY. THE COTTAGE cheese container was almost completely empty, and there were no croutons or imitation crab either. Victoria felt uninspired as she surveyed her options, making a mental note not to meet Holly here on the weekend again.

"He called twenty-seven times in a row yesterday," said Holly, as she piled dry spinach leaves high on her plate with a pair of tongs. "After the thirteenth, I had to leave the house. I couldn't take it anymore. All that ringing. I went for a run. I didn't care about the cold at that point."

"He knows your landline too?" Victoria never understood why Holly bothered with a landline. Even Holly had to admit she rarely got calls on it.

Holly shrugged. "I guess so."

"Tell me you're going to change the number and your locks, Holly. You'd be stupid not to." She dropped a few cherry tomatoes and a dry-looking carrot on top of a blob of macaroni salad.

Holly rolled her eyes, topping her lettuce pile with some bacon bits and a squirt of oily dressing. She looked a little worse for wear, Victoria thought, feeling concern, despite everything. What was she thinking of, wearing that short dress in this weather? Holly had seemed reluctant to meet with Victoria today, even though it was their Friday routine, claiming a busy day at work. In the end she agreed to come, but only for a quick bite.

At that moment, a group of people speaking Chinese appeared. Holly gestured that she was going to the cashier. "See you at the table."

Victoria carelessly added a few olives to the unappetizing mish-mash on her plate and hurried behind Holly, hissing, "Don't roll your eyes at me. I know you're scared."

Holly passed her plate over the counter to be weighed, not answering, then handed over a twenty-dollar bill to the cashier.

Victoria tried again, while her plate was being weighed. "I mean, what are you waiting for? Do you want the guy to show up at your door in the middle of the night?"

"Fourteen seventy-two," the cashier said.

Victoria sighed and searched through her purse for her wallet. "I feel like this place is getting more and more expensive," she complained, but when she looked up, Holly had already turned around with her tray in search of a table.

Victoria hastened behind her. Holly had found a table for two in the middle of the cafeteria-style room. It hadn't been wiped down and was right next to one with a mother and two screaming twins in matching outfits. It was as though Holly picked the most unpleasant table on purpose.

Holly's face was flushed. She removed her jacket in angry jags, thrusting it on the back of her chair. She was wearing a colorful scarf, inexpertly tied, that Victoria had never seen on her before. "I don't need you to . . . to . . . *badger* me about this," she spluttered, her small blue eyes bright and shiny. "I'm not *stupid*, you know. I know I shouldn't have given him my key, okay? But I'm not going to let that asshole change my life. I'm not going to change my phone number, the only one I've had since I got a cell phone, like . . . twenty years ago! I'm not getting rid of my landline, either. It's the one my grandmother calls me on every Sunday. I don't want to change my locks. What if someone, the right person, who still has my key, wouldn't be able to get in one day? Like you, Victoria! I know you think I'm stupid, don't even try to deny it. I know what you think. But I'm not going to let him bully me!"

One of the twins shrieked after the other pulled her hair. Victoria rested her arms on the table, right into a pool of beet juice that quickly soaked into the sleeve of her cream sweater. She ignored it, because Holly had tears rolling down her angry face, tears that started after she mentioned "the right person."

"I don't think you're stupid. I don't. Okay? I understand. I really do. I'll drop it, if you want. But I'm just worried. I'm worried he's going to try to hurt you."

Holly softened a little. She brushed her tears away carelessly. "I know. I'm a little worried too, but I'm just hoping he'll get bored with it. I haven't responded . . . how fun could it be for him?"

As Holly rearranged her scarf, a blotch that resembled a hickey appeared briefly in Victoria's vision. Victoria felt disgust, deep in the pit of her stomach. It all made sense, the scarf serving a utilitarian purpose. Holly was more of a plunging neckline kind of girl.

And then a vision came to Victoria, one of the toppled bookcase, and Eric under it. This time, though, he had company. A bright ribbon of scarf trailed out from underneath the wooden wreckage. A second pair of feet too—Holly's. Good. Together at last!

She blinked the thought away. It was just too disturbing to contemplate.

"Maybe. You could be right, it could just fizzle out. But, what if it doesn't? What if he attacks you?"

"If he's still bothering me in a couple weeks, I'll consider changing the locks," Holly said with reluctance. "But . . . I gave those keys to people for a reason, and I don't want to have to chase them all down to give them a new one. I know you don't understand. But those people in my past, they aren't nothing to me. I'm not going to lock them out."

"Okay. I get it, sort of. But in the meanwhile, until he goes away?"

"In the meanwhile, I'll go running a lot, I guess."

Victoria gave a little gasp. "Ooh! I just remembered! I have a client who's being stalked, long story. I just saw her yesterday. Know what she does? She keeps a baseball bat under her bed."

Holly put her fork down. She raised her eyebrows but didn't say anything.

"I think it helps her, to have it there. Like a plan of action, in case he comes in. Especially at night. I mean, she's just a little thing, but you can do a lot of damage with a bat."

Holly nodded. "I actually have a bat, from back in high school. A good one—aluminum."

"It's just a thought, Holly. I'm sure you'll never need to use it. I mean, it wouldn't come to that. But it could help you sleep better."

"Well," said Holly, stifling a yawn. "I might see if I can dig it up. I had a few bad nights, I'll admit. My imagination gets away from me."

"I know just what you mean."

Holly narrowed her eyes. "What do you have to worry about?" she asked, her tone taking on a harshness. "I bet you sleep like a baby every night in your king-size bed and five-hundred-thousand-thread-count sheets."

Holly had always oohed and aahed about king-size beds for some reason, like they were the holy grail. If you had one, you'd made it in life. She'd said on more than one occasion that for Victoria to share such a bed with Eric was over-the-top good fortune. Victoria noticed that this time, Holly hadn't mentioned Eric. And previously when she gushed about how lucky Victoria was, it was with an envious smile on her face, not this petulant, angry one. Maybe hickeyland wasn't everything it was cracked up to be for Holly.

Victoria took a deep breath and waited a few seconds before replying in an even voice. "Everyone has bad nights, Holly, no matter the thread count in their sheets."

"You have no idea how cheesy you sound. You could be on Oprah with that line," Holly said dismissively, returning her attention to her salad, taking vigorous, wolfish bites. "Let's hurry up. I have to get back soon."

THIRTY-NINE

T THE REGISTER, AS SHE WATCHED THE LADY IN THE BEEHIVE hairdo put the finishing touches on her latte, Victoria wondered if had been a mistake to stop by the café before meeting Luke for their date. She would have coffee breath. She rustled through her purse for mints, knowing it was a futile effort. She would have to pick up gum or something before seeing him, but then, would she want to show up chewing like a cow?

The café was busy, but her usual table in the corner was empty. She sat and surveyed the room before taking a tentative sip of her coffee, careful not to drip onto her dress—a simple number made of cotton material that hugged her body like a second skin. Yes, she'd have wicked coffee breath. Today's brew was strong. But she had needed to get out of the apartment. She didn't want to run into Eric. He would disapprove of her outfit, and that would kill her buzz. She was too happy to let him ruin it—and he definitely could, with one judgmental sweep of his eyes. He would look at her and see her unwholesome, duplicitous intentions, as clearly as if they were written in capital letters across her forehead. How could she hide the energy that coursed through her veins, even now causing her palms to pulse?

She would soon be at Luke's house, soon drinking from a glass he handed to her, soon leaning toward him over a table set for two. She could say and do all the wonderful things that she'd been dreaming of for months now. She felt like she was on the verge of a defining change, this the moment before her life truly started. Everything would count, from here on out. With Luke in her life, everything in her life, even the drudgery (dishes, cooking, cleaning), would be a joy. Her hand trembled slightly as she set the cup back down on the table.

From her purse she pulled an item that would cause further Eric disapproval—a 1970s paperback edition of *The Sundial* by Shirley Jackson. She had found it in the lobby of their building, on a table where people left books they were finished with. Prior to the book ban, she found the discarded volumes unanimously uninteresting. She knew they weren't for her, with their battered covers that boasted in large, tacky metallic letters uninspiring titles that usually contained the word "prey." But this morning she had stopped to look, out of desperation for a novel—any novel—and she was rewarded with this vintage beauty. The clouds parted for a moment and the theme song of *Jesus Christ Superstar* rang through her mind in victorious refrain. *Do you think you're what they say you are?* Well, she was just being herself, actually. The rest of the day would be perfect. She would spend time with Shirley Jackson and her wonderful cast of gothic weirdos before having dinner with Luke.

And, of course, she would people watch now, which was something she couldn't seem to help herself from doing.

A woman was wandering the café in search of a table, a heavy woman who Victoria's mother would have described as "gone to seed." Her frizzy brown hair bushed out behind her, too long for a woman her age, and showed a good two inches of gray roots. The woman sniffed and pulled her orange pants from her crotch without any subtlety whatsoever, then used one finger to shove her smudged glasses higher up her nose. Victoria saw that the woman lived alone in vagabond style, surviving off a limited variety of takeout options. Chinese wontons, potstickers, Colonel Zho's sizzling beef, all in oily paper cartons stacked in the sink. She was kind—didn't kill spiders, or even the mice that were attracted by her lack of cleanliness—but had preferred her own company ever since she was jilted as a young woman by Martin Sally, a chatty middle-aged bus driver who managed slummy buildings on the side. Buildings built in the 1960s, in which illegal basement suites with windowless rooms were rented to silly women like her who didn't mind the paper-thin Astroturf carpet and stinking, dirty walls. Martin Sally jilted her and also screwed her out of her damage deposit, the scuzzball. She rarely ventured out to restaurants, preferring to eat alone. Today, however, her bossy sister, Louise, had insisted on meeting her to discuss their father's estate, and the café was a better place than her apartment, which, though it was not in one of Martin Sally's buildings, was still smelly, dirty, and had carpets that had rarely been acquainted with a vacuum. With the selling of her father's estate, a move would be just the thing.

Victoria sipped her latte again. A man in a beard and shabby suit jacket brushed by the woman, drawing Victoria's attention. She saw he, too, was meeting someone, his soon to be ex-wife, Constance. They were going together to mediation to determine the custody details of their divorce agreement. They had twin sons, Lunar (Lu) and Solar (So-So), who were now almost two. Bernard and his wife had met as mates in a house that practiced "conscious community." Constance, a dancer with the most magnificent dancer's body, Bernard a philosophy student at McGill. Their love had been sweet, wide-eyed, naked, smiling. There had been delicious weekends together by the lake, meals cooked side by side, a clear, open honesty running like a river between them. Everything changed after the boys though. Everything became tight, and life was no longer free. Constance never recovered her dancer's body or spirit. Her mouth was now always drawn together tightly as though it had a drawstring sewn into it. When Bernard told her haltingly that their marriage was no longer his true and healing destiny, she had thrown a pot of kombucha at him, the babies screaming in the background. Always the babies. They had begun as seeds, planted in pure, loving intention. How could they have resulted in warping his perfect, blissful life? Bernard was meeting her at the café in order to tell her his truthful proposition: that the babies needed their mother and that they should live with her full time, but that he would be "on call" whenever she needed him (outside of working hours, of course). Bernard hoped she would recognize the transparent sweetness of his heart again and wouldn't clench up her mouth like an angry fist.

Victoria consciously drew her eyes away from him, not interested in watching his family-law situation unfold. No more lonely people today, she vowed, a day when her domestic life would be taking a serious turn for the better, when all the signs would be confirmed and connections anchored, when Luke would know, just as strongly as she had known since she first laid eyes on him, their undeniable, shared fate.

She opened *The Sundial* and read the first page. Lionel Halloran, dead after a fall—or was it a push?—down the stairs. Now everything belonged to Orianna, his cold and ambitious mother. The haunting but meaningful inscription in the main room of the Halloran mansion caught Victoria's attention: WHEN SHALL WE LIVE IF NOT NOW?

Victoria felt a regret that their apartment was all on one floor. No stairs. She had never taken particular notice of stairs before. They could be so useful, so convenient, their downwardness practically made for deathly purposes, doing all the work for you. Well, not *all* the work. The whole idea would require an initial physical force that, she had already admitted to herself, she lacked. That oh-so-definitive *push* necessary for the fall to happen. The vigorous shove, her hands violent against Eric's body, making momentary contact, feeling the fabric of his shirt, the flesh and bone underneath it. She knew with dismay that this vital, final, killing touch would be impossible for her. It was a major frustration, really, to be forever stuck in inaction like this. She would have to accept that she and Eric would part ways like over 50 percent of married couples did, and that she would be left with nothing but what she'd come with—actually, less, now that she knew just how firmly her parents' camp was pitched with her husband's. There would be a nastiness that would be difficult to get through, but she had to take comfort knowing she would have Luke as compensation.

After she read a few more pages of Jackson's sniping misfits, she found herself wondering about Luke's financial situation. He was an artist, which usually meant lots of instant ramen noodles and ruined friendships over unpaid loans. But he was also a business owner who demanded high prices for his work. Not that it mattered so much. It didn't. They could live off the ramen together. Ramen and a Dickensian love was all she needed, when it came down to it.

FORTY

VICTORIA SUCKED ON A CURIOUSLY STRONG MINT AS SHE STOOD in front of His apartment. Luke lived in an upper-story walk-up in St-Henri, a neighborhood that real estate agents would describe as "gentrifying." It looked pretty shabby from outside, with a peeling brown facade that had a 1970s air to it, and an old, rusty clawfoot bathtub parked on the lawn, but at least he was in an upper corner unit. Victoria recognized his bedroom window immediately, the one she'd flown to those nights.

She shivered and cast her eyes to the sky, where she saw endless gray. The moon was hidden. It would snow tonight, if the weather report was right. It had warmed a little, from previous days. There were overflowing trash bins under the stairs leading to his apartment. A corkless bottle of champagne sat next to one of the bins. Luke's? She heard rustling and thought she caught a glimpse of a rat tail.

Taking a deep breath, Victoria clutched the metal railing. She imagined that when the snow and ice came, this staircase would be very slippery indeed. She'd have to be careful when she left tonight. Ascending the staircase, she thought about the black bra and panties she was wearing. She thought about how men didn't usually drink champagne, unless they were in the company of women. She thought of a dark-haired woman, or yes, Alexia, wearing silver hoop earrings, smiling as she brought a champagne flute to her mouth. She shook the thought away, and instead, *WHEN SHALL WE LIVE IF NOT NOW?* marched through her head. Good question, Shirley Jackson, she whispered to herself.

She pressed the doorbell but heard nothing. After waiting a minute, she knocked. Footsteps came, and soon Luke was at the door. He was effortlessly casual, wearing the same faded jeans he had been wearing when she saw him at his shop, and a navy long-sleeved shirt with a waffled texture. He looked good. She was prepared with a nervous smile and felt momentarily mute, but he had his cell phone at his ear, so no greetings were exchanged aside from his mimed "sorry" and a shrug of his shoulders. He guided her inside and took her coat, which he then draped over a chair.

"Oh yeah?" he was saying, as she stood awkwardly, trying not to appear like she was waiting for him. "Well, like I said, I looked around, but it's not here. I think I'd have noticed it. That porcelain horse, for god's sake." He rolled his eyes apologetically. She smiled.

She turned away from him and took in the room. It was tasteful, warm, and comfortable, if a bit worn. Much of the furniture was wood, including a beautiful coffee table and a unique high-backed chair with carved armrests. An old, pea-green velvet couch with tufted cushions provided some color. The main wall was covered with dozens of frames of different sizes, in them photographs of Luke with various scenery in the background, and undoubtedly what were postcard versions of famous works of art. The effect was pleasing, if a little strange. Luke standing shirtless on a Thai beach next to Seurat's *Bathers at Asnières*. But the wall was nicely arranged.

"Of course I didn't 'give it away,'" he snarled. "I know it belonged to your grandmother."

The dining area was behind the couch. The table wasn't set; it was covered with papers and two of the light bulbs on the track lighting overhead were burned out. Her stomach gurgled, reminding her of the lattes she had consumed. She reached into her purse for another mint. It burned her tongue.

Luke ducked into another room, the kitchen, which had a sliding pocket door that stuck halfway shut. He made a frustrated hand gesture.

"Francesca, I'm not going to argue with you about it," he said. "I paid my lawyer a lot of money so that I wouldn't have to argue with you anymore."

Francesca. Only beautiful women with ample, goddess-sized breasts had names like Francesca. *Oh, Francesca, I must have you. Now.*

"No. No. I have no idea where those are either. Look, if I see them, I'll give you a call. I have to go now, sorry, but you'll have to look somewhere else. Well, we both can agree that was a mistake. Look, I have a guest now, so I'm not going to say it. Yes, I do. Goodbye, Francesca."

She pretended to be interested in a magazine on the table. When he came around it, he tossed his phone onto the couch with a rueful smile. His cheeks had a ruddy quality. With the flat of his hand, he swept his hair off his forehead.

"Really sorry about that. My ex. She was always so into her STUFF. So much goddamned stuff."

"That sounds—"

"As though I would keep some porcelain statue a hundred years old! More than likely it was smashed in one of our 'discussions.' Let's just say she has a flair for the dramatic."

Victoria nodded mutely, hoping her expression showed the right amount of sympathy, but not too much so as to encourage a big debriefing. She didn't want to know yet how often he sparred with Francesca.

Whatever she was doing seemed to work. The stormy expression in his eyes broke. His face cleared and spread into a smile.

"You know what? This is *not* how I wanted this to go. Can we start over, please?"

He walked her back to the door, handing her coat over on the way. She giggled as he opened the door, letting a whoosh of cold air in.

"Well hello there, beautiful," he said, looking at her properly for the first time that night. He cupped her face with his hands and kissed her on both cheeks in Montreal custom, lingering deliberately on each side. His hair smelled woodsy, like pine.

"Hello," she breathed. Her legs felt wobbly.

He closed the door and took her coat, draping it again over the back of the chair. "And how are you this fine evening?"

"I couldn't be better," she said, feeling the truth of her words with exhilaration.

His eyes scanned her body. It was clear he liked the dress, but even more so what was under it. "Hungry?"

She wasn't, but she said, "Starving. Rumor has it you're a good cook. I've been saving my appetite all day."

He smiled. "I hope you like pasta. I'm going to make you my famous pesto penne."

It wasn't the most original-sounding dinner, but it was wonderful to be cooked for, for a change. And at least it wasn't chicken, she thought.

"Wonderful! I love pesto."

"You'll love this, then," he said, leading her into the kitchen.

She watched as he filled a pot with water and put it on the stove, sprinkling in an extravagant amount of salt. "The Italians really salt their pasta water," he explained. "I took a cooking class years ago given by an Italian guy who sang opera the whole time, and you wouldn't believe the amount of salt he used."

He ducked into the fridge and brought out a jar. "This is hands down the best pesto I've ever had. It's made by a guy who has a stand at the Jean-Talon Market. Everything's organic, even the pine nuts. I can't get enough of this stuff, it's magic."

She watched him as he opened the jar, twisting the lid open with ease. His sleeves were pushed up to his elbows, exposing strong, capable forearms.

He brought the jar over to her where she was leaning against the counter, put it under her nose. "Smell."

She inhaled. It smelled like pesto, all right.

"Wow, that is . . . great."

He looked expectantly at her. "Did you notice? He uses lemon juice in his recipe. Unusual, right? It adds a . . . zing."

"Oh, that's what I was smelling. So fresh."

He smiled. "Exactly. You're gonna love it. So, can I get the pretty lady a drink? Your hands are empty. I've got beer, beer, and more beer. Oh and I have a bottle of white somewhere too."

The two of them standing shoulder to shoulder, Victoria accepted the wine, feeling prissy doing so, but mortified at the thought of "beer, beer, and more beer" and the possibility it brought of stinking burps or worse during a romantic moment. She had a vague impression that Luke would have liked her to choose the beer—he was proud of the selection of microbrews in his fridge—and he might have been impressed to see her drink straight from the bottle, deftly manipulating the neck. It had sort of the same effect as a woman smoking a cigar.

But his smile was warm when they clinked glasses, and her doubts quickly evaporated.

"Cheers, bookworm," he said, winking.

He went back to his work, which consisted of boiling the pasta and putting together a Caesar salad from a large bag of precut romaine lettuce, and everything else from a box adorned with a cartoon of Julius Caesar (the dressing was made in Canada, and he promised her it would be the best she had tasted too). She watched him, enjoying the sight of him in his natural environment, like a zoologist might when entering a chimpanzee habitat for the first time—not wanting to draw attention to herself and noting his every act. She enjoyed his casual, easygoing manner, the ease with which he laughed, and the tender and worn patch of skin right below his Adam's apple.

When the pasta had been boiled and the spoonfuls of pesto were mixed in, she helped set the table while he hastily cleared the clutter away and redistributed it to the kitchen counter. He also produced a few candles, which he lit with a lighter from his pocket.

"I know I already have mood lighting," he said, glancing up ruefully at the burned-out bulbs overhead, "but I thought these might be nicer."

She laughed. They sat across from each other, and she felt a quietness between them descend, like they were now alone for the first time. She felt an unexpected prickle of fear. She had never felt frightened in any of her nighttime visits—she had felt powerful and confident those times. But tonight she felt like a girl on a date at a guy's house, a guy she didn't know all that well. She wondered momentarily why they weren't at the movies, doing things most people do on first and second dates.

She pushed those thoughts away, dismissing them as nerves. What she and Luke had was not typical, so why should they behave that way? This may be their "second date" by the outside world's standards, but their connection was far deeper than dates. They were anything but strangers. She recalled the certainty she felt the day she first saw him in the café, how thunderstruck she had been by the recognition she felt in her mind, body, and heart. The instant love. This memory calmed and reminded her why she was here. She smiled and raised her glass to his. He smiled too.

"Cheers," he said. "Sorry, no martinis tonight."

"Oh, I think that's all right. I don't think I'll be drinking a martini again anytime soon."

He snickered as he put his glass down, and using tongs, started serving salad on their plates. "But you've gotta admit, it's fun to tie one on every so often, isn't it? Don't worry, I won't be pouring you into a cab tonight. I guess I should have asked if you're okay with Caesar salad. I won't have any unless you do . . . it's one of those things we have to do together, or not at all."

"Let's do it then," she said, spearing a leaf of romaine with her fork.

"Okay," he said, doing the same, never taking his eyes from hers.

She felt the magic from their first date reappear. She was smiling, she was at ease, she was in his gaze, and it felt so good. He got up at one point and put an old record on a turntable. It was Billie Holiday, much to Victoria's approval. The sultry cadences made time go by more slowly, at a reluctant pace, making her feel like there was no rush and nowhere else to be.

"So," she said, when they had finished eating and he was pouring her second glass of wine, "have you sold any more bookcases lately?"

"Bookcases? No," he answered easily. "That doesn't happen as often as you might think. Only very special people buy those."

She blushed, and thought, *Yes, I was right to buy it.* He stood, taking their wineglasses, and gestured that she join him. They left their plates on the table and moved over to the couch, which was old and smelled of mildew. She sank deeply into the cushions. He lifted her feet from the ground and placed them on his lap so she could stretch out a bit while he massaged her feet, which sent waves of pleasure through her. Victoria hadn't had her feet rubbed in years and couldn't believe how good it felt.

"Alexia was shocked that you bought one, actually. She calls the bookcases 'permanent fixtures' in the shop."

"She's very beautiful, Alexia." The words slipped out before she could rethink them. "I mean . . ."

"Yeah, she is, but she knows it," Luke answered. He dropped her feet softly to the floor and reached for his wineglass. "And she uses it."

She had no desire to know how Alexia used her beauty, or how Luke knew about it. Why had she said that?

"Well, as long as she uses it to sell your beautiful pieces, then I don't mind."

"Yeah, but you know what I'm talking about, right? Women who know they are beautiful, they use their beauty like a key to unlock the world. To get what they want. To give them permission, forgiveness, whatever. My ex was like that too."

Victoria nodded, lashing herself inwardly. Somehow, through her idiocy, she had managed to invite both Alexia and Francesca to be part of their romantic evening, which just now was no longer. She had to admit, his gushing stung—so much so, a brittle silence filled the room. She held her breath, willing it to turn in her favor.

"But then there are women like you," he tilted his glass toward Victoria, "who really don't know just how beautiful they are. You don't know, do you? You don't notice how men look at you when you enter a room. It's amazing, really."

Victoria felt her face become hot. Luke had lifted her feet back into his lap, where she felt something stirring there.

"Oh, you're just being charming," she purred.

"No, I'm telling you the truth. I've given it some thought, actually. I think you don't know, and it's all because of the books."

"The books?"

Snow was coming down on the window behind him.

"Yes, you've got so much in your mind. From all the reading you do. You're a thinker. And you've got better things to think of than your hair or nails, or hatching plans to get a man to do something you want."

"That's a very nice way of calling me a nerd," she said, still smiling.

"It's a compliment, believe me. It's so nice to be around a smart woman. Someone who thinks on a . . . higher level, I guess. Someone who's not trying to manipulate. I mean, I can handle, uh, complex situations, if people are up front. But I don't like being tricked."

Victoria felt a wave of goose bumps as Luke's hands continued to caress her calves, and the tender part behind her knees.

"That's very nice of you to say, and I'm glad that you think I'm smart, but in the spirit of honesty, I should admit something: I don't *always* think about books," she said in a low voice.

He smiled and his eyes took on a hungry look that, she imagined, matched hers. He put the wineglass down.

"How did you know that's exactly what I wanted to hear?" he said.

FORTY-ONE

H E DIDN'T WASTE ANY TIME. INSTEAD OF KISSING HER, WHICH she thought was probably a natural progression from the foot rubbing and flirting, he surprised her by rapidly unbuttoning the front of her cotton dress and lifting up her bra without even stopping to look at it. His kisses to her breasts were fevered. She tried to enjoy them, tried not to feel cheated of whatever had been skipped over, tried to remember that he and she already had so much history on their nocturnal visits. They had already had many "firsts" together, and he more than likely knew this on some level, though they had never talked about it.

She found herself bringing his head up, though, in an attempt to slow him down a little. "Kiss me," she breathed.

His mouth was full and warm, and they kissed a few times while his hand moved over her breasts. Squeezing, pinching. Soon he was pulling at her dress, trying to get the whole works down. She stopped him gently.

"Let's go to your room," she suggested, standing up and drawing her bra back over her breasts.

He led her through the kitchen and into the room that she had been in on those nights before, washed in the blue light of night. His bedding was rumpled. She turned her head and suddenly he was kissing her. Teeth and tongue and mouth working, it was hungry and animal and brought to mind for her two fighting wolves. Animals do not use foreplay. Before she knew it, he was sucking her breasts again, she was gulping for air, she was grasping at his shirt.

"I can't believe I'm really here," she gasped as they staggered toward the bed. She searched for his eyes. "This is really happening. Don't you think it's amazing?"

"I think you're pretty amazing," he said, licking her neck.

Luke was pulling at her dress and decided to peel it off, right over her head. As he did so, it caught on one of her earrings, which she heard tinkling onto the wood floor.

"My earring," she said, touching her naked earlobe. It stung a bit, pulsing between her fingers.

"It happens," he murmured between kisses, leading her to the bed. "Don't worry, I'll get it for you after."

He was suddenly naked, and she felt a wave of discomfort at the unfamiliar body in front of her. She thought briefly of the nocturnal visits she had made to him, and they seemed almost chaste, in slow motion compared to what was happening now.

She got into the bed and shimmied under the covers. Before she knew it, he was next to her, unsnapping her bra. He dropped it on the floor, probably somewhere near her earring. She thought it was a shame that he never noticed her carefully chosen (and expensive) lingerie from Agent Provocateur. Well. There would be other times. She just wasn't used to this level of animal passion.

"Tell me," she said breathlessly, her eyes still trying to focus in the darkness. "When you met me. Did you . . . just know? Like really know more than anything else?"

"I knew you were sexy as hell," he murmured into her hair. She could feel him press against her. His body was more muscular than she remembered.

"But . . . didn't you get the feeling . . . when you saw me . . ."

"Yes," he answered, before she had a chance to finish. His hands were moving over her panties quickly, missing the delicate ribbon ties at the sides, the little peek-a-boo cutout at the back. He pulled them down to her knees and used his feet to remove them completely.

"And you don't mind that I'm not divorced yet? Because that's going to change. It's going to change soon. I promise."

At this, he stopped and drew away slightly. She was sure that if it hadn't been quite so dark that she would have seen an amused look on his face.

"Of course I don't mind. It's your . . . situation. Everyone has their own situation. Life is complicated." She felt him shrug, then lean back toward her. "Now, missy. Anyone ever tell you that you talk too much in bed? Cuz you do. Shhhhh . . ."

She giggled nervously, and then his mouth was on hers, his body's weight pinning her firmly on her back. She felt him move against her. He moaned. She could smell the intimate sourness of sweat coming from his underarms. She reached down to touch him, and he responded with a low growl and kissed her, for a moment his mouth more slack and gentle.

She told herself to remember everything, every detail, a catalogue to return to later when she wanted to recall their first coupling. Time was going by too quickly, she was going to miss something if she wasn't careful.

"Victoria," he breathed, just as he pushed himself inside her.

She felt underwater, she was aroused, and too hungry herself, but behind her arousal, she was running hard to catch up. She pushed against him and he pushed back with fierce strokes, she almost howled, and like fighting wolves, they made love.

Afterward, she arched her neck to look out the window, but the moon was still hidden behind the clouds.

She lay against his chest, playing with the small patch of hair at his sternum, fighting a strong tug to close her eyes.

"Thank you, Victoria," Luke said, his breath acidic from the wine. She tried to inhale it instead of being repelled.

It was strange, being thanked. She felt shy. She felt the wetness between her legs; it was lucky she was on the pill, because he hadn't asked and they hadn't used a condom.

"Where's the bathroom?" she asked.

"Just down the hall, to the left."

She touched the cool walls gingerly as she made her way down the hall. Sitting on the toilet, as she released his seed into the water, she rested her head in her hands, and the floor rocked below her. She realized: it had happened. And: it was over. Their first time together had happened. It happened with the trajectory of an arrow striking a target, and while she was, somewhere in her heart, elated, right now she was keening with a feeling that her brain wouldn't name, and it was familiar. She was visited with the same feeling every time she had been with a man. Her arrow, again, was more like a spinning top. Going round, and round, and round. Name it, she commanded her brain.

All the dreaming in the world didn't conjure the reality of what happens when men and women get together. Bodies mingled, sharing space for minutes, invited intrusion, there is pleasure, there is heat. But she still found herself incomplete, longing for what she did not know.

Disappointment. That was the word, the sense that flashed so quickly across her brain.

Immediately, she shook her head, in disagreement with herself. It was a case of being used to being unhappy. She just didn't know how to be otherwise. She needed to stretch those never-used muscles and lift the corners of her mouth, gaze in appreciation at someone else for a change, instead of being the eternal critic. Who did she think she was?

She closed her eyes, replayed the carnal scene that had only just ended minutes before, felt heat in her breast. He had crawled on top of her like a beast, he had no shyness or restraint or patience. She wondered if he had looked at her as he entered her. Her eyes had been closed, she had been moaning. When she had finally opened them, he was panting above her, his canines bared. By instinct, she had reached up to touch them, and he bit her hand. More heat rolled through her in remembrance.

Hold on to that, she told herself. Stop looking for faults, there are none. This is Him. He. He knows, he understands.

She would focus on the positives from now on. Neither Doris Lessing, nor, equally bad, Shirley Jackson, had intruded in the bedroom this time, not for a second. Though, if they had, she had the nagging idea that the two of them would have had their criticisms.

She returned to the bed and checked the time on his alarm clock, the only item on his bedside table. It was almost eleven.

She turned toward him.

"You need to get back, don't you," he said, more as a statement. His voice sounded far away.

"Yes," she said, sighing deeply, feeling pangs of anxiety and unease. She wished she could stay longer, but it would be better if she got home before Eric.

Luke called her a taxi. "You'd better get dressed now," he advised. "They never take long to get here."

He pulled on his shorts and a T-shirt. She wondered if this was a walk of shame, the steps to the front door, the minutes looking out the window for car lights that stopped. She thought of Holly.

It was still snowing. Everything looked fresh, untouched, but slippery.

When the cab did arrive, he pulled her to him and kissed her tenderly on the forehead. "What are you doing tomorrow, beautiful?"

"Seeing you?"

He smiled. "I'll call you." He opened the door for her and watched as she carefully descended the metal staircase, which was already covered in white. She waved from the taxi, but he had already shut the door behind her.

FORTY-TWO

HINDSIGHT WAS USELESS, LIKE A FISH ON A BICYCLE. HINDSIGHT couldn't have told her not to rush out of Luke's bed, like a princess about to turn into a pumpkin. But Hindsight was a bitch who, after the fact, only ever said, "If you only knew . . ."

After Victoria's cab ride home, she showered hastily and changed into modest, flannel pajamas. Ugly purple plaid, suitable for the doldrums of winter. She would have looked blameless had there been anyone to see: the good wife, home from a work function at a very respectable hour. It was amazing what she had accomplished, and all before midnight.

But it was all for nothing, because then Eric's text came, at 11:43.

ERIC: Don't wait up. Crashing here. See you tomorrow.

She moaned in disappointment. She could've been in Luke's bed, starting a slower, more sensual round two right now. Shoulda, woulda, coulda. Damn Hindsight. She replied with Where's "here?" but there was no response.

Victoria replayed the night over and over in her mind until she finally fell asleep. Everything felt sexier and sexier the more she thought of Luke's insistence, his single-mindedness. The disappointment she had felt sitting on his toilet faded with each mental replay, until it was something in the past, something that she would eventually forget altogether.

She awoke with the sound of Eric's key in the front door.

He popped his head in the bedroom. He was pale and his shirt looked rumpled, lending him a little-boy quality that was oddly likable. Maybe he had slept in it?

"Hi," he said. "Sorry to wake you." Sorry? Eric never apologized.

"No problem. Did you have fun last night?"

He brushed his hand through his hair absently. "Yeah, I guess too much fun. I crashed at Steve's."

"Oh, okay."

"There's like ten feet of snow out there."

"Oh, shit."

"I'm just going to get a shower. Feel disgusting."

"I understand."

His head disappeared from the doorway.

Victoria's phone buzzed. She immediately grabbed it, hoping it was Luke. Maybe they could make plans today. The snow would be a pain, but they could get around it. There were plenty of things lovebirds could do on a snowy day in Montreal.

It wasn't Luke, though. It was Holly.

HOLLY: OMG. You were amaaaaaaazing last night, lover! Four times??? Hope you got home ok!

Victoria stared at her phone. She reread the message a few times in confusion. Her heart felt quite still, almost dead. Her whole body felt hollow, like a cheap chocolate Easter bunny.

Holly had obviously sent this text to the wrong person. She hadn't sent it to her amazing lover. The silly goof had sent it to his wife by mistake.

It wasn't as though Victoria was surprised. How could she be? This was what she had known, at least on an intellectual level, for a while now, with an aloof air of feigned disinterest. It was what she had even hoped for, a distraction for Eric while she hatched her own escape plan.

She heard traffic buzzing outside, the sound of cars honking. A siren in the distance. She heard Eric's shower door close. She sat with her phone in her hand, identifying the still, hollow feeling engulfing her as blinding, singular rage.

FORTY-THREE

IT WAS WEDNESDAY, THE DAY THAT HAD TAKEN A FORTNIGHT TO arrive. Victoria luxuriated on the couch, all but swooning at the paper's texture between her fingers as she turned another page. She was reading a paperback edition of *The End of the Affair*, one of several volumes she had picked up at a used bookstore close to her work. Not only reading, but the unthinkable: underlining and note-taking! So far she'd filled the pages with satisfying markings made in strong, blue ballpoint.

She'd also purchased a battered copy of John Updike's *Couples*, and, for good measure, *Rebecca* by Daphne du Maurier. The books were on the coffee table and she gazed at them lovingly whenever she took her eyes from Greene's pages.

Eric grimaced when he entered the room, seeing her stretched out with her undoubtedly new purchases. She met his eyes with daring. The book ban was over. So, they both knew, were a lot of things. He opened his mouth to say something, but decided against it. He fixed himself a glass of Perrier and drank from it, leaning against the kitchen counter.

His thinning Pete Sampras hair looked dry and unkempt. What

was he doing to it? She'd thought she heard a blow-dryer going after his shower, but that would have been a first. He must have forgotten to put in product after his shower. This happened a few days ago too. He had become absent minded, almost lighthearted, in recent days. If she hadn't known the reason why, she would have enjoyed it. This new Eric didn't nitpick, didn't insist they watch terrible movies together, didn't even expect that she prepare him dinner. In fact, he had worked every night of the week, and sent her considerate, apologetic texts to this effect.

But she did know the reason, and though she was certain she had no right to be, she was furious, plagued with Technicolor visions of Eric and Holly together. Holly's augmented breasts bouncing as she screamed in delight astride Eric. *Four times, lover!* Holly's pink nails scratching Eric's shirtless chest, his puffy nipples not bothering her in the least. Both of them joined in ecstasy in various adulterous positions. Holly praising Eric in steamy postcoital analysis. Holly stretching out on a king-size bed—*Victoria's bed?*—with an expression of accomplishment. She'd really made it.

Given her own extracurricular activities with Luke, Victoria knew her indignation was hypocritical at best. But she couldn't seem to tame the boiling fury in her chest, the molten sparks that leapt up and burned at each unbidden imagining. That Holly and Eric could—effortlessly, it seemed—find joyful connection together was a constant source of bewilderment and, yes, resentment, if she was going to be honest with herself.

Victoria tried to imagine Eric and Holly instead in the midst of an awkward embrace. Teeth knocking against teeth, a tongue too forceful down a throat, a shirt pulled up and caught roughly in the mouth, the failure of a vital organ at the most inopportune moment. A giggle at the failure, then—oh, what's *that*?

Small red dots on Eric's skin upon closer inspection revealed tiny hairy insects burrowed in. Neither Eric nor Holly could name what they were looking at, but Victoria recognized them from horror stories told by colleagues at the spa. Chiggers.

When the red dots were found on Holly's skin, too, the giggling stopped. The parasitic insects usually lived on the surface of the skin, but these seemed unsatisfied, burrowing underneath. Holly screamed. Looking at her own arm, watching insect activity under the skin, the trajectory of the chiggers hectic and all too visible to her widening eyes, she pleaded hysterically "GET . . . THEM . . . OUT!!" transfixed on the raised lines made by the tunneling insects, one line aimed determinedly for her heart. She jumped off the bed, eyes wide, brain fighting to decide whether to scratch in an attempt to get the chiggers out or kill herself to get rid of them completely. Comically frozen in indecision, she let out a childish wail. Eric jumped up and down, his deflated, forgotten parts jangling, his face nothing but a pained grimace.

"A funny book?" he asked now.

Victoria jumped a little. She reoriented her gaze to the page, then to Eric, who had asked his question in response to her quiet laughter. He had drained his glass of Perrier and regarded her with an expression of confusion.

She bristled, the amusement draining from her face. "Hardly," she said, showing irritation with an expression of disdain she rarely allowed herself, then flicked her eyes back to the page. "I was thinking of something else."

He nodded and shook his head a little, eyeing the books on the coffee table, no doubt interpreting her mood swings as brought on by the reinfusion of all things literary. But he said nothing, which was also unusual, and infuriated Victoria all the more. He put his glass in the sink and started down the hall.

"You should put something in your hair. It's frizzy again, like a clown's. You don't look like any lawyer I'd hire." Her voice rang out, louder than she had intended, and sounded like her mother's.

His footsteps halted, then started again.

Victoria didn't feel any better having said it, and muttered further insults under her breath—"Shlup, moron, fucktard"—when no retaliation came her way. His failure to put her in her place served to goad her on.

It was so strange, this new meekness of his. He must be operating out of a fear that she knew something. Victoria hadn't immediately responded to Holly's accidental text from a few days ago. Later, Holly had realized her error and backpedaled with:

> **HOLLY:** Oops! So embarrassing! Meant to send this to my date, Enrico, not you. Sorry!

Victoria had gawked at Holly's use of the name Enrico, and then left her (and Eric, presumably) hanging for several hours before replying.

> **VICTORIA:** I thought so. Back on the wagon, I see. Let's guess, a professional idiot this time?

Holly had replied with an overly jolly LOL It's nothing serious! Ha ha ha!!, to which Victoria didn't respond. She didn't want to make Holly lie to her further. She wished her friend had been smarter, had gotten away with it all, had been smoother in her betrayal. She should have been better at lying and worse at the sex part. (*Four times, lover?*) She should have had a long and ultimately unsatisfying affair that left her unavailable and bound in a silent contract. Blue-pill moments, maybe a sneeze that left them both unsatisfied. Victoria would have forgiven her that. Maybe even thanked her for it. That way, Victoria's joy would be unmarred by the inky, cancerous stain that now infected her mind. Gone were the days of linking arms with that girl and believing the clear expression in those small blue eyes. How dare Holly, effortlessly, it would seem, turn Victoria's personal hell into some kind of pornographic filmmaker's dream, too good to wake up from?

Victoria consoled herself by texting with Luke brazenly, with Eric in the room.

> VICTORIA: I'm looking for a hardwood banquet set. Got any of that?
> LUKE: Hardwood here a plenty, do you want it oiled or natural?

Once she even took his call when she and Eric were having their morning coffee.

"It's just work," she said, leaving her cup on the counter and letting her friendly "Hello?" echo down the hall as she disappeared into the bedroom, closing the door behind her.

She and Luke hadn't seen each other since their dinner date. He wanted to, he assured her, with many complimentary (and two X-rated) assurances. There were a lot of things he needed to "take care of," workwise, the most pressing of which was a commissioned premodern dining set—a huge table with twelve chairs. He had his hands full, for the time being.

"I'm my own boss," he had explained ruefully, "but I'm a slave to my work."

She had hoped he'd be a slave to love, but she would be patient. He wanted to see her in a few days. She would show him then why he should make dates with her more often.

Now she heard the click of the front door and knew she was alone in the apartment. She put down Graham Greene and strolled around the room, as though there were suddenly more space in it than there had been before. Standing in front of the Bose sound system, which was virtually never used, she scrolled through an old playlist she had made when they had first set it up. She turned on one of her favorites, John Lennon's *(Just Like) Starting Over*, and cranked the volume up to an adolescent pitch.

Lennon's post-Beatles voice rang out, his Elvis-y swagger encouraging her to dance away her dark mood. Hips swayed, hips that had found their purpose again, Victoria imagining Luke holding her in his arms. *But when I see you darlin' / It's like we both are fallin'. . . .*

In Luke's arms, she felt effervescent, light as air, right in place. He swept her across the room with the dancing prowess of John Travolta, she as demure and compliant as a Disney princess.

As she danced, Victoria decided to adopt John Lennon's hopefulness, to wrap it around her like a cloak, despite what had happened to him later.

She three-stepped up the hall, sashaying to the dreamy chorus of *"over and over and over . . ."* and into Eric's bathroom. She never entered this room, as a rule. He had emphasized, from the beginning of their relationship, how important his/her bathrooms were. How it preserved "the mystery," whatever that meant.

There wasn't much mysterious about Eric's bathroom. It was the same as the rest of the house. Spotless, white, orderly, aside from a few toothpaste flecks on the mirror. After scanning the room and still moving to the music, she noticed with some amusement that there *was* a blow-dryer on the vanity counter.

Ensuring it was still plugged in, she moved it from the vanity to the edge of the bathtub. It was mainly hidden behind the white shower curtain, precariously so. Only an accidental nudge would be required to send it tumbling into the bath. Did Eric take baths? Sometimes. Would it work if he was taking a shower? Would he turn it on, and *then* tip it into his own bathtub?

It *could* happen. He could decide, after a grueling badminton game, that a bath was in order. He could wash his hair while in the bath, using the convenient telephone nozzle thing that hung next to the tap, then he could notice the blow-dryer where she had left it, remember Holly's suggestion that blow-drying would give Enrico's locks "more body." Lazily, he could stand in the bathtub, letting the hot air blast at his wispy strands, heating his scalp more than anything. Then what? A ding from his phone? An unexpected knock at the bathroom door? Whatever, it could send a ripple of surprise through his body, an unforeseen jolt of adrenaline that could cause him to spasm and drop the blow-dryer into the water. And his brain could go fizzzzzzzzzzz.

It was a long shot. But Victoria decided it didn't much matter as she flounced out of Eric's bathroom, feeling lighter than she had in days. It was the possibility that counted. It was the possibility that lightened her heart. Possibility—she would hang on to that. Goodness knew there was enough pessimism in the world. She was making a delectable suggestion to the universe. Maybe, just maybe, it would listen.

FORTY-FOUR

THE HORSES' HAUNCHES FLEXED AND WORKED IN FRONT OF THEM, and Victoria pulled the scratchy blanket higher around her throat. When she had suggested meeting at Old Port so Luke could have a few hours' break from work, she had envisioned a walk along the water, then ducking into a cozy crêpe place to warm up, sitting side by side on a banquette the way people did when they were really in love. She hadn't foreseen that Luke would be a horse-and-buggy guy, who paid God-knew-what to trot around on cobblestone, while they froze their asses off and pretended to be in the 1800s, as Teslas shot impatiently past.

She'd always scoffed at the gesture of the horse-drawn carriage ride. You'd see them offered in any city. It was unoriginal. For tourists. For high school couples. The woman invariably held a single red rose with babies' breath wrapped in cellophane.

"Who actually *does* that?" she'd asked Holly, on one occasion.

"Oh, I think it's kind of romantic," Holly had said wistfully. "You're so hard to please, Victoria! If a guy took me on one of those rides, I'd know he was really trying, he must really like me."

Victoria tried to invoke Holly's generous way of thinking. She tried to summon a scene, or at least a feeling, from something Edith Wharton, say, *The Age of Innocence*, in which lovers in a simpler time feel the complications of a secret love. It was an excuse to snuggle up to Luke, not that he was any warmer. He stiffly put his arm around her as she leaned into him, then took it away to adjust the blanket and surreptitiously wipe his nose with the back of his sleeve.

He laughed, his breath making little cloud puffs. "I'm so sorry. This falls under the category of 'it seemed like a good idea at the time.' Why the hell aren't we indoors?"

She laughed and shivered. "Ah, the indoors. We would be a lot warmer AND wearing far fewer clothes. Just imagine!"

"You make it so difficult to be a gentleman when you say things like that," he said, bringing cold lips to hers, lips that were waxy with Chapstick. He pressed his hand, thick with the padding of his mitten, against her breast, and trailed it down between her legs.

"If only I had any feeling in my body," she joked, "that would be so sexy."

He really laughed now, and any annoyance she'd been feeling melted away. His smile was the best she'd ever seen. The crooked tooth so perfect, the lines by his eyes creased after years of good humor and optimism.

"Oh, you, you're so . . ." She trailed off, her own breath puffing tiny clouds that evaporated. She leaned forward and kissed him again, feeling a romance burning deep inside her despite the clopping of the horses' hoofs and the rumbling of the wooden wheels on the cobblestone.

FORTY-FIVE

HOLLY WAS STANDING IN THE WAITING ROOM AT THE SPA WHEN Victoria's shift was over. Her back was turned as she examined the rows of nail polishes, but Victoria instantly recognized her neon-pink gym bag.

"Holly?" she said, trying to keep her tone neutral. The Calming Fountain behind her cascaded and tinkled, a contrast to her erratic heartbeat.

Holly turned, alarm on her face, which was makeup-free and showing fatigue. She stepped toward Victoria and hugged her. Victoria responded, woodenly.

"I was hoping I'd catch you! Sorry, I hope that's okay?"

Victoria shrugged. "I'm just heading home. Something wrong?"

Holly opened the door, deferentially letting Victoria through first onto the busy street. "No, nothing's wrong. Just been awhile, you know? Just wanted to . . . see you."

Against her better judgment, Victoria met Holly's eyes. They looked smaller than usual. Maybe a little puffy, but that could have been the lack of makeup, which was really strange. Holly always wore makeup, even if she was working out. Victoria felt a pang of pity for Holly, which was annoying. She didn't deserve anyone's pity, least of all Victoria's. But she had a simple innocence about her, as though nothing bad she'd ever done was actually her fault. Like Lenny from *Of Mice and Men.* Holly wasn't about to accidentally strangle any bunnies, but Victoria felt a twinge of guilt, granted Holly had been led unawares into her current predicament by people smarter than she, and wasn't savvy enough to get herself out.

"Well, I figured you were just too, too busy," said Victoria.

Holly looked confused.

"With . . . *Enrico?*" It enraged Victoria to even say the name. Her pity had shrunk by about fifty percent now.

A maniacal, twittering sound came from Holly. "Oh! Hahaha!" It caused Victoria to give her a sidelong glance as they walked past the entrance to Holt Renfrew, where a display of mannequins proclaimed that real fur wasn't completely out of style. Strangers, mainly older women with expensive handbags, turned their heads at the unnatural laughter. It was already dark at four thirty, and Sherbrooke was crowded with commuters waiting at bus stops or hurrying to a metro station.

"Did I say something funny?" Victoria asked, her voice sharp.

"Oh, no," and Holly's giggles ceased with bizarre immediacy. "No, no, no. Not funny."

"O-kay then . . ." Maybe the whole thing with Eric was over. Maybe that was why Holly had shown up like this, out of the blue, no makeup. "Sorry if Enrico's a sore subject." And in this moment, she was truly sorry. If Eric had inflicted some of his soul-destroying black magic on Holly, Victoria knew too well how that felt.

"No worries," Holly said, her voice artificially high. "Oh, do you mind if we stop in here? I love this store."

It was a shop that sold the kind of loose tea that was trendy about a decade ago, but now had a has-been vibe to it. They were assaulted by a strong odor of musk and fruit mixed together as they entered the shop, but Victoria was relieved to be out of the cold.

Holly busied herself by opening tins of tea, poking her nose in, and sniffing dramatically. "Oh do you remember this? Mango Wango Island Punch! We drank this constantly that year I was getting over Philippe-Etienne, remember?"

Victoria stood to the side, rather impatiently. She did remember—the tea was a bit of a letdown, much like Philippe-Etienne, and they drank gallons of it—but she only shrugged.

"Something you'll be happy to hear," Holly said as she groaned in pleasure over a chocolate-and-mint tea that had tiny red peppermint candies shaped like lips sprinkled throughout, "that freak of nature has finally stopped bothering me."

"What freak of nature?"

Holly rolled her eyes. "You know. *Todd*. The bouncer with the small . . ."

"Oh, yeah, sorry. I forgot. Yes, Todd. He's left you alone now? How do you know?"

"Well, it's been, like, a week, or almost, since I heard from him. And the last time he called, I picked up and let him have it."

"Really. What does that mean?"

Holly brought the tin of the lips tea to the counter. She indicated to a mammoth ten-ounce container, and a girl with four facial piercings started to shovel tea into it.

"I told him he and his tiny dick needed to leave me alone or my big brute of a boyfriend would teach him a lesson." Holly's weird laugh bubbled up again. The girl with the piercings looked up, startled.

"A big brute of a boyfriend?" Victoria said. "Really? You actually said that? How did Todd take it?"

Holly paid for her tea, which was almost fifty dollars, and far too large to fit in her purse. She looked a bit shocked at the whole transaction, and Victoria worried she would start giggling again, but she didn't. Instead, she snapped her purse closed, and they turned to the door and went out into the cold.

"He was all bravado, of course. Said a ton of horrible things. Like, really terrible, horrible things. He said he wanted to . . . well, I actually don't want to repeat what he said. And that he knew where I lived and that both me and my boyfriend better watch it. I told him I'd moved, but he said he didn't believe me because he saw my dog in the window. That was really creepy."

"Oh my god. He said he saw Brando?"

"Well, he just said 'that black mutt of yours,' not 'Brando,' but yeah."

"He's been watching you, Holly!"

Holly looked straight ahead. "It scared me too," she said, her voice sounding normal for the first time. "But then he stopped calling. He hasn't called once, not even to breathe or hang up. I think he got scared off."

"I think you're crazy," Victoria said irritably. She had wanted to hear about Enrico breaking Holly's heart and earning a mean nickname, like "Rico-Not-So-Suave," but she was certain that no such story existed. Enrico and Holly were alive and well.

"Well, the proof is in the pudding," Holly declared, her voice high again.

"What does that even mean? I don't understand why you don't file a police report, at least."

"I was going to. I really was. But I waited it out, and it looks like he's given up."

"Unbelievable."

"Are you—are you mad, Victoria? Please don't be mad." Holly tugged at the sleeve of Victoria's down jacket. Their eyes met. Holly's looked old and sad.

FORTY-SIX

THE WIND WAS HOWLING OUTSIDE, PICKING UP THE SNOW IN AN exhausting swirl, never letting it rest on the ground. Victoria watched the violent dance in the streetlight. It was a disgusting winter night, the kind that gave Montrealers PTSD-like reactions when they thought about winter. Any sensible person would be indoors.

It was past midnight, Eric still wasn't home, and Victoria was in the kitchen, baking again. Ever since she extricated herself from Holly, she'd had a craving for cake, the kind with a sweet, crumbly topping, best eaten with a mug of coffee (not tea) in the other hand.

Eric interrupted her during the final stages. He came into the room gingerly.

"It's pretty late. Where have you been?" she asked, mixing the sugar into the softened butter with a fork.

"Uh, work. I had an important meeting," he said, focusing on the harsh, jabbing movements of her fork.

"Lots of those these days," she observed.

"Did you talk with Holly?" he blurted.

She looked up from the bowl, her eyes flashing. "Yeah, I did, after work. Why?"

"Oh, I don't know. I don't. Just that, you sometimes see her, that's all."

She smiled at his nervousness. "Ah. Yes. So I do. Today she surprised me at the spa, full of giggles and talk of her new lover."

He looked confused, his brow creasing at the word "lover," a word best suited for novels and not said aloud in an echoing kitchen.

"You know," she prompted in a conspiratorial tone, "*Enrico?*"

Eric frowned at this, the veins in his neck standing out.

"But," she said, smiling, "I'm sure he'll improve with time."

"Improve? How?"

"Oh Holly wouldn't say much, but she did say, well . . . *fake it till you make it!* Let's just say Enrico's magic act could use a little wand work."

Eric seemed to be at a loss for words.

"I suppose you see I've turned into a little Martha Stewart here," she continued. "You liked the last cake so much, I decided to make another."

"What kind is this one?"

"Cinnamon coffee cake. You like cinnamon, don't you?"

He nodded. She dipped a teaspoon into the spice jar and held out a generous mound as though offering him a taste. The spoon quivered a little in her fingers as it hovered near his mouth.

The tip of his tongue lightly touched the reddish substance. "Mmm. Yes. I like cinnamon."

She urged the spoon at him again. "Have it. You've licked it, I'm not about to put it back in the jar now."

"No, thanks."

"Come on."

"I'm not going to eat a spoonful of cinnamon, Victoria," he said, stepping back.

"I thought you liked it."

Eric squinted at her with an old derision. "People don't eat spices by the teaspoon. I heard people can actually choke and *die* doing that. Anyway, what the hell is wrong with you?"

Victoria scoffed. "Oh, come on, 'death by cinnamon'? Aren't you spicing things up? C'mon, I dare you."

She prodded the spoon against his firmly closed lips a few times before he knocked it from her hand and it clattered onto the floor in a dusting of rust-colored powder.

"Enough!" he said. "Goddamnit, Victoria, you're so fucking crazy! You always ruin everything, you know that?"

"Oh, I do, do I?" her voice was very calm, like all the truth was there ready to say, as though it always had been.

"Yes!" he said, raising his voice. "Yes, yes you do! You're always hovering around with this . . . possessed look in your eyes, like you haven't slept in a week, your face always in a book. Just LOOK at this place, would you? Who else gets to live like this?"

He swept his hand across the sea of white in demonstration, and to her books on the coffee table.

"Don't start picking on my reading again. I'm not giving that up for you, not ever again."

"Oh, I wouldn't dream of it! Not now, not since you bought that . . . THING that you've been hiding in the guest room. Wait till I tell Deirdre about that latest development."

"Oh, there you go, running to Mother again. Now I've done something really crazy. Ooooh. I bought a bookcase."

Eric drew back at Victoria's tone. "Well, it actually IS crazy. People who have no BOOKS don't buy BOOKCASES that are as big as the damn *Titanic*."

"The only reason I don't have any books is because my loving husband doesn't allow it! He actually forbade me to read for two weeks. How's that for crazy, *Enrico*?"

Eric's face paled. He pressed his lips together so that they turned white.

"I knew you'd find a way to ruin us," he said quietly. "It's what you want, really, isn't it?"

She didn't answer.

"I came home to tell you that after all this time, after all the hours and the meetings and the ass-kissing and the sleepless nights, I made partner. Bravo! Job well done! But you don't care, do you? That's fine. You can get out of this, of us, Victoria. That's fine. I won't stop you. But you're not taking a single thing. Not even that godawful carbuncle in the spare room."

Victoria was about to reply when her phone dinged three times in quick succession. She picked it up and scanned the texts on her screen. She looked up, expression urgent, all malevolence wiped away.

"Holly. It's Holly. She's in trouble. She's in real trouble."

Eric's eyes registered alarm. Instinctively, he glanced toward the window, and the cold, blind darkness of the night.

"That guy, the bouncer," she said, her voice clipped, "Todd. He's going to hurt her."

FORTY-SEVEN

HE TOOK THE KEY THAT VICTORIA OFFERED TO HIM, THE ONE that had been in residence in the little white dish in the junk drawer since they moved in. He accepted the hat and second scarf (it was awful out there).

"Just help her," was all Victoria said, and he nodded, then dashed out, a black blur, without saying goodbye.

She didn't bother to text Holly back, because Holly hadn't messaged. Luke had.

She cleaned up the cinnamon from the floor, spread the streusel on the top of the cake, then put it in the oven to finish. By the time she took it out a good thirty minutes later, she knew Eric had probably arrived at Holly's. The cake smelled sweet and warm. She'd have some tonight.

As she had those nights visiting Luke's place, she now visited Holly's. She closed her eyes and leaned against the quartz countertop, inhaling the cake-perfumed air, allowing each breath to wash over her in comforting calm. The dark promise of this evening, which she had concocted like a demonic conductor of some sort, stayed her heart. She felt the euphoric lift from her body in no time at all, and knew exactly the airborne trajectory to take to her friend's apartment building. The only heartbeat she needed to follow was her own, this time. She soared over neighborhoods, parking lots, then long stretches of highway, lit by yellowish streetlights. Everything was covered in snow, giving it a pristine, peaceful appearance.

When she got to Holly's building, she saw Eric had parked and was rushing from his car, like a superhero without a costume. She saw him clutching the key in his gloved hand and stopping suddenly to pat his pocket for his cell phone.

The front door to the building was propped open slightly as it always was, with an ancient wooden doorstop. The lobby was not much more than a hallway, in the corner a fossilized potted plant abandoned by a former tenant. It was eerily quiet.

She followed Eric, who raced to the stairway with speed that indicated a familiarity with the building. Eyes bugging out, he charged up the four flights with relative ease. When he reached the top, he slowed down, panting, perhaps listening for the sounds of an intruder.

It was pretty quiet, except for the hum of traffic from outside and the occasional footstep that was impossible to source. The movement could have been coming from any of the six apartments on this floor. He had probably anticipated a less serene situation. There were no crashes or yells, no bumps and thumps from the drunken dance of two people, one pushing, one resisting. The building felt like any other in the middle of the night.

His eyes still had that hyperthyroid look to them, darting this way and that. Fear. He minced up to the door like a cat burglar in his black getup. He put the key in the lock, quietly as possible, turning it with a click that seemed to echo throughout the building. Wincing, he pushed the door open. It betrayed him with a creak. It closed behind him quickly, taking with it the comforting light of the hallway.

Victoria hovered over him in the darkness, both of them taking a moment to let their eyes adjust to their deep black surroundings.

"Holly?" he whispered, his voice an unrecognizable croak.

BRANDO WAS THE FIRST TO HEAR THE SOUND OF THE DOOR. HE HAD been in his usual position on Holly's bed. After hearing the door, he sat up, and a low growl started in his throat. He barked, his dog's voice ringing out loudly in warning.

A silhouette appeared in the doorway of Holly's bedroom at the end of the hallway, a form exaggerated by the angle and dimness. The long outline of a baseball bat was perched on the person's shoulder. The dog continued to bark. Brando, such a goofy, sloppy dog every other day of his life, had morphed into a hell hound, snarling and blood hungry. Victoria thought she glimpsed teeth bared. Was that possible in this blackness?

"I've come for Holly," she heard Eric say through the noise, but his voice came out strange and forced, much lower than usual. Victoria could almost smell his fear, could sense the acidity in his belly.

It was hard to know if the person holding the bat heard him, with all the sound from the dog, which was decidedly louder and closer. The figure stood poised in position a few moments, as if undecided. Eric determinedly moved down the hall in small, lurching steps.

"Holly," he grunted, again, forcing air out of his throat as though the word was choking him.

The figure, still cloaked in darkness, advanced. Eric ducked and dived like he did on the badminton court, making himself as small as possible, in an attempt to hide from view. But what this really served to do, and what he wouldn't know until it was too late, was to offer his head to his attacker in the most genteel way, like a knight on bended knee.

When the bat came down, glinting metallic in a quick flash as it made its arc, Victoria watched Eric fail his heroic task. He glanced up at just that moment and, though she knew it was impossible, it was as though he were seeing her, Victoria, bitter fear and dislike in his expression. His eyes flashed open in shock. He then closed them. He made an animal's groan.

Victoria heard a woman's guttural scream, Holly's, in the moment before his skull split.

WHEN THE TIMER FINALLY CHIMED, ANNOUNCING IT WAS TIME TO frost the cake, Victoria found herself back in her kitchen. She stood up from where she had been leaning on the counter and began methodically to drizzle on a glaze, giving great care and attention to the even distribution. When she had finished, she smiled in contentment and licked the spreading knife on one side, then the other. At the same time across town, Brando, too, was licking something sticky, from the floor.

FORTY-EIGHT

T WAS THE BRIGHTEST, MOST SPARKLY WINTER DAY VICTORIA could imagine. Walking hand in hand with Luke along Sherbrooke Street, she felt their shared power bouncing back and forth. She felt the exhilaration of a thousand suns. She was an octopus, freed from the tank. She had made it through that two-inch tube, that white-lacquered tube that no one thought she could fit through. Crystal-line diamonds sparkled everywhere she looked. Ah, the wonder of winter!

Her synapses were firing one after another, her future life in front of her. She could see them reading books in the evening, with a fire-place roaring. She would get up for a few minutes to fix tea, and then they would lapse into the most comfortable silence two people could share. He would look up at her and mention something about the undeniability of Coetzee's brilliance, and she would agree. They'd discuss the meaning of the dogs in *Disgrace*. They would discuss the other novels under two hundred pages that changed their lives. Then they would return to their books.

This was the dream, and now she could live it. They would laugh, and make love, and look across rooms at each other, and live happily ever after. Every step was a shimmy and a shake. She was walking down a church aisle toward the heart of her life.

It was Him, and He wanted Her. And this time, she would be happy.

He looked at her, sharing the moment, not needing to describe it. Surely he knew what she was thinking; he was probably thinking the very same thing.

"Want to stop for a coffee?" he suggested.

A great idea. They were close to her café, the one where they had met the first time. They wouldn't stay long. Brando was still getting used to the apartment—*her* apartment, rather.

Of course, it would soon be *their* apartment, hers and Luke's, when Luke moved his things over at the end of the month. He'd been so understanding, a permanent fixture, ever since that night. That night when she had picked up the phone, mouth full of cake (it had turned out so well!), and it was Holly, hysterical, gurgling.

"I thought it was HIM, I thought it was HIM!" she had screamed over and over through gagging sobs.

Victoria had taken a cab over and found her friend in the hallway. The hems of Holly's pajama pants were soaked in blood, her tank top was a red and white Jackson Pollock. Her forehead was smeared with red, and in her blond hair sat a gray, slimy lump that was beginning to congeal.

Victoria had glimpsed Eric through the open door to Holly's apartment, around his neck the extra scarf she had given him. She could see from a distance, from the crumpled condition of his head, that he would not need an ambulance.

Holly hadn't moved until the police came. She remained unresponsive to Victoria, who had patted her hand and said with all the sincerity in her heart, "You were so brave."

Now, Victoria and Luke, the wonder couple, ordered twin lattes.

The woman in the beehive hairdo nodded at Victoria with an approving smile.

"You get a table," Luke said, reaching for his wallet. "I've got this."

She squeezed his hand and sought out a table in the middle of the room. No people watching today. Today she was one of them. She sighed in contentment as she watched Luke approach.

He put the mugs on the table, careful not to spill. He took off his army-green bag and slung it over the back of his chair and sat. They were side by side. His phone buzzed and he looked down at it.

She glanced over at him and was startled to notice how weak his chin was from this angle. She hadn't noticed it before. It melted into his neck too soon, with too many folds. The skin was speckled red, from a careless swipe of the razor. A pinprick of disgust surfaced. Suddenly she could see exactly how he would look when he was old. She turned away, trying to push the image out of her mind. That chin! This wasn't helpful, wasn't something to focus on right now, this most perfect day of all days, when she'd finally gotten exactly what she wanted. And wasn't he here, right here with her? As if it had all happened according to plan. A plan, it occurred to her, she could return to, if need be.

She shook her head out of this thought. Of course there would be no need. What was she thinking?

Recalling that she had a copy of *The Great Gatsby* in her bag, she eagerly reached for it, knowing it would clear her head, reacquainting herself with one of the most sympathetic characters she'd ever read. Oh, how well she understood the allure of that green light at the end of the dock.

ACKNOWLEDGMENTS

EACH BOOK IS A COLLABORATIVE EFFORT, AND YOU NEED GOOD people around you. I couldn't be more fortunate to have found my people (or did they find me?). So, thank you, to the three who have all my gratitude and admiration:

Wayne Johnson (teacher, editor), without whose singular insight and support none of this would have happened. Madison Smartt Bell (agent), whose willingness to take me on is one of my life's greatest honors. Sara Nelson (editor and champion), whose steadfast belief in and vision for this story cracked open my dreams and made them reality.

Thanks also to: the Iowa Summer Writing Festival; the city of Montreal; my Goodreads community; my dear friends, Myra, Tamsin, and Fiona; my parents; my sister Vanessa; and, of course, to Will, Georgia, and Julian, with love.

ABOUT THE AUTHOR

Robin Yeatman is a shameless bookworm who was born in Calgary, Alberta, and raised in Vancouver, Canada. Educated in British Columbia and England, she studied literature, trained as a broadcast journalist, and worked in radio as a morning show producer. After a dozen years in Montreal, she lives in Vancouver. *Bookworm* is her first book.